Bestsell:

P
JO

presents

The PARENTI MARRIAGE

Power, privilege and passion
The worlds of big business and
royalty unite…

The epic romance of Saul and Giselle…
Two fabulous novels, together at last

Penny Jordan is one of Mills & Boon's most popular authors. Sadly Penny died from cancer on 31st December 2011, aged sixty-five. She leaves an outstanding legacy, having sold over a hundred million books around the world. She wrote a total of a hundred and eighty-seven novels for Mills & Boon, including the phenomenally successful *A Perfect Family, To Love, Honour & Betray, The Perfect Sinner* and *Power Play*, which hit the Sunday Times and New York Times bestseller lists. Loved for her distinctive voice, her success was in part because she continually broke boundaries and evolved her writing to keep up with readers' changing tastes. *Publishers Weekly* said about Jordan, 'Women everywhere will find pieces of themselves in Jordan's characters' and this perhaps explains her enduring appeal.

Although Penny was born in Preston, Lancashire, and spent her childhood there, she moved to Cheshire as a teenager and continued to live there for the rest of her life. Following the death of her husband she moved to the small traditional Cheshire market town on which she based her much-loved Crighton books.

Penny was a member and supporter of the Romantic Novelists' Association and the Romance Writers of America—two organisations dedicated to providing support for both published and yet-to-be published authors. Her significant contribution to women's fiction was recognised in 2011, when the Romantic Novelists' Association presented Penny with a Lifetime Achievement Award.

PENNY JORDAN

The *P*ARENTI MARRIAGE

MILLS & BOON

Published in Great Britain 2014
by Mills & Boon, an imprint of Harlequin (UK) Limited,
Eton House, 18-24 Paradise Road, Richmond, Surrey, TW9 1SR

THE PARENTI MARRIAGE © 2014 Harlequin Books S.A.

The Reluctant Surrender © 2010 Penny Jordan
The Dutiful Wife © 2010 Penny Jordan

ISBN: 978 0 263 24585 1

009-0314

Harlequin (UK) Limited's policy is to use papers that are natural, renewable and recyclable products and made from wood grown in sustainable forests The logging and manufacturing processes conform to the legalenvironmental regulations of the country of origin.

Printed and bound in Spain
by Blackprint CPI, Barcelona

THE RELUCTANT SURRENDER

PENNY JORDAN

CHAPTER ONE

As SHE turned into the underground car park, shared by
the architectural practice she worked for with several
other businesses in the same modern block, Giselle saw
a car reversing from one of the precious spaces. Quickly
she turned the wheel of her small company car against
the arrows, driving up an exit lane, her brain and body
automatically focusing on getting to the empty space
before anyone else spotted it. She only realised as she
swung round the end of the exit lane and up to the space
that an imposing, expensive, polished sports car, with
an equally imposing, expensive and polished, far too
harshly good-looking man at its wheel, was stationary
just down from the space. He had obviously been waiting for the space's occupant to leave.

He looked at her, his expression one of arrogance
mingled with open male disbelief. For a second she
hesitated, her resolve almost failing, but then she saw
how his glance moved deliberately from her face to her
body, as though she was a piece of merchandise he was
looking over and then rejecting, and a spurt of pure
female fury had her turning into the spot for which he
had been waiting.

She could see the cold savagery of the look he was

giving her, and lip-read the words, *What the hell—?* as they were formed by the sensually chiselled hard male mouth as she swept past him, her whole body shaking, her hands damp with perspiration as she clung to the wheel.

It wasn't just because his arrogance had infuriated her that she was doing this. This morning she'd received an unexpected call asking her to get to the office early, to be present after the senior partners' meeting. She could not afford to be late; necessity overruled and squashed the guilt she would normally have felt at her lack of good road manners. Then he had given her that look—that assured, arrogant, hateful glance at her body—that had said so clearly exactly what kind of man he was: predatory, callous, completely fixated on his own desires and needs.

Her need for the parking space was far greater than his, Giselle told herself. She had to be in the office— fifteen minutes ago. He, on the other hand, looked the sort who normally had a driver to attend to such mundane things as parking his car.

Inside the car, she started to change her driving shoes for her office heels. The sound of an engine revving furiously made her exhale in relief. He had obviously driven away—at high speed and in high dudgeon, no doubt.

Having moved his car a few yards, to let another vehicle pass him, Saul Parenti stared with furious disbelief at the thief who had just taken his parking spot. The fact that this deed had been commited by a woman added insult to injury. Saul had the blood of generations of powerful men running through his veins—men in control, in authority, absolute rulers—and right now that blood was running very hot and fast indeed. Saul would never have described himself as a misogynist, far from it—he liked women. He liked them a lot. But generally speaking the place where he liked them most was in his bed—not in a parking spot for which he had been waiting with a patience that went against his nature.

With no other parking space available, he parked swiftly to one side, obstructing two vehicles, and switched off the car engine. He pushed open the door, unfolding his muscular six-foot-four length from the driving seat of his car.

Giselle was unaware that her theft was about to be challenged until she was out of her small car. Making the short walk from the car park to the lift that would take her up to the office was the time she normally used to get her professional mask firmly in place—the one that hid the fact that she disliked the male interest so often directed at her at work. Because of this she was too involved in adopting her cloak of defensive hauteur—straight back, straight-ahead focus, and a lift of her chin that said she was untouchable—to be aware of the danger until it was too late and she was forced to rock back on her heels in mid-stride or risk walking straight into the man standing between her and the exit.

'Not so fast. I want a word with you.'

His English was excellent, and somehow slightly at odds with his darkly male looks.

Well, she certainly did not want to exchange any words with *him*. Giselle stepped past him, and then gasped in outraged shock when he blocked her, stepping closer to her, until she felt as though each breath was filled with the raw masculine smell of him—all dark, erotic mastery spiked with something sharper, like the touch of a velvet glove spiked with hidden danger.

'You're in my way,' she told him as she fought to keep and sound cool—not realising the dangerous opening she had given him.

'And you are in my parking spot,' he retorted.

That might be true, but she wasn't about to give it or anything else up to him.

'Possession is nine-tenths of the law,' she quipped, and then wished that she hadn't when he seemed to move even closer, his presence somehow paralysing and imprisoning her.

'Possession belongs to those who are strong enough to take what they want and hold on to it—whether that applies to a parking space—or a woman.'

And he was a man who *would* possess *his* woman. The knowledge of that had somehow got under her protective armour, and now that it had… She was beginning to feel dizzy, weak, filled with a febrile excitement brought on by the clash of words between them, a dangerous desire to go on pushing him, to test his self-control.

A shudder ripped though her. This was madness. Just because he was a man. And *what* a man, she was forced to acknowledge dizzily. For a start there was his height—easily over six feet, so that even in her heels she had to tilt her head back to look up at him. Somehow, despite the fact that she had worked for years never to allow herself to be physically aware of men, this one had such a powerful aura of raw male sexuality about him that she suspected it would be impossible for *any* woman not to be aware of him. Her own unexpected and unwanted vulnerability set off a chain reaction of panic and anger inside her, and those emotions were intensified by the fact that they could not block out the effect his maleness was having on her.

Unfamiliar and definitely unwanted thoughts were springing up inside her head with such vigour that it was impossible for her to cull them. Dangerous thoughts, all allied to the fact that he was a man. And not *just* a man but the architectural equivalent of instant visual gratification via the perfection of the design of his outer form. In fact looking at him could easily become a female compulsion, Giselle suspected helplessly. That expensive-looking shirt he was wearing must surely have been made to measure for him, to cover those shoulders and that chest. No surplus fat there. His body looked as though it would be all hard muscle over silken flesh. How would it feel to touch such a man? What would it be like to have such a feast of male sensuality spread out for her delight and the enticement of her senses? A quiverful of molten aching darts of longing were piercing her body, lethally infecting it with tiny stings of desire.

Protectively Giselle lifted her hand to her heart in an attempt to steady its increased beat. She must *not* feel like this. Not now and not ever. Not for this man or for any man. She tried to look away from him, to break the spell his sexuality had cast over her, but instead her gaze slid recklessly to his face and became enmeshed there.

His genes were not derived from any Anglo-Saxon ancestor, she was sure. Not with those arrogant, almost

Roman Byzantine features, with that hint of cruelty stamped into them. No. His was an intensely masculine face—intelligent, educated, arrogant and elegant. The Mediterranean olive flesh was drawn smoothly against high cheekbones, a strong jaw, and the Roman strength of his nose. If it hadn't been for his unexpectedly silver eyes she would have said that this was a man whose bloodline came from the darkest mists of time—from a race of men destined by birthright and their own strength to sweep aside all opposition to their will.

One blast from those grey eyes was like having a laser gun applied to her icy shield. This was a man with a capital M—all-male, all-powerful, a man who believed that his will, his needs and desires should be free to rove and take possession of whatever they and he wanted.

The shock of being confronted by him was definitely having a dangerous effect on her. Somehow her senses had managed to break through the mental chastity belt in which she normally locked them to behave like a group of hormone overloaded teenagers, all too ready to feast themselves on the banquet in front of them. Only of course she had no intention of allowing them to do any such thing. And she had years of practice in ensuring that they obeyed her, she reminded herself as she struggled to retain her air of icy uninterest.

She didn't like him, Giselle decided. She didn't like him one little bit. He was far too arrogant. And far too male for her own comfort. Was that why she didn't like him? Because she knew instinctively that his brand of male sexuality was very dangerous to her and that she was not as protected from it as she knew she had to be? Of course not, she assured herself determinedly.

Saul studied the woman standing in front of him with a practised male gaze. Medium height, slim—although the combination of the almost uniform-like dullness of her black skirt suit, worn over a plain white shirt, and the fact that her clothes were cheap and ill-fitting, as though they were a size too big for her, made it impossible to judge accurately how feminine her body shape might be. Her blonde hair was drawn back tightly into a smooth chignon that revealed the delicate bone structure of her face, with its femininely pronounced cheekbones and luminous skin. The gold tips to her eyelashes revealed by the overhead lighting suggested that they were neither dyed nor covered in mascara. Some men might find her cool, touch-me-not Grace Kelly-type looks a sexual challenge, and be curious enough to see just how much applied male interest her ice would take before cracking, but he was not one of them. He liked his women subtly and seductively wanton and willing—not playing at being ice maidens so that they could demand their ice was melted.

However, even if she had been his type, right now his attention was focused on retribution rather than seduction.

'Let me past,' Giselle demanded, asserting herself in an attempt to remind herself of the reality of the situation.

Her sharp demand added to Saul's impatient fury. She had stolen his parking space, and she was argumentative, stubborn, and refusing to admit that she was in the wrong. Her whole attitude made him want to put her in her place.

He wasn't going to move, and she was going to be

late. Determined to make her escape, Giselle stepped quickly to one side of him—but as she did so he reached for her, taking hold of her forearms in a fiercely hostile grip. She could feel their bruising pressure on her flesh, male and alien and burning away the layers of cloth between them, so that it was almost as though he was touching her bare skin. A shocking sensation seized hold of her body as powerfully as he seized hold of her, panicking her into curling her hands into fists that she wanted to beat against his chest.

'Let me go,' she insisted furiously.

Let her go? There was nothing he wanted to do more. She'd already caused him more trouble in five short minutes than he'd ever allowed any woman to cause him. He looked directly at her. Her face was white and set, her eyes burning with temper, her mouth…

Still holding her with one hand, he removed the other from her arm to reach up and very deliberately wipe the lipstick from her mouth with his thumb, as if in preparation to kiss her.

She stood frozen, shocked at the intimate gesture, and the moment stretched as their gazes locked. Unable to move, Giselle was stunned by the leap of sensation his gaze shifting to her mouth conjured within her, and with it the hunger to—to what? To lean in to him?

The sudden blaring of a car horn close to them had Saul releasing his prisoner, thrusting her away from him as he did so. What had possessed him? And what would have happened if they hadn't been disturbed? he asked himself as Giselle took advantage of the interruption to run from him.

To Giselle's relief he didn't follow her to the

lift—which thankfully was empty. In it, on the way up to her office, with her heart thudding and racing and her mind in turmoil, she had to force herself not to think about what had just happened but instead to focus on the reason everyone had been called into the office.

For the past two years—in fact virtually since she had joined the prestigious practice of architects—the firm had been working on a lavish and costly project for a Russian billionaire, which involved turning a small island he had acquired off the coast of Croatia into a luxury holiday resort for the very wealthy. The financial downturn had led to the project being put on hold, much to the dismay of the firm's senior partners, but then late yesterday they had received news that the island had a new owner, in the shape of another billionaire—a very successful entrepreneur, who had seen the plans for the island and now wanted to discuss them.

This news had galvanised the senior partners into swift action. Everyone connected with the plans—no matter in how lowly a capacity—had been instructed to make themselves available after the preliminary early-morning meeting, in case the island's new owner wished to discuss any aspect of the plans with them. The hope was that he would give the green light to the stalled project, but of course there was no guarantee of that. With the threat of potential redundancies looming over them, naturally the more junior architects, like Giselle, were keeping everything crossed that he would look favourably on the plans.

The lift had stopped at her floor. Giselle exited the lift and headed for the office she shared with several other junior architects—all of them male, apart from her, and all of them in their different ways determined to show both her and the senior partners that they were a better financial investment for the firm than she could ever be.

'It's all right,' said Emma Lewis, their shared PA, as Giselle stepped into the office. 'The meeting's been put back an hour. Apparently the new owner has been unavoidably delayed.'

Giselle exhaled with relief and told her, 'I thought I was going to be late. I had to come in my car, because I've got a site meeting this evening, and the traffic was appalling.'

Emma, thirty-four to Giselle's twenty-six, and married to a surveyor who was working on a contract out in the United Arab Emirates, treated her juniors in much the same way as she did her two children—mothering them with fond affection and doing her best to break up any quarrels between them. Giselle liked her, and was very grateful for the support Emma gave her.

'Where's everyone else?' Giselle asked Emma, only to groan and go on, 'No, don't tell me—let me guess. They're all in the gents, trying to work out how to avoid any blame that might be handed out whilst claiming any plaudits that could be going.'

Emma burst out laughing.

'Something like that, I expect. I'll bring you coffee, and then I'll tell you the latest I've heard about our possible new client.'

Giselle nodded her head, and tried not to grimace inwardly. If Emma had one fault it was that she was devoted to gossip magazines charting the lives of the rich and famous, and Giselle suspected that 'the latest' was probably going to be some kind of information she'd gleaned from the pages of one of those dubious sources.

Five minutes later, sipping her coffee whilst she listened to Emma, she knew that she was right.

'I'd never have seen it if I hadn't had to take Timmy to the dentist, because the magazine was months old, and I couldn't believe it when I opened it and right in front of me was an article about Saul Parenti. You'd think he was Italian with that surname, wouldn't you? But he isn't. Apparently his family actually own their own *country,* and his cousin is its Grand Duke. It's somewhere near Croatia, and only small, but apparently he—Saul Parenti, I mean—is fabulously wealthy in his own right, apart from being the cousin of a duke, because his father was involved in loads of business deals with the middle East.'

'Fascinating.' Giselle applauded obligingly.

'I just love knowing all about people's backgrounds and their families, don't you?' Emma enthused. 'His mother was American, and high up in one of the overseas aid agencies. She and his father were killed in South America whilst she was working there, in the aftermath of an earthquake.'

Giselle nodded her head, to show she was following Emma's story, but inwardly the last thing she felt like doing was listening to gossip. Her comment about the death of Saul Parenti's parents had caused an all too familiar panicky swell of nausea and defensive fear to rise insidiously inside her.

The door to the office opened to admit one of the other junior architects, Bill Jeffries. Stockily built and confident, he swaggered into the office looking pleased with himself. Bill considered himself to be something of a ladies' man. He had made advances to her when she had first joined the practice.

Because she had rebuffed him, she was now on the receiving end of increasing animosity and sexual hostility towards her, and Giselle knew perfectly well what he was getting at when he gave a fake shiver and protested, 'Brr…it's cold in here!' before pretending to notice her and then saying, 'Oh, sorry—I hadn't seen you there, Giselle.'

Giselle said nothing. She was well accustomed to Bill's malice and baiting, which she knew sprang from the fact that she had so resolutely refused all the attempts of both him and the other men she worked with to flirt when she had first joined the practice. Bill had chosen to take her chilly manner personally, and she had no intention of telling him that, far from being personal, her icy reserve was a defensive mechanism she used against *every* man who attempted to show any kind of sexual interest in her. If Bill and other men like him chose to be offended because she didn't welcome their attentions, then so be it. The truth was that a long time ago she had sworn that she would never allow herself to date men—because dating could lead to falling in love, falling in love led to making a commitment, and making a commitment led in turn to becoming a pair, and from that pair would come children…

'Bill, I've just been telling Giselle what I've read about Saul Parenti.' Emma broke the hostile silence. 'Giselle, I still haven't told you everything. Apparently he's fabulously wealthy, with a reputation for driving a very hard bargain where his business and his romantic interests are concerned. When it comes to women he likes to play the field—he's supposed to be a wonderful lover—but he's said publicly that he never intends to marry.'

'Hear that, Miss Ice Queen?' Bill mocked Giselle. 'Sounds like our new client is just the man to get you warmed up so that you'll drop your knickers.' He gave an unpleasant snicker. 'Mind you, I don't envy him if he does—all that ice would freeze the balls off any man.'

'Bill!' Emma protested.'

'Well, it's true,' he said, unabashed.

'It's all right, Emma,' Giselle assured the PA. 'My chosen profession is architecture, Bill,' She pointed out calmly. 'Not prostitution.'

'You mean it is if you can keep your job. And, let's face it, you certainly won't win any commissions with your female wiles,' he sneered in response.

'I don't need to use *any* wiles, female or otherwise, to keep my job,' Giselle couldn't resist coming back at him pointedly, causing him to colour up angrily.

Bill was one of those employees who liked to play the good team player in front of those he thought it would impress, whilst being very much a person who put himself first. Bill liked to use their shared gender to get the other men in the office on side with him, and to exclude her, but Giselle had never seen any real evidence that he was the team player he liked to claim he was.

In the senior partners' office the atmosphere was thick with a mixture of tension and determination—the tension coming from Mr Shepherd, one of the senior partners, and the determination from Saul Parenti, the man he needed to satisfy that his firm was up to the challenge being set.

'Yes, of course I accept that you wish to meet and speak with the team who will be working on the changes to the plans you have requested. Perhaps lunch with the other senior partners involved in the plans?'

'I wish to meet *everyone* involved in the project—senior and junior,' Saul stressed briskly.

He did not have time to waste. He was already running late, thanks to the woman who had stolen his parking space and a telephone call from his cousin. Aldo, five years his junior and recently married, might be Grand Duke of Arezzio, thanks to the fact that his father had been their grandfather's eldest son, and his own the younger, but he still turned to him when he needed financial advice. Saul shrugged inwardly. He had done his best to help his young cousin build up some reserves for the royal coffers of Arezzio, the small country on what had once been the border between the old Austrian Empire and Croatia, but Aldo was not a businessman—he was more of an academic. He did not like the harsh cut and thrust of modern business, and preferred to spend his time cataloguing the rare books in the library of his castle in Arezzio.

Saul was grateful for the fact that his father had not been the elder brother, and that he had been spared the onerous duty of becoming Arezzio's Grand Duke, being forced to marry and produce an heir. He might not have approved when Aldo had married Natasha, because he didn't think Natasha loved his cousin, but

he would be very pleased when their marriage produced the child that would mean that he would be not
just one but two steps removed from the Dukedom. He
was, he believed, like his mother. Like her, he loved
the excitement and adventure of new challenges and
demands on his energy. Her life had been her aid work.
She had loved his father, and no doubt she had loved
him too, but parenting a child had not been the focus
of his mother's life.

His own view now was that it would be wrong for him
to bring a child into the world when he knew how little
time he would have for it. He was driven in his work, in
his need to explore the outer boundaries of creating the
most exciting and enticing of luxurious holiday destina-
tions which at the same time supported the environment
and the local population. It was a purpose to which his
emotional time as well as his physical time was given
over wholly. He would not have a child and leave it to
be raised by others, and he did not need or want an heir.
When the time came for him to hand over the business
he would find the right hands to hold it safe.

Given all that, financing his cousin—and thus in part
the country itself—was a small price to pay for his personal freedom.

A personal freedom he never intended to relinquish,
either via a public commitment or a private one—of any
kind.

Saul could see the senior partner of the architectural firm who had been commissioned to design the
complex its previous owner had planned to create on
the island did not approve of Saul's demand. It always
irritated him when people failed to grasp why he made

the decisions he did and delayed executing the orders
that related to those decisions. Their failure betrayed a
lack of vision and foresight, as well as poor financial
acumen. Which was no doubt why the firm was on the
point of bankruptcy—or would have been if he hadn't
just confirmed that he intended to keep them on and go
ahead with the redevelopment of the island.

At the back of his mind was the thought that, should
he increase his financial interest in such projects, adding
an architectural practice to his portfolio of business hold-
ings would be financially beneficial. For now, though,
he intended to make it plain that he would *not* be paying
them the kind of fees they had previously anticipated,
and he would be keeping a far tighter control of both
budgets and plans for the venture. Taking and keeping
control was why he was a billionaire, with his fortune
growing every day, whilst other rich men were losing
money.

'I wish to see them all because I want to make it
clear to them that from now on it is *my* instructions they
will be following and *my* approval they must win,' he
informed the senior partner. 'The previous plans were
spouting wasted money like a leaking colander.'

'Our original brief was that no expense be spared,'
Mr Shepherd protested defensively.

Saul gave him a cool look.

'Which is no doubt why one of your junior staff
elected to have the floor of a summerhouse that is open
to the weather tiled in handmade tiles that are not frost-
proof.'

'An error which of course would have been picked
up,' the senior partner assured him.

'Of course. But I prefer those who work for me not to make such errors in the first place.' Saul looked at his watch, and this time the senior partner stood up.

'I believe all our staff are in the building. I will arrange for all those who worked on the plans to be summoned,' he said unwillingly.

'I have a better idea,' Saul told him. 'Why don't you show me round the office instead, and introduce me to them that way?'

It often paid to see what people were working on. Fortunes could be built—and destroyed—by such means.

The whisper had spread through the office. 'The project's going ahead and he's keeping us on.' And naturally everyone's mood was upbeat and buoyant, with all the staff relieved to have the worry of the last couple of months, when they hadn't known whether or not they would end up being made redundant, finally removed.

Giselle was as relieved as everyone else. She'd worked hard to get where she was, to qualify for and get a job that would enable her to support herself all through her adult life—because she *would* have to support herself. She knew that. There would never be a man, a partner, a husband who loved her and whom she loved in turn to share the burden of providing a roof over their head with her. How could there be when—?

The door to their office opened, and everyone fell silent as Mr Shepherd, one of the senior partners, came in—an unheard-of event. But it wasn't the sight of him that had driven the colour from Giselle's face, leaving it bleached of colour as she stared into the face of the man accompanying him.

It was the man from the car park. The man whose space she had stolen—the man who was now their most important client, Giselle recognised as she heard the senior partner introduce him.

'Mr Parenti wishes to meet all those who have worked or will be working on the plans for the island project,' the senior partner announced.

'Saul,' their new client corrected the older man. 'Not Mr Parenti.' Respect, as far as he was concerned, was something that was earned, not bestowed, and he had no doubt at all about his ability to earn the respect of others.

Whilst he was speaking he was studying the occupants of the room, his gaze cold and analytical, giving nothing away—until he saw and recognised Giselle. On her he allowed his gaze to rest just that little bit longer, so that she would be aware of his recognition of her and be forced to recognise the mistake she had made when she had stolen his parking spot.

Giselle felt the anger in his gaze scorching her conscience, but years of forcing herself never to appear outwardly vulnerable had her lifting her head and meeting his gaze head-on.

She was daring to challenge him? Saul was a recognisably formidable man, whom no one defied—especially not someone who was in the wrong, and especially not when that someone was financially dependent on him, as this woman most decidedly was. He was used to women attempting to bring themselves to his attention because they desired him and his wealth, not so that they could challenge him.

Twice now she had angered him, which meant that she now had two debts to repay—and he would see that she settled up, Saul decided as the senior partner began to introduce his junior architects to him.

Why, *why*, of all the men parking their cars in London had she had to steal the parking spot of *this* man? Giselle agonised inwardly. There was no point in telling herself that her behaviour had been out of character and born of desperation—that would not mean anything to the man slowly making his way towards her.

One by one he spoke to all the juniors, asking them which part of the plan they had worked on. Bill, of course, immediately went into his 'I'm a team player and I get everyone onside with me' routine, whilst at the same time managing to send a look in her direction which said that *she* was not part of that team. Little did Bill know that he had no need to try to make their new client have doubts about her. She'd already done a wonderful job of that herself.

Her stomach tense with apprehension, Giselle waited, and waited, knowing that retribution was going to fall, and knowing too that he was enjoying drawing out her torment.

And then he was standing in front of her, the powerful magnetic quality of his personality causing her to take a step back from him

'And you, Ms…?'

'Giselle,' Giselle answered. 'Giselle Freeman.'

'And your contribution to the plans was…?'

'Cold storage, wasn't it?' someone laughed, but Giselle ignored them.

'I worked on the air conditioning, with an ecological brief to be incorporated,' she said stiffly.

'A brief which I think I am correct in saying is currently running over-budget?' Saul pointed out as he allowed his gaze to slide slowly and thoroughly over her.

He'd picked up on the look Bill had given her and had guessed that she was as unpopular with them as she'd made herself with him. That would mean that she was not an effective team player, and that would hinder work on any project in which she participated. He was surprised that the practice kept her on.

Giselle's heart pounded with fear. She'd been transferred to work on the air conditioning because it had run over-budget and because she was known to be good at working within budget—but she could hardly say so when not even Mr Shepherd had come to her defence.

Saul Parenti was playing with her, she knew. He was going to ask for her to be removed from the project, she could tell, and then she would probably be sacked. A cold sweat began to break out on her skin, and her stomach was churning with nausea. She couldn't lose her job. She mustn't. And beneath her fear was an angry contempt for this man who was using his power to torment her that she dared not let him see.

'I am not happy with the car parking arrangements for the complex,' Saul continued, turning back to the senior partner and breaking the tense silence that had gripped the room. 'Perhaps Giselle should work on those, whilst

someone with more experience takes over from her with
the air conditioning.'

Giselle could feel her face burning. He had both in-
sulted her professional ability and scored a point over
her for her morning run-in with him. He had humiliated her publicly, she admitted helplessly, as the senior
partner hastily assured him that, yes, indeed, she could
do exactly that.

As Saul Parenti left the office with Mr Shepherd,
Giselle lifted her chin. She wasn't going to let anyone,
least of all him, know how hurt and afraid she felt.

She was still daring to challenge him, Saul thought
furiously as he saw her lifted chin. Well, she'd soon
learn that that was a dangerous mistake. Dangerous
for her.

CHAPTER TWO

SEVERAL hours later, still seated in one of the senior partners' offices, whilst they thrashed out the details of the revised plans, Saul found that his thoughts were still straying irritatingly to Giselle.

It was unheard of for any woman to occupy his thoughts when they should be focused on more important matters, and turning this project from the disaster it had been heading for into a financially successful venture was important to him both on a business and a personal level. His success as an entrepreneur had brought him plenty of competitors who resented his success and would be happy to see him fail.

But he was not going to fail—as he had already been making plain to the senior partners via his caustic condemnation of the excesses proposed by the island's previous owner and what Saul considered to be the firm's lax attitude to the control and costing of the plans it had been responsible for drawing up.

'I do not have the time to sift through every detail of each part of the plan and its costing to ensure that your people are doing what I have instructed them to do,' Saul pointed out acerbically. 'And yet it is essential that they do exactly that if this project is to be successful and ultimately financially viable.'

'I accept that.' Mr Shepherd nodded.

'Good. To ensure that my wishes are carried out what I propose is that you second to me one of your best junior architects—someone who would be directly responsible to me for ensuring that the plans adhere to my requirements, and for alerting both me and you should they fail to do so.'

'That sounds an excellent idea,' the Senior Partner agreed.

'I shall require someone well qualified and able to carry out such a role,' Saul told him warningly.

'Of course—and I think I know exactly the right person. You met her earlier—Giselle Freeman.'

Saul looked sharply at the senior partner to assure himself that the other man was not attempting some kind of ridiculous joke. The last person he would want for such a role was Giselle Freeman. The older man's expression, though, was completely serious and free from humour, leaving Saul to battle with a variety of unfamiliar emotions. It was very rare for him to be caught off-guard, and even more rare for him to find that he was in a situation he did not wish to be in and could not easily get out of. Shepherd might not be joking, but Saul's suspicions were aroused that he could be trying to offload an unwanted and ineffective member of his staff off on him. He certainly wasn't going to allow *that* to happen, and thankfully—because of his suspicions— Saul could now see a way of rejecting the other man's recommendation.

'Yes. I remember. She's been working on the air

conditioning plans. I gained the impression that she isn't very popular with her colleagues. Anyone seconded to me in the role I envisage will have to be able to work well with other people.'

'There is some hostility towards Giselle in that office,' the senior partner agreed. 'But it is not her fault.' He sighed, and then continued, 'The truth is that Giselle is far better qualified than her colleagues. She graduated with honours and won an internationally acclaimed prize for her final-year project. She's a dedicated, hardworking professional with the qualifications to have a glittering career in front of her. The reality is that because of the downturn we simply don't have the work for her here that would put her skills to their best use. She's extremely loyal, though. An exemplary employee. I happen to know that in her first year here with us she was approached by two different headhunters working on behalf of international concerns. One job offer was in the Arabian Gulf, the other was in Singapore, but she chose to stay with us. She's only been working on the air con plans because the chap who was doing so before made such a complete hash of things that we had to move him on to something less demanding.'

Saul's expression had grown more grim with every word of praise the senior partner had given Giselle. Praise for her was not, after all, what he had wanted to hear—but now that he *had* heard it, and if she was as good as the senior partner was claiming, it would look decidedly odd and unbusinesslike if he refused to have her working for him. Saul was too good a businessman to allow his personal feelings to affect his business decisions. She might not appeal to him as a woman, but as an architect she was apparently very much 'best in class'. And he simply did not have time to waste sifting through a whole raft of possible candidates with potentially inferior abilities. The reality was that the project needed to get underway and be completed with some speed if he was to make the profit he wanted from it.

'Very well,' he agreed, before warning, 'but if I find she isn't up to the job then I'll expect you to take her back and supply me with someone else.'

Having dealt with the senior partner, Saul resolved grimly that if Giselle was to be seconded to work for him then there was one thing she would have to be taught—and speedily. The rules he made she would have to obey, or face the consequences.

'I imagine you will want the secondment to commence as soon as possible?' said the senior partner.

'Yes,' Saul confirmed. He suspected that Giselle Freeman would want to work for him as little as he wanted her to, and that would certainly afford him a certain amount of cynical satisfaction—that and making sure she knew just how much she had transgressed by stealing the car parking space for which he had been waiting so patiently. He already had a plan to make sure she knew that, though. He had already confirmed that the Human Resources department held copies of the keys to all the company cars, and now the spare keys to Giselle's car were in his pocket.

Not that he should be wasting his valuable mental energy on Giselle, Saul warned himself. He had far more important things to think about—one of the most pressing of which was the financial problems currently being experienced by his cousin.

Normally Saul enjoyed problem-solving. He thrived on juggling a variety of problems and then finding solutions to them. Doing just that had been his way through the bleakness of his despair in the long months after his parents' death, when he had struggled to cope with their loss.

They had been killed when a building had collapsed on them after they had gone to the aid of victims of an earthquake disaster in South America. The pain his parents' death had brought him had shocked him. Like their deaths, he hadn't been prepared for it. His overwhelming emotion initially had been anger—anger because they had risked and lost their lives, anger because they had not thought of how their deaths might affect him, anger because they had not loved him enough to ensure that they would always be there for him. It had been then that he had recognised the effect the loss of parental love and simply 'being there' could have on a child—even when that child was eighteen and officially an adult.

He had sworn then that he would never have a child himself, in case he unwittingly caused it to suffer the pain he himself was suffering. That was when he had also fully recognised just how glad he was that it was his younger cousin who was heir to the family title and lands and not him, that it was on his cousin's shoulders that the responsibility to do his duty would rest for putting their small landlocked country before his own desires.

Aldo wasn't like him. He was a quiet, gentle academic—no match for the scheming daughter of a Russian oligarch who was now his wife, and with whom he was so obviously and desperately in love. Poor fool.

Saul did not believe in love. Desire, lust, sexual hunger—yes. But allying those things to emotion and calling it love—no, never. That was not for him. He preferred his emotional freedom and the security it gave him—the knowledge that he would never again suffer the pain he had experienced when he had lost his parents.

Where Aldo thrived on tradition and continuity, Saul thrived on mastering challenges. And the Kovoca Island project was turning out to be a very considerable challenge indeed. Under-funded and over-budget, the original project had contributed to the financial downfall of the island's previous owner—who, it seemed to Saul, had wanted to outdo Dubai in his plans for the island.

Saul had already drawn a red line through his predecessor's plans for an underwater hotel, complete with a transparent underwater walkway, and for a road connecting the hotel and the island to the mainland. Just as he had drawn a red line through an equally over-ambitious plan to turn the island's single snow-capped mountain into a winter ski resort, complete with imported snow.

It was a pity that for now at least he could not draw a similar red line though Giselle Freeman's involvement in the project.

Everyone else might be celebrating the fact that the new owner of the Kovoca Island had given the go-ahead to the previous owner's project and was keeping them on as its architects, and were keen to show their commitment by working late into the evening, but Giselle had another client to deal with—which was why right now she was on her way to the car park to collect her car. She would drive over to the shabby offices of the small charity which, having been left a plot of land, was now keen to develop it into a community centre and accommodation for homeless people. The charity had appealed for architectural help with the project and Giselle had taken it on as a non-fee-paying commission, in her own free time, with the agreement of her employers that she could use their facilities.

It was important not only that the new building blended in with its surroundings and provided the facilities the charity wanted, but also that it would be affordable to build and to run, and Giselle had spent a great deal of her spare time looking into various ways of meeting all three of those targets.

Then tonight when she got home she would have to e-mail the matron of the retirement home in which her great-aunt lived to see if her aunt had recovered from her cold yet.

Meadowside was an excellent facility, and its elderly residents were really well cared for, but it was also extremely expensive. The invested money from the sale of Great-Aunt Maude's house paid half the monthly fees and Giselle paid the other half. It was the least she could do, given what her great aunt had done for her—taking her in, looking after her and loving her despite everything that had happened.

Giselle felt her stomach muscles starting to tense. It was always like this whenever she was forced to think about the past. She knew that she would never be able to forget what had happened. Even now if the squeal of car tyres caught her unawares the sound had the power to make her freeze into immobile panic. The memories, the images were always there—the wet road, the darkness, her mother telling her to hold on to the pram containing her baby brother as they turned to cross the road. But she hadn't held on to the pram. She had let go. She was starting to breathe too shallowly and too fast, her heart pounding sickly. The sounds—screams, screeching tyres, breaking glass—the spin of the pram's wheels as it lay there in the road, the smells—petrol, rain, blood.

No!

As always, the denial inside her was silent, as she had been silent, digging her nails into the palm of her hand. The hand that should have been gripping the pram handle—the hand which she had pulled away, defying her mother's screamed demand that she stayed where she was, holding onto the pram.

Giselle could see her mother's face now, and hear her screamed command; she could see her fear, and could see too the sleeping face of her baby brother where he'd lain in the pram just before it had left the pavement, straight in the path of an oncoming lorry.

It was over…over… There was no bringing back the dead. But it could never really be over—not for her. But at least no one else apart from her great-aunt knew what she knew.

Initially after the deaths of her mother and baby brother Giselle had continued to live with her father, an overworked GP, with a kind neighbour taking and collecting her from school along with her own children. That time had been the darkest of Giselle's life. Her father, overwhelmed by his own grief, had shut her out, excluding her, not wanting her around—as she had always felt—because she'd reminded him of what he had lost. His emotional distance from her had increased her guilt and her own misery.

And then her great-aunt had come to visit, and it had been arranged that when she returned home Giselle would go with her. She had longed for her father to insist that he wanted her to stay, just as she had longed for him to hold her and tell her that he loved her, that he didn't blame her. But he hadn't. She could see his face now— the last time she had seen it—as he'd nodded his head in agreement with her great-aunt's suggestions, gaunt and drawn, his gaze avoiding her. He had died less than six months afterwards from a fatal heart attack.

As a child Giselle had felt that he had chosen to die to be with her mother and brother rather than live and be with her. Even now sometimes, in her darkest and most despairing moments, she still thought that. If he'd loved her, he'd have kept her with him… But he hadn't.

Not that she'd been unhappy with her great-aunt. She hadn't. Her great-aunt had loved and cared for her, building a new life for her. Of course it had helped that her great-aunt had lived nearly a hundred miles away from the home Giselle had shared with her parents and her baby brother.

Giselle started to walk faster, as though to escape from her own painful memories. Even now, after nearly twenty years, she couldn't bear to think about what had happened. Her great-aunt had been wonderfully kind and generous in taking her in, and Giselle wanted to do everything she could to make sure the now very elderly lady was well looked after. Without her job it would of course be impossible for her to find the money needed to keep her aunt in her excellent retirement home. And

that meant that, no matter how much she might personally resent Saul Parenti and his attitude towards her, she
had to be grateful for the fact that he was continuing
with the project and keeping the firm on. These were
hard times, and to lose such a valuable source of income
would have meant redundancies.

Giselle had never imagined when she had been studying and working so hard for her qualifications that there
would be such a deep downturn in the economy—one
that would affect the construction industry so badly. She
had chosen architecture as her career in part because she
had believed that she would always be able to find work.
Work—and getting paid for it—were vitally important
to a woman who had already made up her mind that
she would have to provide for herself financially all her
life, because she was determined never to share her life
with a partner. And in part she had chosen it because
she had fallen in love with buildings—great houses and
other buildings owned by the National Trust which her
great-aunt had taken her to visit so often whilst she had
been growing up.

Engaged in her own thoughts, Giselle headed automatically for her parked car, but as she approached the
bay instead of seeing her own car all she could see was
the highly polished bonnet of a much larger vehicle in
the space where hers should have been. Automatically
her walking pace slowed, and then she stopped as she
looked round, wondering if she had been mistaken about
where she had parked. The click of a car door opening
caught her attention. She turned in the direction of the
sound, her heart plummeting as she saw Saul Parenti
getting out of the car with the long bonnet, the one that

was parked where she'd expected to see her own car, and coming towards her.

Her reaction was immediate—a gut-deep instinct that went beyond logic or reason, making her confront him and demand, before she could think about the recklessness of doing so, 'Where is my car? What have you done with it?'

For sheer blind arrogance he doubted she had any equal, Saul decided, listening to her and witnessing her immediate hostility.

Her response confirmed every judgement he had already made about her, and reinforced his growing determination to put her in her place.

'I had it removed from my parking space,' he told her meaningfully.

'Removed?' Giselle felt the file she was holding slip from her grasp as the shock hit her, disgorging papers as it fell. 'Removed?' she repeated 'How? Where to?'

She knew her voice was trembling under the weight of her shocked emotions, but as she dropped to her haunches to pick up the contents of her file she was helpless to control it. She hated the effect this man seemed to have on her. She had hated it from their first confrontation and she hated it even more now. It made her feel vulnerable and afraid—it made her behave with a defensive antagonism she couldn't control. It made her want to turn and run away from him. But most of all it made her so acutely aware of him as a man that she hardly dared even breathe, for fear he would somehow sense how physically aware of him her body was. It wasn't just the shameful stiffening of her nipples, nor even the shockingly purposeful beat of the gnawing

pulse aching through her lower body. No, it was the
feeling that a whole protective layer had been ripped
from every inch of her skin, leaving it so sensitive and
reactive to his physical presence that it was as though
he had already touched her so intimately that her body
knew him—and still wanted him.

How had this happened to her? Giselle didn't know. It
must be because of Saul himself—because of the intense
aura of male sexuality he gave off. No other man had
ever affected her like this. It shocked her that she could
be so vulnerable so quickly to a man she didn't know
and didn't think she'd like if she did know him. She'd
controlled her emotions and her desires for so long that
she'd believed she was safe. She must have let her guard
slip somehow without realising it. But she could make
things right again. She could make herself safe. All she
had to do was keep away from Saul Parenti—and that
should be easy enough. At least he didn't want her. That
would have been dreadful. She should be grateful for
the fact that he was so obviously furious with her.

'How?' he was repeating tauntingly. 'How are illegally parked cars normally removed? And as to where…'

She'd stepped back from him, giving him a haughty
look that suggested his proximity was something she
wanted to reject, Saul recognised, and his male pride
was now as antagonised by her attitude as his temper.
Women did not step back from him. Quite the opposite.
They clung to him—sometimes far more than he wanted
them to do.

Just for a moment Saul mentally allowed himself the
pleasure of picturing Giselle clinging to him, her face
turned up beseechingly towards his own. That would

be a *pleasure?* Having her want him to bed her? Was he going mad? There was nothing about her that aroused him sexually, nothing at all. He liked his women softly feminine, not challenging and aggressive. He liked them warm and welcoming, not icy cold and rejecting. The thought of taming such a shrew might excite some men, but he was not one of them.

Having stepped back from Saul to what she hoped was a safe distance from the lure of his sexuality, Giselle managed to drag together the determination to insist, 'My car was not parked illegally, and if you've had it clamped and towed away then *you* are the one who is breaking the law.'

Oh, yes, she was definitely a shrew, Saul decided as he bent to retrieve a stray sheet of paper that had fluttered close to his feet. Automatically he scanned the print on it and then paused to read it more slowly before demanding, 'You're working on this project free of charge?'

Desperate to retrieve the paper, Giselle reached for it, almost snatching it from him in her fear of accidentally coming into physical contact with him.

'And what if I am?' she defended herself sharply. 'It doesn't have anything to do with you, and you have no right to question me.'

There she went again, challenging him with her open animosity to him, when by rights she ought to be humbling herself, admitting her previous fault and seeking his forgiveness.

He had, Saul decided, had enough.

The history of his genes meant that he was not a man who allowed anyone to challenge him, and for a challenge to go unanswered was unthinkable. He might not rule Arezzio, but his ancestors had. They had ruled it and held it against all those who had challenged their right to it. Their blood flowed in his veins and those who defied him—in any way—did so at their own risk.

'You think not?'

The silky tone of his voice had an electrifying effect on her, causing the fine hairs at the nape of her neck to stand on end, her flesh to react as though he had touched it, caressed it.

'I understand from Mr Shepherd at the practice that your job is very important to you?'

'He told you that?' The words were spoken before Giselle could hold them back. She shivered inwardly with apprehension, unable to conceal the shocked fear that darkened her green eyes to a deep jade. She hadn't realised that Mr Shepherd even knew how much her job security mattered to her, never mind discussing it with someone else.

So he had found something that made her feel vulnerable. Saul applauded himself.

'He said that you had turned down far more prestigious job offers and career opportunities to remain with the firm—something which he appears to consider a mark of employee loyalty. I, on the other hand, believe your motivation must be something far more powerful, and am curious to know just what it is.'

He was curious about her? Even as he had spoken the words Saul had felt the jolt of wariness that had shocked through him.

What was it about this woman that was having such an unprecedented effect on him? First she antagonised

him and aroused his anger. Now she was arousing his
curiosity. Deep within him a normally silent voice was
asking him the unthinkable. If she could touch the emotions he normally controlled so tightly that they were
immune to being touched, and if he allowed himself to
be aroused physically by her, then what would happen?
Did he really need to ask? He knew, after all, what happened when someone put a light to a keg of dynamite.
The result was destruction. *Destruction?* Did this infuriating woman have the power to arouse him to the point
where that arousal could destroy the barriers he had put
in place to keep him immune to the weakness of needing
one specific other person in his life? Impossible, Saul
reassured himself.

Saul was waiting for her response, Giselle knew—just
as she knew that she didn't want to answer him.

'Why stay in a job for which you are over-qualified
and I daresay underpaid? Unless, of course, you fear
that all those qualifications of yours are merely pieces
of paper and that in reality you are not up to the work
you would be required to do at a higher level.'

Saul pressed her, determined not to step back from
his probing just because of an inner warning he refused
to give credence to.

His accusation jolted Giselle into an immediate
repudiation.

'Of course I'm up to it.' Angry pride reflected in both
Giselle's voice and the look she gave him. 'And I am
confident that I could do any job I was offered.'

'Are you now?' Her assertion showed him yet another
strand to her personality. With the revelation of each
new strand he felt increasingly compelled to know more

about her. Because she infuriated and antagonised him. Because she was so unlike any other woman he knew. Because she didn't treat him as they did, with delight and docility, eager to please him and pleasure him, his own inner voice dryly mocked him.

She was obviously determined not to answer him, but Saul was equally determined that he would have an answer. He changed tack, saying silkily, 'Correct me if I am wrong, but the Kovoca Island project is, as I understand it, all that currently stands between your employers and insolvency—and with that insolvency the loss of your job?'

Giselle's mouth went dry and her heart started pounding wretchedly heavily as she recognised the threat in his words. She was forced to concede. 'Yes, that is correct.'

'Given your employer has suggested to me that it will facilitate matters if you are seconded to me, to ensure that in future all redrawn plans and costings are in line with my requirements, I should have thought that it is only natural that I would have the right to enquire into your reliability and your probity—in all professional matters.'

Silenced by the shock of what she had just learned, Giselle could only stare at him in appalled dismay.

This couldn't be happening. He—her tormentor— could not be standing there saying that she would be working directly with him, that she would in effect be responsible to him and thus in his power. But he was, Giselle acknowledged as she fought against the panic washing through her at full flood force. If only she could tell him to find someone else to be seconded to him.

If only she could turn on her heel and walk away from him…if only he didn't affect her in the way that he did. So many if onlys. Her life was full of them—heart-sickening, cruelly destructive words that spoke of what could never be. She was trapped, by duty and by love, and she had to hold on to this job even though that now meant that she would be in Saul's power.

At least he did not know how vulnerable she was to him as a woman, Giselle tried to comfort herself. A man like him must be so used to arousing desire in her sex that he simply took it for granted—just as he seemed to take his pick of the beautiful women who flocked around him, from what Emma had told her. Well, he'd certainly never want to pick her. Thank goodness.

'It is not my choice that you be my point person on this project,' Saul pointed out. 'And given what I already know about your inclination towards theft I must warn you that you will be very much on probation. The first sign I see that you are using the same unscrupulous methods you used to gain access to my parking space in your work, you will be out of a job.'

'I made a mistake—' Giselle tried to defend herself, but Saul wasn't in any mood to be compassionate.

'A very big mistake,' he agreed. 'And you will be making another if you don't show some honesty now and tell me why you turned down two prestigious jobs. I won't have someone whose morals I find suspect working for me in a position of trust.'

His meaning was perfectly plain, and it caused Giselle to blench.

Watching her, Saul felt confident that now she would tell him what he could do with his job. That was certainly what he wanted her to do. Loath as he was to admit it, somehow or other she had got under his skin in a way that he was finding increasingly hard to ignore—like an annoying, irritating, unignorable itch that needed to be scratched. He didn't want that kind of intrusion in his life.

Giselle was trying not to let Saul see how vulnerable and anxious she felt. He wanted her to hand in her notice, she suspected. But she was not going to do so. She couldn't.

His accusations might be unjust, and she might feel angry, but anger was a luxury that she couldn't afford, Giselle was forced to concede.

She took a deep breath and said, as calmly as she could, 'Very well. I will tell you.'

Her response was not what Saul had been expecting—and very definitely not what he had wanted.

Lifting her head, Giselle continued, 'I turned down the other jobs because the great-aunt who brought me up now needs full-time care, and in addition to helping fund that I want to be here to ensure that the care is as good as the care she gave me. I can't expect her to leave Yorkshire after she's spent her whole life there, but I do expect myself to be here for her, doing everything I can to ensure that she has all the comfort and care she deserves. Working in London means that I can see her regularly. If I worked abroad that wouldn't be possible.'

Against all his own expectations Saul felt an unwilling tug of grudging respect—and something more.

'You were brought up by your great-aunt? What

happened to your parents?' he felt impelled to ask, the words almost dragged from him against his will.

'They died, and I was orphaned,' Giselle answered as steadily as she could, proud of how calm she managed to keep her voice.

Damn, *damn*. Saul swore inwardly as the result of his forcefulness was made plain to him along with something else—something that touched the deepest part of him, no matter how much he might wish that it did not. That single word 'orphaned' had such resonance for him—such personal and deep-rooted private emotional history.

He might have forced a confession from Giselle Freeman, but he wasn't going to be able to force a resignation from her, given what she had just told him.

He started to turn away from her, and then something stopped him. 'How old were you when…when you lost your parents?'

His voice was low, the words betraying something which in another man Giselle might almost have thought was a hushed, respectful hesitancy. But this man would never show that kind of compassion to anyone, Giselle was sure—much less someone he disliked as much as he had made it plain he disliked her.

'Seven.' Well, nearly seven. But there hadn't been a party to celebrate her November birthday that year—just as there hadn't been the year before either. A picture slid remorselessly into her head: coffins, two of them, one for her mother and one for the baby brother who had been buried with her, his coffin heaped with white flowers. And the house she had returned to with her father, filled with the agonising silence of his grief and her own guilt. She had longed so much for her father to hold her and tell her that it wasn't her fault, but instead he had turned away from her, and she'd known he did blame her, just as she blamed herself. They had never talked about what had happened. Instead he had let her great-aunt take her away because he couldn't bear the sight of her.

Seven! A thought, a fleeting memory of himself at that age, hazy and shadowed: his mother laughing as she stroked a smear of dirt from his cheek, how as that child he had felt his love for her and his happiness because she was there spill out of him to mix with the sunshine.

Saul felt the sour taste of his own revulsion against whatever it was that allowed children to be deprived of the love of their parents. He had been eighteen and he had found it hard enough to cope, even though by then he had thought himself independent and adult.

More memories were surging through the barriers Giselle wanted to put up against them. The other children at the new school she had gone to when her great-aunt had taken her in, feeling sorry for her because she didn't have parents. They had meant to be kind, of course, but then they hadn't known the truth.

In her desperation to close the door on those memories, Giselle made a small agonised sound of protest. She wished desperately that her car was here. If it had been she could have stepped past him and got into it and escaped, putting an end to her present humiliation.

Saul, hearing that sound and recognising the pain it contained—a pain he himself had felt and knew—heard himself saying before he could stop himself, 'I lost my

parents when I was eighteen. You think at that age that
everyone is immortal.'

Silently they looked at one another.

What was he doing? Saul derided himself. This wasn't
the sort of conversation he had with anyone, never mind
a woman who rubbed him up the wrong way and whom
he'd already decided he didn't particularly like. It had
been that word *orphaned* that had done it. Seven years
old and taken in by a great-aunt she now had to help
support. That explained the cheap suit, Saul reflected.

She'd implied that there wasn't currently a man in her
life, but she must have had lovers. She might not be his
type, but he'd be lying to himself if he didn't admit that
physically she had the kind of looks that turned male
heads, and that mix of stitched-up coldness allied to the
suppressed passion that flashed in her eyes when she
couldn't quite control it would have plenty of members
of his sex keen to pursue her.

Fire and ice—that was what she was. How many
lovers had she had? he wondered, the question sneak-
ing up on him before he could stop it. Two? Three?
Certainly no more than could be counted on the fingers of one hand, he suspected. What was he thinking?
Whatever it was he must stop now—must not allow it
to get hold and take root.

'What happened to your parents? Mine died carrying
out aid work at the site of an earthquake, when a huge
aftershock destroyed the building they were in.'

Giselle's muscles clenched—both against what he
was saying and against the shock of his question.

'After my parents' death I wanted to talk about it, but

no one would let me. I suppose they thought it would be too...' he stopped.

'Too painful for you.' Giselle supplied, her voice cracking slightly, like an unhealed scab over a still raw wound.

What had been a hostile confrontation between them had somehow or other veered sharply into something else and somewhere else—a territory that was both familiar to her and yet at the same time unexplored by her. Because she was too afraid? Because it hurt too much?

She spoke slowly at first, the effort of speaking about something so deeply traumatic and personal making her throat feel raw.

'My mother and...and my baby brother were killed in a road accident. My father died from a heart attack eleven months after the accident.'

'I'm sorry.' He was, Saul recognised. Sorry for the child she had been, sorry for her loss, sorry he had asked now that he knew the full extent of the tragedy.

'Life is so fragile,' Giselle heard herself telling him. 'My baby brother was only six months old.' She shuddered. "I can't imagine how parents must feel when they lose a child—especially one so young—or how they cope with the responsibility of protecting such vulnerability. I'd never have a second's peace. I could never...I would never want that responsibility.'

There was a finality in her words that found an echo within him.

She had said too much, revealed and betrayed too much, Giselle recognised. Not that she had told him everything. She would never and could never tell anyone everything. Some things were so painful, so shocking and so dark that they could never be shared—had to be kept hidden away from everyone. She could just imagine how people would treat her if they knew the truth, how suspicious of her they would be—and with good reason. No, she could never speak openly about her guilt or her fear. They were burdens she must carry alone.

But she must not dwell on the past, but instead live in the present, with her duty to her great-aunt. Determinedly she focused her thoughts on the issue that had led to this unexpected and far too intimate conversation, telling Saul, 'If you want to cancel the secondment now that you have the answer to your question…'

She wanted him to cancel the secondment, Saul recognised, ignoring the fact that he had wanted to cancel it himself as he let his male drive to win take over.

'You wouldn't have been my choice. However, I don't have the time to interview other applicants. Of course if you want to withdraw…' He let the offer hang there.

'You already know that I can't,' Giselle said stiffly.

Saul shrugged.

'I doubt that either of us is happy with the situation, but for different reasons it seems that we shall have to endure it and make the best of it.'

Giselle exhaled. Talking about her past had drained her emotionally and physically, and now she felt dreadfully weak and shaky—but there was still something she needed to know.

'My car—' she began, and then stopped when she realised how thin and thready her voice sounded. She was perilously close to the limits of her self-control, she knew. Her head was beginning to ache from the stress of their confrontation. Her lips felt dry. She moistened them with the tip of her tongue.

Saul watched the telltale movement of her tongue-tip, his gaze sliding unwillingly down to the small movement of her throat as she swallowed. Her upswept hair revealed the length of her neck and the neat shape of her ears. Mauve shadows lay beneath her eyes like small bruises; her face was drained of any other colour. Something inside him ached and twisted, an emotion he didn't recognise giving birth to an impulse to reach out and touch her, hold her.

Hold her? Why?

Why? He was a man, wasn't he? And the way she had just drawn attention to her own mouth had had its obvious effect on his body. That was why he felt impelled to touch her. Right now, if he leaned forward and pressed his thumb to that special place behind her ear, if he stroked his fingertips the length of her throat, if he ran his tongue over the soft pillows of flesh that were her lips, he could make her pale skin flush softly with the warmth of arousal. He could make the pulse beat in her throat with desire for him. He could make those green eyes darken to jade and the breath shudder from her lungs. Saul took a step towards her.

Immediately Giselle stepped back from him, with a gasp of sound that brought him back to reality. What the hell was the matter with him? Saul castigated himself. The last thing he felt for her was desire, and the second last thing he wanted was her desire for him. Stepping back from her, he reached for his mobile and spoke into it, announcing, 'You can bring the car back now.'

Less than five minutes later Giselle watched as her

car was driven into the car park towards her. A uniformed driver got out and handed over the keys to Saul before heading for Saul's own gleaming car.

Without a word Giselle got into her car. She had no idea how they had acquired keys for it, and she wasn't going to ask. She was beginning to suspect that for a man like Saul Parenti anything and everything was achievable.

Saul watched her drive away. Fire and ice—a dangerous combination, designed to tempt the strongest-willed man when combined in a woman. He, though, could and would resist that temptation.

CHAPTER THREE

IT WAS nearly two weeks now since Giselle had begun her new duties in the impressive modern office building that was the headquarters of Saul Parenti's business empire, and of course she wasn't in the least bit disappointed that not once during those two very busy weeks had she seen Saul himself and that the glass-fronted office his PA had pointed out to her as his had remained empty. Far from it. She was delighted that he wasn't in evidence, and that she had been able to take up her new role without having to contend with his presence.

Or at least she had been until something had come to light this morning, whilst she had been checking over the latest batch of reworked plans couriered over to her.

Was what she had picked up a simple mistake? Was it a trick to try and catch her out, instituted by Saul himself? Or was it—and her stomach tensed at the thought of this—a deliberate attempt to defraud the Parenti Organisation, put in place by one of her own colleagues?

Whichever of the three options she chose to believe, the initial outcome was the same, and that was that she would have to report what she had seen to Saul Parenti.

Giselle looked towards the office of Saul's PA, Moira Wilson, wondering if she should discuss her concern with her.

She liked the older woman, who had gone out of her way to make her feel at home in her new environment. On her first morning here, Moira had gone through everything with her, informing her with a smile, 'I'll just run through a few things with you. First, we are all on first-name terms here—Saul insists on it. But don't mistake that for a lack of discipline or respect. He demands and gets both. I've got some forms here from HR for you to fill in—personal details, that kind of thing. Whilst you're here your salary will be increased in accordance with the levels Saul pays those who work for him, and you will be eligible for an annual bonus, medical insurance, and a car allowance. Any expenses you incur in the course of your work should be submitted to the accounts department on a monthly basis, and I should warn you that here we do not have a culture of fudging such expenses—if you take my meaning.'

This last piece of information had been accompanied by a grim look which had ensured that Giselle knew exactly what she meant.

'I never fudge my expenses. It would go against my principles to do so,' Giselle had responded truthfully.

'Excellent. I am sure you will fit in very well here,' had been Moira's response, before she had added, 'Oh, and when you complete your personal details form I shall need your passport details.'

'My passport?'

'Yes. You do have one, don't you? If not we must sort one out for you, just in case you are required to

travel abroad on behalf of the company with Saul—to
site meetings and that kind of thing. Saul takes a very
personal and keen interest in all his projects, and is very
hands-on about checking their progress.'

'Yes,' she had a passport, Giselle had confirmed.
She was also used to travelling abroad to conferences
and site meetings with clients—so why on earth had
that tingle of something she refused to name zipped
down her spine? It was doing so now, at the memory—
as though someone had feathered a touch against her
bare skin. What was happening to her? Nothing, Giselle
assured herself fiercely. Nothing was happening to her
and nothing was going to happen to her. Normally she
enjoyed visiting the various sites she worked on, especially when they were abroad. It made up for the fact that
she had missed out on the kind of foreign trips enjoyed
by most of her peers when they had been growing up.

Her great-aunt simply hadn't had the money for
that kind of luxury. Additionally, the circumstances
of her life—the dreadful tragedy that still haunted her
and filled her with guilt—meant that she had always
been wary of allowing others to get close to her even
as friends, so she hadn't joined in the group holidays
abroad enjoyed by her peers during her early twenties,
even when she could have financed them herself. Instead
she had concentrated on getting the very best qualifications she could. Then, when she had started to think
about taking solo holidays to explore the architecture
of other countries, her great-aunt had needed to move
into residential care, and once again there simply hadn't
been the money for such unnecessary expenses.

Giselle judged Moira to be somewhere in her early

fifties, which had surprised her. From Emma's comments about Saul's lifestyle she had imagined that his PA would be glamorous and nubile, not a woman of Moira's age, even if she was a very smart and elegant fifty-something. Her appearance was much like that of the other women Giselle had seen in the offices, making her acutely conscious of the shabbiness of her own clothes. There was nothing she could do about that, though. Only two days ago she had received a letter informing her that regrettably the fees for her great-aunt's care and accommodation were to be increased by twenty per cent—not far short of the unexpected increase in her salary. There were cheaper care homes, but Giselle was determined that her great-aunt would go on enjoying the level of comfort she had where she was—even if that did mean she herself would have to go without the new clothes she had been tempted to buy, having seen how smart the other women working here were.

Now, as she looked round her spacious office, Giselle admitted that in many ways she preferred her new working environment—even if she would rather have worked for the devil himself than Saul Parenti. She doubted that she would be missed by her old colleagues. The men she worked with had shown quite plainly prior to her departure that they resented the fact that she had been selected over them for what they considered to be a prestigious and career-boosting opportunity, and of course her own pride had not allowed her to tell them that she would have preferred not to be chosen. However, it was the well-meaning Emma's words that were still sending scalding waves of humiliation burning painfully through Giselle's emotions.

She had spoken to her in private. 'It's just as well that it's you who's been seconded to go and work for Saul Parenti. If it was anyone else then all the other girls would be seething with jealousy at the thought of someone getting the opportunity to work closely with such a fabulously sexy man. But of course they won't be jealous of you, because they all know that there's no danger of you attracting him—not with your attitude to men and the way you give them the cold shoulder. Especially not with a man like Saul, who can have any woman he wants.'

Giselle knew it was ridiculous of her to feel humiliated by Emma's remarks—somehow less of a woman. After all, Giselle herself had always made it plain that she wasn't interested in flirting with or attracting men, cold-shouldering their advances and retreating into herself whenever they showed any interest in her. The last thing she wanted was a man pursuing her—any man—and especially a man like Saul Parenti. Why especially him? Because she was afraid that she might be vulnerable to him? Because she was afraid that she might actually want him?

Giselle stood up, panicked by her own thoughts, and then subsided back into her chair. Of course not. It was nothing to do with anything like that. She knew that she was perfectly safe from desiring Saul Parenti, and even if by some foolish misjudgement she did, she also knew that it was impossible for anything to come of that desire. Because, as Emma had made clear, Saul Parenti would never find her desirable? No! Because she did not *want* him to desire her—just as she did not want *any* man to desire her.

She had taken refuge in angry disdain, demanding of Emma, 'Does everything have to come down to sex?'

Emma had laughed and told her, 'For most of us—yes.' Before adding, 'Men can't help being men, and they are predatory by instinct. It's in their genes. But in your case... Well, what I'm trying to say, Giselle, is that...'

'That a man like Saul Parenti wouldn't find me desirable enough to want to go to the trouble of trying to seduce me?' Giselle had supplied for her colleague.

'Well, you do send a keep-your-distance vibe to men, you must admit, and men like Saul Parenti have plenty of women all too ready to give them what they want to be bothered with a woman who freezes them off. I haven't hurt your feelings, have I?' Emma had asked anxiously.

Giselle had shaken her head.

'No, of course not.' Giselle had assured her. And that was the truth. Of course she wasn't hurt because Emma had spoken the truth and said that Saul wouldn't be interested in her. She didn't want him to be. She didn't want *any* man to be interested in her. She couldn't afford to allow any man to become interested in her because she knew that she could not and must not become interested in them. She could never have in her life the relationships that others took for granted. She could not fall in love. She could not commit to anyone, and most of all she could not within that commitment help to create a child. She must never have a child. Never.

Anyway, how she looked and whether Saul Parenti did or did not see her as attractive were not subjects she should be paying any mind to. Instead she must focus on the reason she was here and on what she was being paid to do.

The office provided for her was well planned out and perfect for her duties, with its large windows flooding the room with natural light. It contained all the equipment she might need, including a good-sized table in the middle of the floor on which she was able to spread out paper copies of architectural drawings and plans—just as she had done earlier, with the new drawings and costings that had been sent over.

Uncertainly Giselle looked back at them. She had been worrying about them for so long, going back to check and then recheck them just in case she had made a mistake, that she hadn't realised how late it was. Scanning the office, she saw nearly everyone else had gone home. Moira had gone too, no doubt, without Giselle having taken the opportunity to speak with her and seek her advice.

The anomaly was definitely there. The non-frostproof terracotta tiles for the summerhouse and the area surrounding it, leading to the first of the staggered-level swimming pools, had been changed as Saul had instructed. But the tiles used in substitution were considerably more expensive, and from a supplier whose name Giselle could not remember having seen on their approved lists. As a precaution she had e-mailed a couple of approved suppliers, and they had both come back with costings far lower than the one quoted—which meant that either by accident or design the person responsible for the changed plans and materials was recommending a purchase that would cost far far more than it needed to. To make matters worse, the tiles recommended had a non-standard raised pattern, which meant that in future, should any one of them need replacing, they would have to be specially produced at a very high cost. And, worst of all by far, the person responsible for the recommendation and costing was her male colleague and adversary Bill Jeffries.

She'd e-mailed him to check discreetly with him that there hadn't been an error but it appeared that he was on leave for a week, and with Saul due back from his overseas trip in the morning there was no way Giselle could hold the plans and costings back from him until Bill Jeffries returned to the office.

She needed someone else's input and advice, she decided, making up her mind. Through the plate glass that fronted all the mezzanine offices she was delighted to spot Moira, putting on her suit jacket and preparing to leave. It had been a warm day for mid-April, with the sun streaming in through the windows, and Giselle had removed her own jacket to work more easily. She looked hesitantly at it, and then, seeing Moira heading for the door, scooped up the papers from the desk instead and hurried to intercept her.

'From what you've told me, I rather think this is something you need to discuss with Saul,' Moira judged firmly, once Giselle had reached the end of her story.

'I know he isn't due back until tomorrow, and I expect he'll have a full diary. Perhaps you…?' Giselle began, only to have Moira shake her head.

'He's actually just arrived and he's in his office,' she told her. 'Why don't you go and have a word with him now?'

Giselle's heart sank. This wasn't what she had expected or wanted to hear.

Witnessing her hesitation and reluctance, Saul's PA insisted, 'I really do think you should, Giselle. This sounds like a potentially serious matter to me, and Saul won't thank you for delaying informing him about it.' Moira looked at her watch. 'I'm sorry—I must run. I've promised to take the notes for a committee meeting of our Gardening Club this evening, and I mustn't be late. But I know Saul's planning to work late, and I can assure you that he will want to know what you've just told me. That's why you're here after all.'

It was too late now to wish that she'd kept quiet and not sought Moira's advice. Taking a deep breath, Giselle headed towards Saul's office.

Like the other offices on the mezzanine floor, Saul's was fronted by plate glass 'walls'. It might be larger than the other offices, and it might have a private inner sanctum, but that apart it was no more prestigiously furnished than her own office, Giselle noted, and it was equipped as a practical working office. Apparently for business meetings Saul used the hospitality suite on the top floor of the building.

Since Saul operated an 'open door' working policy, Giselle only knocked briefly on the glass door, which was in any event half open, before stepping into Saul's office. The brilliance of the late-afternoon sun shone into the room, momentarily blinding her, so that she didn't realise until her vision cleared that Saul wasn't there—despite the fact that his laptop was open on his desk and his suit jacket was hanging from the back of his chair. Why was it that only a certain type of very male European man seemed able to wear that particular shade of light tan successfully, whilst looking as though they could have stepped out of an Armani ad? Giselle found herself wondering distractedly. She tried very hard not to picture Saul in just that role—only to be betrayed by her traitorous imagination which suddenly, out of nowhere, managed to create an all too realistic image of Saul standing in for one of the designer's male underwear models.

Battling with her own imagination, Giselle almost dropped the papers she was hugging to her when the door connecting Saul's inner office with the outer one suddenly opened, and Saul himself stepped through it.

His easy words—'Moira, if you could manage to rustle up some coffee and a sandwich whilst I have a shower I'll be eternally grateful to you...'—changed to an abrupt and far less welcoming, 'Oh, it's you,' when he realised that it was Giselle who was standing in his office and not his PA.

It wasn't his abrupt manner that was driving hot, self-conscious colour up under her skin, though. Giselle knew that as she struggled to retain her equilibrium under the increased pounding of her heart when she realised that when he had initially come into the room Saul had been starting to unfasten his shirt. The cuffs were already loose, revealing the sinewy dark-hair-covered flesh of one arm as he reached up to push his hand into his hair in a gesture of irritation. His tie was missing and the top buttons of his shirt were unfastened, so that she could see the fine criss-crossing of the beginnings of his body hair. The rush of female awareness that

flooded through her almost knocked her off balance
with an alien, almost frightening power. She wasn't used
to feeling like this, and the fact that she was doing so
affronted and angered her, causing her to clutch the
papers even more tightly to her body.

The crackle they made focused Saul's attention on
her. She was breathing too fast, her lips parted, her hands
trembling slightly as she gripped some papers in front of
her. Her pose was almost that of an ancient civilisation
virgin slave, facing the master who had bought her for
his pleasure—and with it her own.

The direction his thoughts were taking didn't please
Saul one little bit. He'd spent the last ten days engaged
in hard negotiation to secure the prime Chinese sites he
wanted for his expanding hotel chain—hard negotiation and also what had seemed at the time easy refusal
of sexual favours from the socialites his hosts had introduced him to. Perhaps his body hadn't been as on-
message with that refusal as he had believed, he decided
grimly as he attempted to banish the images his mind
was now busy conjuring up—images of a green-eyed,
blonde-haired beauty wearing next to nothing, offering
him the welcome and the pleasure battle-scarred war-
riors like his own ancestors had expected to receive as a
matter of course. He, on the other hand, whilst returning
triumphant from his own battle, couldn't get so much
as a drink and a sandwich, and was being confronted
by the abrasive secondee he had no wish to have in his
life.

Giselle's voice cut across his thoughts. 'I can come
back tomorrow if you're too busy to see me now.'

'I'm leaving for New York tomorrow. If it's urgent

enough for you to come and see me now, then you'd better tell me whatever it is that's brought you here. Sit down,' he commanded, before speaking into the intercom. 'Charlie, would you mind getting me a double espresso and a sandwich from across the road? Put it on my tab. I'll be in my office.'

Charlie was the doorman, as Giselle knew.

'Right,' he said to Giselle when he had finished. 'What's the problem?'

'I'm a bit concerned about a costing on one of the new plans,' Giselle answered. 'I've got the paperwork here.'

Saul made an exasperated sound.

'I can't see it whilst you're clutching it like that, can I? Bring it here and put it on the desk.'

A shaft of sunlight penetrating the shadows around his desk gave the cheap white tee shirt she was wearing an opacity that drew Saul's gaze automatically to her breasts as she dropped the papers on his desk. Her actions dragged the thin fabric against her body, so that her nipples were outlined in erotically sharp relief. His gaze lingered where the shaft of light was probing the cheap fabric, as though it possessed a male need to strip back the covering from her flesh and explore the sensuality beneath.

She must focus on why she was here and forget about the way her proximity to Saul Parenti was making her feel, Giselle told herself. But how could she when she could almost *feel* Saul's critical gaze, underlining Emma's comments about her?

The arrival of the doorman with Saul's coffee and sandwich was a welcome relief, allowing her to straighten the papers and then step back from the desk whilst Saul thanked Charlie, rewarding him with a warm smile and a few words of male banter about the doorman's favourite football team. So there was a human side to Saul Parenti—even if she was never likely to see much of it. Giselle had no idea why that should bring her such a sense of loss and exclusion. She didn't *want* him to be nice to her. Not one little bit.

'So what exactly is the problem?' Saul demanded, sitting back in his chair and drinking his coffee.

'It's this reworked plan, here,' Giselle told him. She had to lean across the desk to point out the part of the plan in question, too intent on getting the ordeal of what she had to say over and done with to be aware of the way in which her pose had brought her breasts in line with Saul's gaze.

Saul was, though. And so was his body. And it was reacting very specifically indeed to those soft teardrop-shaped curves with their tip-tilted nipples. He eased his chair closer to the desk, to conceal the giveaway tightening of his trousers as his erection swelled demandingly against the fabric. His hunger for the sandwich the doorman had brought him had suddenly been replaced by a very different and even more insistent kind of hunger.

'And your conclusion?' Saul interrupted Giselle curtly. He needed to get her out of his office and get his body back under control—and the sooner the better.

Giselle's face burned. It was obvious that Saul didn't want to listen to her and thought that she was wasting his time.

'There are three possibilities,' she answered crisply, straightening up and stepping back from the desk. 'One:

the person who drew up the plan and its costing made an error. Two: they knew what they were doing and this is a deliberate attempt to defraud your company...'

'And three?' Saul queried, recognising now that she had moved back from him that she had spotted something that could be very serious indeed. He was in no mood to thank her, though. Not whilst his body's reaction to her was so intense and unwanted.

'Three: you are deliberately testing me by setting up an error to see what I will do.'

Saul stared at her, anger driving out his desire to get rid of her.

'Let me get this straight. Are you actually suggesting that I would stoop to that kind of game-playing?'

Giselle lifted her head

'Why not? You had my car moved.'

Saul came out from behind his desk and walked towards her. Immediately Giselle took a step back from him. She could smell the hot male scent of him and it was making her dizzy, weak, igniting a low, dull, pulsing ache that was taking over her whole body.

'That was nothing more than an indication of my irritation on the day,' Saul told her flatly,

Giselle defended her suspicions. 'You don't want me here.'

'No,' Saul agreed, 'I don't.'

And then he did what he had sworn he would not do, cursing himself beneath his breath as he reached for her, pulling her fiercely into his arms and kissing her with all the pent-up fury she had aroused in him from the moment he had first seen her.

Giselle tried to resist him. She certainly *wanted* to

resist him. But the hand she raised to push him away
had developed a will of its own and was sliding along
his bare arm beneath the sleeve of his shirt, and the
body that should have been arching away from him was
instead melting into him.

She was all fire, nectar and ambrosia, heated by her
desire to run intoxicatingly through his senses, until he
was filled by his need for the scent, the feel, the taste
and the sound of her as he coupled her desire to his own.
His hand reached for her breast, pushing away the fabric
that came between her flesh and his touch with all the
urgency and impatience of a young untried youth. The
dying sunlight embraced her pale flesh, firing it with its
caress, and the ruby darkness of her nipple was a hard
thrust of flesh that mirrored in its own way his own taut
arousal.

Beneath the pressure of his kiss he could feel and
taste her gasp of undeniable response to him. He wanted
to devour her, consume her, take her and drive them
both until they were equally satiated—even whilst the
anger within him that she should make him feel that
way roared and burned its resentment of his need.

She was helpless, Giselle recognised, totally unable
to withstand the storm lashing at her, able only to cling
to the man who was the cause of it and pray that she
would survive whilst her body opened all its gateways
and let down its barriers to admit the rolling, roiling
ferocity that was now possessing her.

This was what she had feared, what she had denied
herself for so long, and she had been right to do so,
because to suffer what she was suffering now would
surely destroy her.

Somewhere else in the building a door banged. The sound exploded into the sensual tension that had enclosed them, driving them apart. Saul's chest was rising and falling as he fought for control; Giselle's whole body was trembling.

Without a word she turned and ran, fleeing as though she was being pursued by the devil himself, not stopping until she had reached her own office, where she quickly gathered up her jacket and her bag, not daring to look behind her as she fled the building.

Saul watched her in silence. He wanted her to go. He wanted what had happened not to have happened. He wanted—

Saul closed his eyes as his body told him exactly what it wanted—no matter what he might think about its desire and no matter how much he might want to reject it. Rolling up the papers Giselle had left behind, Saul slammed them down on the desk as anger against his unwanted physical ache for her savaged his self-control.

CHAPTER FOUR

GISELLE could see from the illuminated face of her small bedside clock that it was almost half past two in the morning, but sleep was impossible. How could she possibly sleep after what had happened? She had no idea why Saul had kissed her. She could only presume it had been his way of punishing her. He had been so angry when she had dared to suggest that he might have tried to trick her.

What had he expected her to do? He had made it plain that he didn't want her seconded to him. He had even said that he would be waiting for her to prove herself not up to the job so that he could demand a replacement for her. Under such circumstances surely anyone would need to be suspicious in order to protect themselves.

In fact for all she knew her suspicions were correct, and his anger could have been because she had not fallen into the trap he had set for her. Had he kissed her as a way of trying to force her to leave? If only she could do just that. If only she could ask, even beg her employers to send someone else to Saul in her place.

She'd picked up a newspaper on her way home, in the desperate hope that by some miracle she might find a job advertised in it that would offer her a means of escape.

She had even gone online to check out some job search websites, but the reality was that nobody was hiring in the current climate—and, much as she hated to admit it, the increased salary Saul Parenti was paying her meant that it would be impossible for her to find another job in London that would pay her as much.

As much as she loathed the blow her pride would suffer every day she had to step across the threshold of the Parenti Organisation, and despite her suspicions that Saul was doing everything he could to manipulate her into leaving, the debt she owed her great-aunt was such that she would just have to bear it. Without her great-aunt… Giselle dreaded to think what would have happened to her if her elderly relative had not stepped in and offered her a home, a safe haven. She had been so kind to her—shielding her, protecting her—but Giselle had caught the small fragments of adult conversations that had dropped to whispers, and then shaken heads and knowing looks when those adults had realised that she was there. She had known they were talking about her, known too of their suspicions about her. As a child she'd had nightmares, dreaming of ghostly voices reaching out to accuse her, and ghostly hands reaching out to drag her down into the darkness.

It had never been discussed between them, but Giselle knew that her great-aunt knew about the secret that could never be spoken. How could she not know when it had been the direct cause of her mother and baby brother's deaths and the indirect cause of her father's? She didn't know the exact details, though—that Giselle had deliberately disobeyed her mother, that she had let go of the pram, pulling back onto the pavement and then watching as the pram's momentum had carried it and her baby brother, and then her mother, who had clutched desperately at the pram's handle, straight under the front wheels of a lorry.

She would never sleep now. She was too afraid of the memories that would surface if she did. She must not go down that dark and tormenting road. She already knew where it led, and the horrors that waited for her at its end.

If only her life could be different. If only right here, right now, there were comforting, loving male arms waiting to enfold her—a strong male chest for her to lean on, and the protection of a man who understood and forgave all that there was to understand and forgive and still went on loving her.

If only there was a man in her life—a lover—whose desire for her and hers for him could prevent her from suffering the sharp pangs of aching sexual need she had felt earlier in Saul's arms, when her body had been on fire with the intensity of what he had aroused within her.

But there wasn't. There never would be; there never could be. The kind of man she wanted to love, the kind of lover she wanted to share such intimacy with, would be the kind of man who carried in his genes a need for the traditional things in life: a relationship, commitment, children.

Children! A shudder galvanised her body. She could not, *must* not ever have a child. And equally she could not and must not ever put a man she might love in a position where loving her back would mean that he would be deprived of his own right to be a parent.

The wilder shores of sexual promiscuity and the supposed 'fun' they afforded were not for her. Even if her own nature had not inclined her against them, Giselle suspected that her upbringing by her great-aunt would have done so.

Until now—until Saul Parenti—she had been free to believe that her sexuality was under her own control, and that there was no danger whatsoever of her physical desire for a man making her want to break the rules she had set for herself.

Until now.

Those few minutes in Saul's arms, with her senses hungering beneath Saul's kiss, her flesh clamouring for Saul's touch, had changed everything. Like a genie let out of a bottle by a person who did not believe such things could exist, she was now having to deal with something that she had believed could never happen.

How was it possible for her of all people to feel such an uncontrollable flood tide of physical desire for a man she actively disliked? It went against everything she knew and understood about herself. Or rather everything she had *thought* she knew and understood about the person she wanted to be. Inside her head she could see once again the small family group: the mother, preoccupied, tense and impatient, the baby—the good child—sleeping in the pram, whilst she—the bad child—disobeyed her mother's instructions, ignoring them to give in to her inner need to follow her own instincts. As a result of that two members of that trio had died whilst she, the third, had survived.

Since then she had worked unceasingly to be 'good' and to make amends, but now, thanks to Saul, she was being forced to accept that the wilful, reckless side of her nature had not been banished at all.

Nothing could be returned to what it had been before Saul's fierce kiss had ripped from her the protection of her own delusion to show her the raw, physical reality of her desire for him.

How had it happened, when she had always been so careful and so controlled? She didn't know. What she did know, though, was that trying to deny its existence would be pointless—as pointless as trying to hold back the tide. It had seared its reality into her senses and sealed itself there with the pain of its white-hot heat. Perhaps this was her punishment for the past? The agonising price she must pay for what she had done? To be tormented by a need that would never be satisfied.

She might not know why she was being forced to endure the agony of physical desire for a man she disliked, and whom she knew disliked her, but what she *did* know was that Saul must never discover her weakness. He must never know that she wanted him, that the desire he aroused in her was overwhelming—and, most humiliating of all, that it was unique in her own experience and felt for him alone.

Like love.

The treacherous thought slid into her mind, to be instantly and frantically denied.

No! What she felt for Saul was nothing like love at all. It was merely physical—physical and nothing else.

Her only comfort was that Saul did not desire *her* with an equally irrational and overwhelming hunger. Because if he did... But, no—she must not go there.

Her eyes were dry and gritty from lack of sleep and

suppressed emotion, and Giselle warned herself that she must try and get some sleep. It was now gone four o'clock in the morning, and she would have to be at her desk for nine—or risk the consequences to her pride. Taking time off because she couldn't bear to face Saul was not an option she was willing to allow herself.

Broodingly Saul stood staring out of his window and watched Giselle as she entered the building. He should not have kissed her. He wished fiercely that he had not done so. Kissing her had breached his own moral barriers against that kind of intimacy with someone he employed—and, even more disturbingly, deep down inside himself he knew that it had also breached his emotional defences. So why make the hole she had driven through those defences even bigger by spending time he should be giving to other things—far more important things—not only thinking about what had happened but actively dwelling on it?

Because he needed to dwell on it—to focus on it and come up with a plan to deal with it and its potential consequences.

Abruptly Saul turned and strode purposefully across his office.

Apprehensively Giselle headed directly for her office, desperate to avoid seeing Saul, only allowing herself to feel safe when she had closed the door behind her with a sigh of relief—only to realise that she was not safe and that Saul was there, standing in the shadows, watching her.

'We need to talk,' he told her peremptorily, not

looking directly at her at all as he crossed over to the window and stood there, looking out of it. His dark-suited figure was highlighted by the light coming in through the window. His back was to her, so that she could not read his expression, but she knew that if he chose to do so he could turn round and see hers exposed by the merciless beam of sunlight pouring into the office.

'What happened between us was a mistake and should not have happened,' he said.

Giselle could feel her pain fanning her anger.

'Do you think that I *wanted* it to happen?' she challenged him. 'Well, I didn't. Because you are who you are, I dare say you believe that all women want to… to be physically intimate with you, and that they hope intimacy will lead to a relationship. Well, I don't. I don't want that and I never will.'

Her angry claim was heartfelt enough to surprise Saul into turning round to look at her.

'It's easy enough to say that, but show me a woman who doesn't claim she wants to be free and then claims that all she's ever wanted is motherhood the minute she's managed to get pregnant by a man she sees as her meal ticket and I'll show you a liar,' Saul retaliated brutally.

His words hit Giselle as brutally as though they had been physical blows, bringing to life her deepest fear.

'I shall never be that woman,' she told him passionately. 'I shall never have a child. *Never!* And as for… for what happened, I wish with all my heart that it had not.'

She meant it, Saul recognized, and he nodded his

head and informed her crisply, 'That makes two of us. For once it seems we are in accord.'

As he strode past her to the door Giselle turned her back to him and pretended to be engrossed in the plans laid out on the large desk beside her.

Back in his own office, though, Saul discovered that neither Giselle nor their kiss was easy to put out of his mind. Last night in his impressively elegant Chelsea townhouse Saul hadn't been able to sleep, despite the comfort of his bed with its stratospherically expensive Egyptian cotton sheets, changed and smoothed to perfection every day by the small and discreet army of service staff provided by the agency he used, because Giselle had got under his skin as effectively as a handful of grit placed under those sheets to deliberately irritate him. And now he couldn't erase her from his thoughts.

In fact her presence in his thoughts had gone way beyond mere irritation, Saul acknowledged, remembering how he had watched the dawn breaking, its grey light coming in through the bedroom window that he preferred to keep open to the light, etching smudged lines across the glass. That dull dawn light would have suited Giselle Freeman, he thought unkindly, with her too-often-washed black suit and her pale hair and skin.

Too late Saul realised his mistake, as the image that immediately formed inside his head was not one that focused on the shabbiness of Giselle's clothes but instead on the way her shirt pulled against her breasts.

His head might be willing to create an unflattering

image of her, but his memory was not being anything as like as co-operative—and as for his body!

Against his will he remembered what it had felt like to hold her. If he closed his eyes now he would almost be able to feel her body trembling against his own, inciting within him the desire to cover her mouth with his and take the sweet, soft movement of her lips hostage. He could imagine the weight of her slender body leaning against his, producing an effect on him as erotic as if she had physically and deliberately placed her hand on his sex and openly caressed him. He could visualise her breasts, naked and revealed for his pleasure. As a young man one of his first sexual experiences had been with an older woman who had liked him to fill his mouth with ice before emptying it to take her hot, swollen nipple into the icy chill of his mouth. She loved the sensuality of his ice-cold mouth against her sex-hot breast. He thought of Giselle, shuddering wildly under such an embrace, her fingers entwined with his as he pinioned her hands back and suckled on her nipples until she was writhing with the pleasure of his caress.

Abruptly Saul dragged his thoughts back under the control of his mind. He'd never been a fan of cold showers, but right now that was exactly what he needed—and being forced to acknowledge that didn't please him one little bit.

Saul wasn't used to anything whatsoever in his life not being under his control, never mind his own body.

It was as though for some reason his own flesh was rebelling against him. What other logical explanation could there be for its maddening insistence on telling him that it found Giselle desirable when he had strictly forbidden it to do any such thing?

Swiftly Saul mentally reviewed the women he had taken to bed over the last five years. He'd never felt any need to prove himself as a man via a list of sexual conquests, but his sexual appetite had been sharpened on and satisfied by some very beautiful women—women who were skilled and adept at appealing to a man's ego, women who did not steal car park spaces nor fill him with an irrational sense of guilt mixed with compassion which was then laced with anger because they wore shabby clothes that made them stand out from their peers in all the wrong ways.

That was it, Saul decided grimly. Put Giselle Freeman in the kind of clothes the other women in his employ wore and, instead of standing out from them, thus forcing him to focus on her, she would fade into the wallpaper, so to speak. Problem solved!

Impatiently Saul buzzed through to his PA and gave her his instructions. He heard her indrawn breath and demanded, 'What's wrong?'

'Saul, if I may say so, I don't think that being told to present herself at Harvey Nichols' personal shopping suite in order to be provided with some new work clothes so that her appearance fits with that of your other female employees will go down very well with Giselle.'

'If she argues, tell her that she doesn't have any choice,' Saul commanded, before ending the call.

He was pleased—not just because he had solved his problem, but because, even more importantly, he felt that he had found the cause for it. He was focusing on Giselle because she stood out from the other women.

Once she ceased to do that he would cease to notice her
and when he ceased to notice he would cease to… To
want her? He did *not* want her, Saul assured himself.
Not really.

Wanting a woman—any woman—was the first dangerous step down a road he had no intentions of travelling. His father had almost worshipped his mother, and
look where that had got him. Dead because his mother
had refused to give up her aid work and his father had
not been able to bear being apart from her. He never
wanted to risk loving a woman to that extent. Better
by far not to love at all—and that was exactly what he
intended to do. He never intended to love and he never
intended to have a child. Children were vulnerable—
helpless hostages to fate, their emotions so tender that
a parent could with the smallest sentence, the briefest
gesture, accidentally scar them. He did not want the
burden of carrying that responsibility.

His mother, in particular, had been burdened by the
responsibility of having him. He could vividly remember
how, after a wonderful fortnight spent with his parents,
the first summer after he had gone to boarding school,
he had begged his mother to allow him to stay with them
all the time.

'I could learn from books,' he had told her. 'You
could teach me like you teach other kids—you and
Papa.'

'No, Saul,' his mother had refused, quietly but firmly.
'If your papa and I were to devote our time to you, then
how could we do the work that is so important for helping all the thousands of children who do not have the

advantages you have? They have so little and need so much.'

They have you. Saul remembered his eight-year-old self wanting to protest. But of course he had not done so, knowing how much such a comment would have displeased his mother, to whom it had been so important that he understood the needs of the children she worked with from war torn and disaster-struck parts of the world. Children so much more deserving of her time and her love than he himself.

CHAPTER FIVE

'SAUL has done *what?*'

Moira sighed silently to herself as she heard the note of outrage in Giselle's voice.

'He's instructed me to arrange an appointment for you at Harvey Nichols for four this afternoon with one of their personal shoppers. He feels…' The PA paused, trying to find the right words. 'Saul has explained that because of the expense of your great-aunt's healthcare you can't afford to…'

'To what?' Giselle stopped her angrily. 'To buy my own clothes?'

'He simply felt it would be easier for you to fit in if you were provided with some suitable business outfits to wear whilst you are working here. He thought it would help you if—'

'*Help* me? By embarrassing me like this?'

'I don't think for one minute that that was his intention, Giselle.' Moira tried to comfort and placate her. 'In fact I gained the impression that he rather admires you for what you are doing—as indeed I do myself. It can't be easy for you.'

Giselle's body stiffened as she heard the pity in the older woman's voice.

'What can't be easy for me? Wearing cheap clothes? I can think of plenty of things that would be far harder to bear.'

Moira tried another tack.

'A large part of Saul's business comes from the international high finance set, and it is all about convincing them that becoming partners with him and investing in his construction projects will bring them good returns. For that reason he believes that it is important to maintain the right kind of image. We have a mainly young staff, and their standards of grooming tend to be high.'

'So it isn't for *my* benefit that he has given instructions that I am to be shamed and patronised, then,' Giselle challenged her, 'but for his own?'

'For his own *and* for yours,' Moira insisted.

'I won't do it,' Giselle told her fiercely. 'He can get someone else from the firm—in fact I wish he would.'

'Do you? That would mean being sent back to your employers in disgrace. Saul is their most important client. I can understand how you feel, but you have your CV and your future to think of. And with your great-aunt's care to provide, taking any kind of risk with your earning potential might not be a good idea.'

What Moira was saying made good sense, Giselle knew. But that did not mean that she had to welcome hearing it.

The initial surge of adrenalin-boosted fury Moira's announcement had brought subsided now, leaving Giselle feeling emotionally raw and shaky.

Moira put her hand on Giselle's arm. They were in

Giselle's office, where she had come to pass on Saul's instructions.

'I do understand how you must feel, and indeed how I would feel myself, were I you,' she told her calmly.

No, she didn't, Giselle thought inwardly. How could she? How could anyone? *She* was the one who had been subjected to the humiliation Saul was heaping on her. *She* was the one who had been mocked and taunted and…and kissed by him until she was reduced to a molten aching longing.

'I cannot and will not allow Saul to buy my clothes. And since I cannot afford to buy the kind of clothes for myself he seems to deem necessary for those who work for him—'

'It is not Saul who will be paying for them; it is the company. If as an employee you were required to wear a uniform you would not object to your employer providing that uniform for you, would you?' Moira challenged briskly, and continued without giving her time to respond. 'This is just the same. Saul requires you to wear the same "uniform" as his other employees.'

'I won't do it,' Giselle repeated. 'And I shall go and tell him so.'

'You can't,' Moira told her, stepping in front of her as Giselle made to head for the door. 'He isn't here. He's flying to New York this morning. Don't make your mind up right now, Giselle. The appointment isn't until four o'clock.'

This was her punishment for last night, Giselle decided after Moira had gone. She was sure of it.

Her mobile rang whilst she was still brooding on her situation. Her caller was Emma.

'You'll never guess what,' Emma told her without preamble as soon as Giselle had answered the call. 'Bill Jeffries has been called in from annual leave and suspended from work until further notice because Saul Parenti has queried some of his costings. And I should warn you, Giselle, that Bill is blaming you—and gunning for you as well. You're lucky you're working at Parenti's and not over here, I can tell you.'

Listening to Emma, Giselle gripped her mobile more tightly, torn between disbelief that Saul had actually taken her disclosures seriously enough to report them to the partnership for further investigations, the realisation that she must after all have been wrong about him trying to trick her, and the recognition that the door to her escape route from Parenti had just swung closed on her.

An hour later, on her way to the communal coffee machine, one of the other girls smiled at her and asked her if she was settling in okay. Giselle couldn't help but notice how smart Aimee looked. *Her* black suit wasn't shiny from being over-washed—but then it had probably never been anywhere near a washing machine Giselle reflected ruefully. It looked far too expensive for that.

'Saul's gorgeous, isn't he?' Aimee chatted whilst she got her coffee and Giselle queued next to her. 'Pity he's so anti-commitment and settling down. Mind you, if he wasn't I dare say we'd all be trying our best to become the future Mrs Saul Parenti. There's no chance of that, though. Not with him having said so often and so publicly that he intends to remain single and family-free. Oh, it's my birthday at the end of the month—

you're welcome to join us for drinks after work if you're free.'

The other girls here did seem to be welcoming and friendly, Giselle acknowledged, and the drinks invitation was one she would have liked to take up if...

If what? If she could afford to dress like they did?

Some of the coffee she had just made herself slopped over onto the counter as her hand shook betrayingly. It wasn't just expensive clothes that separated her from her co-workers, Giselle reminded herself. There was their differing attitudes to Saul as well. The reason he didn't want to commit and settle down was probably because he couldn't imagine any woman ever being good enough for him, Giselle thought cynically as she made her way back to her office, with her coffee. They seemed eager and ready to adore him, whilst she loathed him.

By three o'clock she had made up her mind what she had to do over the issue of Saul providing her with new work clothes—or rather she had had that decision made for her as a result of Emma's telephone call.

As angry and resentful as it made her, she would have to accept Saul's diktat.

When she went to inform Moira of her decision she couldn't bring herself to meet the older woman's gaze.

Right now there was nothing she longed for more than the financial independence to refuse both this secondment *and* the clothes he deemed good enough to go with it. But of course she couldn't. Not whilst her great-aunt was so financially dependent on her. She owed her elderly relative so much, and nothing—not even her own pride—could be allowed to stand in the way of doing everything she could to repay the debt of loyalty and love she owed her.

Without her great-aunt she would have ended up in a children's home—or worse. Giselle felt the old familiar sickness and fear rising up inside her. It was Saul's fault that she was feeling like this, with her old fears being dragged up from their burial ground to torment her.

Giselle could feel Moira's pity for her in the silence surrounding them.

'It will make your working life here much easier if you can accept that Saul is a law unto himself,' she told Giselle, breaking that silence. 'And that he does not like having his decisions questioned.'

Half an hour later, stepping out into the street, Giselle witnessed a young couple stopping to exchange a tender kiss and her heart turned over inside her chest.

A dangerous emotion was filling her—a sharp, searing feeling of pain and regret because *she* would never be kissed like that, because for her there would never be a time when she was held in a man's arms in an intimate moment of trust and love between them.

That emotion was still worrying her over an hour later, as she sat in the private fitting room of Harvey Nichols' personal shopping suite with a cup of coffee in her hand whilst she waited for the shopper and her assistants to return with a selection of clothes for her to try on.

Why, after so many years of managing perfectly well not to think about all that she would be missing because of her vow to remain single, had her emotions and her body betrayed her now, by reacting in the way that they had done to Saul, of all men?

Her hand shook, spilling coffee onto the skirt of her cheap suit.

What was happening to her? She had always known that there was no escape for her from the burden she must carry. She had known that and accepted it, thankful for the fact that no one else other than her great-aunt knew of the terrible secret she had to conceal. Surely she had been tormented enough by her own guilt? She didn't need the added cruelty of what she had felt yesterday, held against Saul's body.

There was no place in her life and never would be for the age-old instinctive female need for the support of a man strong enough to carry her troubles should she herself grow too weary to carry them. No place either for the white-hot spear of female desire so strong that the ache of it was still pulsing within her.

The problem was that she had grown so accustomed to shutting herself off from what most women would consider 'normal' reactions to the male sex that she had grown complacent, she tried to reassure herself as she drank her coffee. Saul Parenti did not have any special magical powers that made her more vulnerable to him than she was to other men. She had simply allowed her protective guard to slip a little, that was all. Nothing more than that.

The squeak of the wheels of a garment rail being moved alerted her to the fact that the personal shopper was returning. Quickly finishing her coffee, Giselle smoothed down the dark material of her skirt and tried to mask her embarrassment at even being there.

* * *

'We often notice with customers who have lost weight that they find it hard to judge what will be the right fit for them,' the personal shopper informed Giselle with an encouraging smile half an hour later, after she had coaxed her into a black suit, apparently from a designer popular with many working women.

Giselle didn't answer her. She was too busy staring at her own reflection in the full-length mirror. Surely she wasn't really that shape? With that narrow waist and that curve to her hips and her bottom so subtly outlined by the shape of the elegant black skirt? It must be the mirror that was making her look like that. Hadn't she read somewhere that women's fitting rooms had mirrors in them which made customers look slimmer than they actually were?

'Try the jacket,' the shopper encouraged her. 'The skirt's a size eight, but the jacket's a ten because you do have a good bust.'

A good bust? What did that mean?

Giselle soon discovered when she slipped the jacket on and discovered how its shaped shoulders and nipped-in waist accentuated the fullness of her breasts. Panicking, she pulled it off, shaking her head as she told the shopper, 'No, I couldn't wear that.'

'But you looked lovely in it. It was a perfect fit.'

'No. It's too… It was too revealing. I need sensible work clothes that look smart—not clothes that draw attention to my…to my body.'

The shopper laughed.

'I could understand you saying that if I'd brought you some of the more figure-hugging outfits for instance. I have to say that I was tempted, because you have the perfect figure for them. Trust me,' she informed Giselle, 'these pieces will be perfect for you.'

Before Giselle could object again she was producing a crisp fitted white shirt, which she explained had Lycra added to it for a neat fit.

'We recommend a couple of shirts and a couple of plain white short-sleeved round-necked white tees as a basic working wardrobe staple. We're in April now, so I think we should add a lighter-weight skirt—something you can wear with the jacket. Personally I love this black, grey and white patterned skirt.'

Giselle watched with growing discomfort and anxiety as the pile of clothes increased—beautiful elegant clothes—clothes for someone whose life included all the things that hers did not and could not. But there was nothing she could do or say. Saul had given instructions that she was to have a wardrobe suitable for one of his employees, and Moira had warned her not to defy him.

Because if she did he would punish her? How? By kissing her again? By touching her body, her breast, tormenting her nipple until she ached for him to…?

Frantically, her face on fire, her heart thudding, and deep within her that shockingly sensual pulse beating out its message, Giselle struggled to push away her dangerous thoughts.

Three cups of coffee later it was all over, and she and her new clothes—which to her dismay included sheer tights, smart shoes and, most discomforting of all, the underwear that she'd been measured for, having been told by the smiling assistant who did so that despite her narrow back she was a perfect C cup—were being handed into a taxi to be taken home. Even the taxi fare was apparently to be put on the bill, which would be paid by her new employer.

Giselle could feel her face burning afresh at the thought of the accounts department scrutinising the bill for her new underwear. Not so much the thankfully sensible and smooth tee shirt bra, but the other things—the delicate lace and silk bras with matching boy-pant knickers. She had thought at least one of them far too low cut, but the shopper had insisted she was going to need it. How could someone living her life possibly need something so…so sensual and seductive? And as for the two evening dresses that had been included, despite her protestations that she was unlikely to ever wear them…

Her flat was technically in Notting Hill—just. She'd bought it with the money that had been put in trust for her after the death of her parents, which she'd received on her twenty-fifth birthday—just before the recession had really started to bite. On the ground floor of a Victorian house, it included ownership of a tiny back garden, and comprised a good-sized sitting room, two bedrooms—each with its own bathroom—and a kitchen-dining-room which opened out onto the garden.

The previous owners had thoroughly modernised the whole flat, and Giselle hadn't had to do anything other than buy some furniture and move in.

She knew that other women might consider her flat to be bare and lacking in femininity, but she didn't care. A decor that focused on or reflected any kind of female sensual warmth was not for her. It might potentially

arouse yearnings and needs she could not allow herself
to have. She preferred her home as it was—even if others
might think it looked bleak and impersonal.

No photographs or ornaments broke up the flat matt
surfaces of the dark furniture. The wooden floors were
free of rugs, the leather sofa unadorned by throws or
cushions. The bedrooms reflected the same Spartan
decor. The entire flat was as immaculate as though no
one actually lived in it—but then she didn't really *live*
anywhere, did she? Giselle challenged herself as she
let herself into the narrow hall, its small space opened
up by the large mirrors on the walls, and took all the
glossy carrier bags into her bedroom. She didn't really
'live' at all, as other people understood the word.

When she wasn't working or driving north to visit her
great-aunt she spent as much time as she could visiting
London's museums, walking in the city's parks or just
simply sitting in a café watching the world go by. A
world of couples and families and happiness from which
she was excluded and always would be.

The master bedroom of the flat had the luxury of a
walk-in wardrobe. For the first time since its previous
occupants had left it would now have something hanging
in it that suited its expensive designer space, Giselle reflected as she started to unpack her new clothes. Clothes
she knew she would have to force herself to wear.

They were only clothes, she tried to tell herself. She
had not chosen them and they were not a gift—rather,
they were her own form of personal hair shirt, and that
was what she must focus on when she wore them. Not
how elegant and smart they made her look, but how
painful it was for her to wear them. She must think of

them as a penance she was forced to make. A penance forced on her by Saul to punish her.

Giselle's chin lifted. Well, she would make sure that he never knew from her that he had succeeded in humiliating her—again. She would not allow him to know so much as by a look how she really felt. Instead she would make herself act as though she was 'grateful' for his 'kindness', and thus deprive him of any satisfaction he might get from knowing he had got under her skin.

CHAPTER SIX

FROM the glass-sided gallery that ran the full width of his office, Saul could look down into the atrium of the reception area and its busy comings and goings. It was one person his gaze was focused on as she crossed the foyer—Giselle, looking far more smartly dressed than she had done the last time he had seen her.

So she had obeyed his instructions. Good. That of course was the only reason he was watching her—to make sure that she had. So why did the sight of two men from his senior management team turning to watch her walk past with discreet but quite definite male appreciation have his hackles rising like those of a possessive guard dog? Because he did not want flirtations between his staff members distracting them from their work, Saul told himself grimly. That was why.

It was just over twelve hours since he had returned from New York—earlier than he had planned. It was just as well that his business meetings in New York had gone well, Saul reflected, because the situation in another area of his life was going far from well.

He'd received a bewildered telephone call from his cousin whilst he was in New York, from which he had deduced that his cousin Aldo had become the victim of a Ponzi scheme and had probably lost the entire twenty million that Saul had given him when he had realised how hard-pressed financially his cousin was.

Being Grand Duke of one's own country might seem an exalted position, but neither the ducal exchequer nor the country itself was wealthy, and for all his promises of helping out his new son-in-law the Russian oligarch whose daughter Aldo had fallen so deeply in love with and married had so far failed to deliver. Not that Saul *wanted* to see his cousin financially tied to the Russian. It was bad enough that he was already emotionally tied to his daughter.

Saul grimaced with distaste and dislike. There was some history and hostility between Natasha, his cousin's wife, and himself—mainly because he had refused Natasha's advances.

Women! Natasha was a jealous shrew, with no compunction whatsoever about using his cousin for her own ends, and Saul avoided her company as much as he could. Normally he would have tried to sort out the mess in Aldo's affairs without having to visit Arezzio, but on this occasion that would be impossible—which meant that he would have to fly out there. It was a pity he wasn't currently involved with anyone. Another woman clinging determinedly to his side and sharing his bed would help to keep Natasha at bay.

Almost as though it possessed the instincts of a homing pigeon, his attention returned to Giselle and stayed there.

Without him encouraging it to do so his gaze slid over the curve of her hips before travelling upwards, over the white shirt that modestly hinted at rather than revealed the curve of her breasts. What had begun as a mental exercise had turned into something far more personal and intimate with such speed that his body was reacting to his visual scrutiny of her before he could stop it. What the hell was going on? She wasn't his type, her attitude irritated him like that of no other woman he had ever met, rubbing against him like sandpaper, and yet every time he moved to put her in her place something she said or did, something she inadvertently revealed about herself, had him experiencing a pang of sympathy and fellow feeling for her. She was like a thorn under his skin, a pebble in his shoe—an irritant he couldn't escape. Like his growing need to know more about her.

She wasn't just the first but the *only* woman he had ever met who had told him that she wanted to remain single and child-free and meant it. Had she made that decision because, like him, she had been orphaned?

She had stopped still in the middle of the atrium, and was looking round as though she suspected that someone was following her—or watching her? Saul stepped back from the glass. It wasn't like him to allow anyone to get into his head when she had no right to be there. It was because it was well over six months since he had ended his last relationship that he was feeling the increasingly inescapable pulsing ache every time he saw her. Nor could he forget how it had felt to kiss Giselle, to touch her and feel her responding to him as though she too was driven by the same fierce compulsive need that had driven him.

The last woman he had been seeing had started to make assumptions, and with those assumptions demands, which had led to him making it plain to her that he had no intention of making her or any other woman a permanent fixture in his life.

He had thought his parents were permanent fixtures, but they had left him, and their deaths had taught him that nothing and no one could be relied on to always be there. Was that how Giselle felt? Would she understand as no one else had or could that it was impossible for him to risk that level of pain again and survive? If he told her, would she…?

Cursing beneath his breath, Saul reined in his thoughts. He had never discussed his feelings about losing his parents with anyone, and he never intended to do so. It was safer to keep those thoughts to himself. That way it wasn't possible to be hurt, or to feel betrayed when the inevitable happened.

He knew Natasha would undoubtedly hurt and betray Aldo, and probably sooner rather than later. His thoughts returned to his cousin. Yes, Natasha would hurt Aldo— but not through him. Taking another woman with him would definitely help to keep Natasha at bay. His glance returned to Giselle and stayed there whilst he assessed and considered the situation, working with the speed and the focused clarity of a man used to making swift decisions.

'Moira,' he told his PA five minutes later, going into her office, 'I'm going to have to fly out to Arezzio. Fix up a flight with the usual private jet people, will you?'

'When for?'

'ASAP.'

'You've got that lunch appointment with Lord Richards in half an hour,' Moira reminded him.

'Yes. I know,' Saul agreed, and then told her, 'I'll be taking Giselle with me. I've decided I might as well kill two birds with one stone and visit Kovoca as well. I've got some issues with the plans that can best be settled by a site visit.'

After nodding her head, Moira queried, 'Will you be staying on the island? If so, I'll let the caretaker at the villa know.'

'Yes,' Saul confirmed.

It was too late to change his mind now, or to listen to the inner voice that was questioning the reasoning behind what he was doing. Or the reason why she was occupying his thoughts so much. So what if she was? It meant nothing.

Within fifteen minutes Moira was reporting to him that a private executive jet would be waiting on the tarmac at Luton Airport at six o'clock.

Saul looked at his watch.

'I'd better go. I don't want to keep Lord Richards waiting. Tell Giselle she can take the rest of the day off and that I'll pick her up at her home address at three-thirty. That should leave us plenty of time to reach Luton.'

'How long do you expect the trip to last?' Moira asked.

'No more than five days at most—possibly less. I'll be able to be more definite once I've spoken with Aldo and checked properly what's going on.'

Giselle's heart was thudding heavily into her ribs. She was still in shock from learning that she was going to have to accompany Saul on a field trip to Kovoca—a trip she couldn't refuse to go on, since it was quite obviously part and parcel of her work and objecting was out of the question. It would make her look unprofessional and, worse, might lead to Saul guessing that… Guessing what? That she was afraid of being on her own with him because of the way he'd made her feel when he'd kissed her? She couldn't put herself in that position. And she wasn't going to.

Instead she was going to focus on being completely professional. She looked down at her bed and the clothes she had laid out on it. Field trips in her experience usually called for outdoor clothes, which meant jeans, and since she knew from the surveyors' reports that the island's terrain was rugged in places she'd need a pair of sensible shoes.

Moira had warned her, though, that Saul was combining the trip to the island with a visit to his cousin the Grand Duke of Arezzio on what Moira had described vaguely as 'family business'. Giselle looked at her watch. Nearly three o'clock. Moira had said that Saul would pick her up at three-thirty, prior to driving them both to Luton for their flight.

She looked down at the bed again, checking to make sure she'd laid out everything she'd need. Jeans, her two new white tee shirts, undies, sensible shoes—and socks for them—and she would travel in her Joseph work suit and one of her white shirts.

She'd taken the precaution of checking online once she'd got home just to see what the weather would be like in both Kovoca and Arezzio at this time of the year, guessing correctly that it would be warmer than London.

Ten past three. She'd better hurry. The only case she had was the small one she used when she went north for a few days to see her great-aunt.

She had almost finished packing when the doorbell rang. The undies she was holding slipped from her grasp as her heartbeat accelerated. What was she so nervous for? Or was it excitement she was feeling and not nervousness?

Of course it wasn't excitement. Why should it be? The doorbell pealed again, forcing her to hurry to the door.

Saul was standing on her doorstep and a long, dark, polished expensive limousine was parked at the kerb.

'Ready?' he asked her.

'Not quite. Moira said half past three,' she told him defensively, stepping back into her hall and then wishing she hadn't when he followed her inside.

'I won't be long, though, if you want to wait in your car.'

'I never trust a woman when she says she won't be long. Women have a very elastic idea of time, in my experience.'

'That might have more to do with your taste in women than with hard truth about the female sex in general,' Giselle couldn't resist pointing out as she hurried down the corridor, pausing only to turn back towards him and wave her hand in the direction of her living room, inviting him to go in, before assuring him, 'I *will* only be five minutes.'

Saul nodded his head.

He wasn't prepared to admit that he had been curious to see where and how she lived. Picking her up at her home address had merely been effective in terms of the time it would save. Now that he was here, though, he was prepared to admit that it was impossible to learn anything about her life from the impersonal starkness of her decor. Where were the photographs? The cherished bits and pieces of female clutter he was familiar with seeing in the homes of the women he had dated over the years. There was nothing here in this room to tell anyone anything at all about the woman who lived here.

He looked at his watch. Five minutes Giselle had said, and she had one of those minutes left. Opening the door into the hallway, Saul walked towards what he guessed must be her bedroom. The door was open, and he could hear the sound of a suitcase being zipped closed. From the doorway he looked into the room. Like the living room, it was empty of any kind of female frippery, bare and bleak.

'This is your bedroom?' he asked, causing Giselle, who hadn't been aware of his presence behind her until she heard his voice, to spin round immediately to confront him.

'Yes,' she confirmed crisply, almost biting off the word, as though reluctant to make even such a small admission to him.

'It looks more like a nun's cell than a modern woman's bedroom,' was Saul's equally curtly delivered assessment.

The air hissed out of Giselle's lungs as though she

had just taken the full force of a painful blow, but she wasn't about to let him go unanswered.

'That's probably because you're contrasting it with the kind of bedrooms favoured by a *very* different type of woman to me.'

As she spoke both the tone of her voice and her expression made it plain that this 'different' type of woman was, in her opinion, an inferior type.

Reflecting on the women who had shared his bed, and the high value they put on themselves and their needs, Saul had to admit that Giselle had guts—even if she was engaging in a fight for which she was poorly equipped and which, more importantly, he had no intention of allowing her to win.

'Not as different as you might like to think,' he assured her softly, bending down to retrieve from the floor the pair of silk and lace knickers that must have fallen off the bed whilst she had been packing.

Held in Saul's hand, the delicate scrap of nude and cream underwear somehow looked even more deliberately sensual than it had when the personal shopper had insisted on adding it to her purchases.

'A taste for wearing the kind of underwear that a man both likes to see and touch on a woman must be a universal female trait.'

'It wasn't my choice,' Giselle snapped at him as she reached out to take the knickers from him.

But instead of letting go Saul closed his hand round them and enquired, 'A gift from a lover, then, were they?'

'No!' Giselle knew she was losing her self-control to the mix of anger and embarrassment that was storming her, which had been deliberately aroused by this man who was so obviously enjoying baiting her. She wanted to regain that control, but she couldn't. It was like being caught in a fine net—the more she thrashed about, trying to set herself free, the more entangled she became. Like telling lies.

Lies—how they could trick you with their easy offer of security. Like the offer of money from a loan shark. Just like that loan shark, the payment lies demanded for what they had given came with compound interest, to make an intolerable burden that could never be diminished. But how could she ever tell the truth—the whole truth—without being judged and labelled by its darkness herself? She had taken and would continue to take all the steps that needed to be taken to ensure that history could never repeat itself. That was surely all she needed to do?

Saul, watching her, saw the fight drain out of her like blood draining from an open vein. The abrupt change in her from angry adversary to someone who looked too afraid even to breathe didn't bring him any satisfaction, though. His instincts told him that it was not he who had secured a victory, but rather something or someone else.

'You'll need an evening dress,' he warned her, almost absently.

Who or what had caused that almost naked fear he had seen seize her? Why should he want to know or care? He'd always been a man who refused to allow the women he took to bed to bring their emotions into their relationship with him. But he hadn't taken Giselle to

bed, and he wasn't having a relationship with her. All the
more reason not to question her emotional reactions.

'An evening dress?'

'Yes. Moira must have told you that we will be visiting Arezzio prior to going on to Kovoca?'

'She said that you had some family business to attend
to,' Giselle agreed.

'Family business, yes, but you can hardly be expected
to eat alone in your room like some Victorian governess.
And since my cousin's wife enjoys the formality of being
Grand Duchess and dressing for dinner you will need an
appropriate outfit. Or were you imagining that I wanted
you to dress for me?' Saul taunted her unkindly.

'Certainly not,' Giselle flashed back.

'Good. I wouldn't want you getting the wrong idea
just because—'

Gisele stopped him. 'You've already told me that, and
I haven't.' She didn't want him mentioning that kiss—
not here in her bedroom, where since it had happened
there had hardly been a night when she hadn't been
woken from her sleep by her memories of it and how
he had made her feel.

She was glad of the excuse his assertion that she
would need to pack an evening dress gave her to put
some distance between them. The cool privacy of her
walk-in wardrobe gave her a badly needed opportunity
to press her hands to her hot face and try to still her
racing heartbeat. Racing because she was so furious, she
assured herself, and not for any other reason—not for
one minute because her bedroom was now filled with
the male smell of the man who had disturbed her dreams
for the last two weeks and whose touch was already

imprinted on her body and her senses. She reached blindly for the two evening dresses the personal shopper had selected for her, thankful for her sensible advice that the silky jersey fabric wouldn't crush and would be easy to pack.

Whilst he waited for her, Saul studied her bedroom. There was nothing here to give any sense of who or what she was. The room was a blank canvas of anodyne good taste. He wouldn't even have known it was her room apart from one small thing. She might not wear any perfume, but her body carried its own personal scent, recognisable to a man who had held her close, and that scent was elusively and unexpectedly provocatively discernible to him. It reminded him of how she had felt beneath his kiss, of how her body had responded to his touch, her nipples swollen and flushed—

He was doing it again—or rather she was doing it to him again.

Giselle had come back into the bedroom. Saul watched as she unzipped her case and hastily placed the dresses she was holding into it. Her hands were shaking slightly. Watching her, he had a sudden fierce urge to throw the bag onto the floor, then take hold of her hands and place them on his body whilst he stripped hers of its barriers to his possession. What would she do if he did? What would she do if right here and right now he did what his body had been urging him to do virtually from the minute he had set eyes on her?

An overwhelming urge to find out stormed through him, carrying him towards her. He wanted to fill her body with his own. He wanted to take her with him deep into the fire, holding her there until it consumed them both. He wanted… He wanted *her*, Saul recognised.

Giselle refastened her case, and then reached for its handle to lift it off the bed. But Saul beat her to it, picking it up as easily as though it weighed less than her handbag.

Giselle hadn't expected Saul to be driving himself, so was unprepared to be alone with him in the car. It was an unfamiliar experience for her to be sitting in the front passenger seat of a car driven by a man. That was something that couples did—or people who shared some kind of intimacy other than the sort of intimacy they were sharing now, shut away together in the enclosed space of the car's luxurious interior.

Her leather seat seemed almost to shape itself to her body, and the thick-pile carpet was soft beneath her feet. Beneath the expensive leather scent of the car she could smell Saul's skin—not just the cologne he was wearing but his actual flesh, warm, living and male. She could see his hands on the steering wheel, strong and capable hands, with long fingers and clean nails, the skin tanned. Hands whose touch she had felt against her own flesh—but not, of course, in a caress.

What must it be like to sit in a car next to a man, the way she was sitting next to Saul, as his lover? For other women that kind of intimacy—the physical, mental and emotional closeness to a man, a lover—was something they took for granted. But she would never travel through life with a man she loved and who loved her in return. Out of nowhere, a yearning ache of loss welled up inside her. A sense of barren hopelessness that panicked and angered her.

Why should being with Saul Parenti and his…his maleness cause this awareness within her of all that she could not have, all that she could not permit herself to want? He was the very last kind of man she would be attracted to if she was in a position to allow herself to become attracted to someone. Determinedly she dragged her gaze away from him and focused instead on the road ahead, busy now with traffic.

It didn't take them long to reach the airport. As he changed lanes for the airport turnoff, Saul asked, 'Have you already been to Kovoca?'

Giselle shook her head.

'I've seen photographs and video footage of it, and read the surveyors' reports. The land rises pretty steeply on the western side of the island, and with the mountain in the east it makes sense to build the resort on the relatively flat area in between. From the photographs I've seen it looks incredibly beautiful.'

'It is,' Saul confirmed, as the airport buildings loomed up ahead of them. 'Like a green jewel set in a turquoise-blue sea. My grandfather always bemoaned the fact that Arezzio is landlocked, and I suppose that is part of the reason why I bought the island—part, but not all. No man who is controlled by sentiment can ever expect to become successful.'

'And success is very important to you?'

'Very,' Saul agreed, unabashed. 'Any man who denies that he feels the same is lying. Success matters. It feeds the male psyche and it nourishes male pride in much the same way that a man's desire for her nourishes a woman's pride in herself.'

Giselle shot him an infuriated look.

'That is a ridiculously sexist remark, and totally untrue. Women do *not* need to be desired by a man to feel pride in themselves.'

'Maybe not. But when he does, they do,' Saul insisted.

Giselle would have responded and told him what she thought of his ego-bound arrogance if she hadn't suddenly realised that Saul was driving straight towards a gleaming private jet parked only yards away from them on the tarmac.

Giselle had flown in private jets before. The firm had several wealthy clients who thought nothing of flying those they commissioned and employed to wherever they wanted them as speedily as possible. However, there was still *something* about the exclusivity and luxury of stepping out of a car right in front of the plane that was to carry you through the skies that pulled her in two very different ways. There was a distinct thrill and sense of awe about enjoying such privilege, but it came with a feeling of guilt and resentment on behalf of those who could not afford such extravagance.

CHAPTER SEVEN

The jet was coming in to land. Saul, who had spent most of the flight working, switched off his laptop, the movement drawing the fabric of his shirt tightly across his shoulders and chest. Through the cotton Giselle could see the dark shadowing of his body hair. Her stomach lurched, her muscles tightening in protest against her awareness of his sexuality. She tried to look away from him, but somehow her brain misinterpreted the command she had given it because her gaze slid upwards instead. He'd unbuttoned the top buttons of his shirt and loosened the tie he'd been wearing when they came on board. The five o'clock shadow on his jaw was darker now, its darkness somehow underlining the shape of the male mouth her gaze seemed so eager to focus on, despite her attempts to will it to move away.

Her face burning, Giselle pulled her gaze away. Another few seconds and she'd have been reliving that kiss—again. But even though her instincts screamed for her to think of something else, anything else, she couldn't. And then it was too late for her to do anything other than submit to the sensual memories flooding through her. How was it possible to be so affected by just one kiss? Was it because she had starved herself for so long? Denied herself any expression of her own sensuality? Or was it because Saul Parenti had some special demonic power to affect her that she was powerless to resist?

Saul's voice warning, 'We'll be landing in a minute,' brought her back to reality. Her hands fumbled with her seat belt as she looked rigidly away from him, not daring to look at him in case her body betrayed her and he could see in her eyes what she did not want him to see.

Through the cabin window Giselle could see the countryside over which they were flying. The sun was setting against a backdrop of imposing mountains capped with snow, their lower slopes forested, and the dying light streaked across the calm waters of a large lake.

They were losing height now, and she could see towns and villages clustered in valleys, hugging the edges of the lake, their route following the ribbon of a river tumbling from the lake into a manmade dam and from there meandering across a broad valley. To her left she could see a sizeable town, with stone bridges spanning the river, a castle built high on a vantage point where an outcrop of rock had resisted the attempts of the river to smooth it away, the mountains rising up behind it. The town had been built at a good strategic point, Giselle recognised.

Beyond the town on the flat delta plain she could see the runway. The plane touched down smoothly as the dying sun began to sink below the horizon in a blaze of pink and gold, leaving the sky richly blue.

A man in a uniform heavily decorated with gold

braid—an official aide-de-camp of some sort, Giselle supposed—lifted a white-gloved hand in an unsmiling salute for Saul as he exited the plane and reached the ground. A red carpet had been laid out, running from the plane to a waiting car.

Although Giselle kept in the background as Saul greeted the uniformed official and shook his hand, she heard the other man saying to Saul, 'Welcome home, sir,' as he escorted them to the waiting car, climbing into the front passenger seat once he had seen them both safely into the opulence of the white leather rear seat.

Since a glass screen separated them from the driver—who was also in uniform—and the official, Giselle felt free to speak to Saul. 'I noticed he said "welcome home" to you. Did you grow up here?'

She didn't *really* yearn to know all there was to know about him. Not one little bit. No, she was simply making conversation so that she wouldn't keep on thinking about that kiss, that was all, Giselle assured herself.

'Not exactly—although Arezzio was home to my father when he was growing up. I did spend some of my school holidays here, though. I was at boarding school in England, and sometimes it was easier for my parents to fly to Arezzio to spend time with me than for me to go and join them. London is where I spend most of my time, although I have my own apartment in Arezzio within the Royal Palace.'

His life was a world away from her own—so much so that they could be living on different planets. And she was *glad* about that, she told herself fiercely. She welcomed everything that reinforced for her how impossible it was for... For what? For her to want him to take her to bed? Her body shook inwardly with the enormity of what was being revealed to her. She must stop thinking like this. She must break free of the spell she was under.

Determinedly she asked Saul, 'Is that the building I could see from the plane?'

'Yes. It was originally constructed as a fortress—some say as far back as the time when the Goths invaded the Roman Empire. But I suspect that that is more legend than truth. Though certainly it dates back to the time of the great castle-building era in Europe. You couldn't see it from the plane, but a new palace was added to the original fortress during the time of the Renaissance—one of my ancestors made a diplomatic marriage with a supporter of the Medicis, and his visit to Florence to woo and claim his bride resulted in him bringing back with him more than a Florentine wife. It is rumoured that she had in her personal retinue a chef who had trained with the chef Catherine de Medici took with her to France, a perfumier, an artist, and several artisans skilled in creating the kind of buildings admired by the Florentines. Apparently she brought her own velvet and silk bed hangings and a good deal more, including her own men at arms and a chest packed with the gold she had coaxed out of her guardian. She was a very ambitious woman, with a desire to create a dynasty.'

'It sounds fascinating,' Giselle told him truthfully.

'My cousin is an academic whose knowledge of such matters is far more extensive than mine. I am sure he will be delighted to show you the records we have of the Florentine bride's dowry.'

As Giselle moved in her seat next to him, Saul felt

his own body responding to her proximity with a fierce male surge of pleasure and desire that caught him off guard. He had never experienced anything like this before, and his instinct for the survival of his emotional independence fought against it just as he was fighting against his body's need.

Giselle felt the movement of air as Saul moved back from her, very obviously putting a distance between them. His action filled her with a sense of desolation that scorched her pride. Had he thought that she wanted to be close to him? Well, she didn't. She moved closer to her own window and stared fixedly out of it, even though there was nothing to see other than darkness now the sun had set.

The lights of the town were up ahead of them.

The town was obviously very old. They drove into it through a bridge tower, and then over a bridge that reminded Giselle of photographs she'd seen of the old Charles Bridge across the river in Prague. Like the Charles Bridge, this one too was decorated with Baroque-style statues and ornamentation.

Once they had crossed the bridge the road opened out into an imposing square, well lit with decorated lamps, whilst the magnificent frontage of the Renaissance building on the opposite side of the square was illuminated by soft floodlighting.

It all looked very imposing and very regal. There was enough light to reveal the flag flying on top of the building—gold-crowned lions rampant against a deep blue background, a Florentine lily between the lions.

The car had come to a halt alongside a flight of stone steps that led to the entrance of the building, its doors guarded by uniformed men, their blue coats the same colour as the background of the flag.

It would be easy to be over-awed by this kind of pageantry, Giselle admitted to herself a few minutes later, when the enormous polished wood double doors were thrown open with a flourish to reveal a large round entrance hall, flooded with light from a chandelier that Giselle suspected was larger than the entire floor space of her flat.

Several sets of doors opened off the hallway, whose walls were painted with the now familiar blue of the ducal arms, and the light from the chandelier crystals splintered and danced on the highly polished wooden parquetry floor. A flight of marble stairs led upwards to a galleried landing, the walls filled with portraits of autocratic, arrogant-looking men who all bore a strong resemblance to Saul. But it was the woman standing halfway up the stairs who drew and kept Giselle's attention.

She was, Giselle thought, quite simply the most beautiful-looking woman she had ever seen. Tall and slender, with thick, dark shiny hair that fell to her shoulders and framed the perfect symmetry of her face. It didn't need the jewels round her throat and wrists or the fit of the gown she was wearing to tell Giselle that this was a woman who was used to the very best of everything.

'Saul.' Her lips formed a smile as she almost purred Saul's name.

Her eyes were the same shade of rich sherry as the silk dress she was wearing. She descended the stairs with graceful ease, standing in front of Saul in such a way that Giselle, who had been standing at his side, was forced to step back onto a lower step, excluded from the intimate circle the other woman was forming with the angle of her body. Her hand was on Saul's arm, her diamond-set wedding band and the huge solitaire she was wearing with it glittering as they caught the light.

There was a predatory possessiveness about her attitude to Saul, Giselle recognized. An intimacy that brushed coldly against her own senses, causing her to feel an inner disquiet and revulsion—because already Giselle was sure that this woman was Saul's cousin's wife. And she was equally sure that she desired *Saul*.

Without seeing his face it was impossible to see whether or not he reciprocated her desire, but surely no man could fail to be tempted by such beauty—and availability?

Giselle took another step down the stairs, and then went rigid with shock when out of nowhere Saul's hand curled round her arm, pulling her back towards him. Automatically Giselle tried to pull away, but Saul wouldn't let her. She could see the way in which Natasha's gaze had fastened on Saul's hand on her arm.

'I thought you'd be coming alone,' Natasha said to Saul. 'Since Aldo has such important and private family business to discuss with you.'

'You thought wrong.' Saul's answer was unequivocal. 'Where is Aldo?' he added.

'He's in the library—where else?' Natasha gave a petulant shrug. 'I am bored with these books he finds so fascinating, and I have told him so. But soon I shall have some fun as my father has a new yacht and I am to spend the summer on it as his hostess. You must join us,

Saul. My father will introduce you to many influential people. There is good business to be had in Russia for those with the right connections.'

'I'm afraid that my plans for the summer depend very much on what Giselle wishes to do, Natasha.'

Saul's voice held anything but regret, but it wasn't that that had Giselle turning to him with a shocked demand for an explanation on her lips. He silenced it by nipping her arm sharply.

'Goodness.' Natasha's smile was as deadly as arsenic. 'Your new friend really must have some very special talents if you envisage still enjoying her in three months' time, Saul. You don't normally keep your lovers that long.'

If she *had* been Saul's lover then his cousin's wife's offensive remarks would have been bound to cause her distress and anger, Giselle knew, but right now it was Saul who was the cause of those emotions, not Natasha. What on earth was he doing? Why hadn't he told the other woman that theirs was a business relationship? Giselle looked accusingly at him, ready to correct Natasha herself, but there was a look in Saul's eyes that warned her against doing so, reminding her of just how much she was already in his power, and how dependent financially she was on his good will, no matter how much she might resent that reality.

'Tell Aldo that I'll talk with him later, will you, Natasha?'

'Later? Why can't you talk to him now?'

'You've just said that he's busy—and besides, it's been a long week. I've been in New York and Giselle has been in London. We've got a lot of catching up to do.'

As he spoke Saul turned to give Giselle a look that said quite openly that the kind of catching up he had in mind involved a bed and Giselle's body naked for his enjoyment in it. Even though she knew that look was manufactured and meant nothing, and even though she was furious with him, it still had the power to melt through her resistance and leave her quivering inwardly on the edge of a quickening pulse of desire that arced and ached almost painfully inside her.

It was plain that Natasha was equally aware of what Saul had wanted to convey. Her lips pressed together and her gaze hardened on them both—but especially on her, Giselle recognised.

'Dinner is at ten o'clock,' she announced coldly.

'We'll try and make it,' Saul responded. 'But don't hold anything up for us. Go ahead without us. Like I said, we've got a lot of catching up to do.'

Natasha's face was a picture—a furiously angry picture, Giselle acknowledged. And she wasn't the only one who was furiously angry with Saul either. He'd put his arm around her now, and was guiding her towards the stairs, probably refusing to let go of her in case she demanded an explanation for his behaviour in front of Natasha, Giselle decided, reluctant to admit that she might well have done so if she hadn't taken such an immediate dislike to the other woman.

CHAPTER NINE

'I WANT to know what's going on,' Giselle demanded as soon as she felt they were out of earshot of Natasha. As she spoke she tried to pull away from Saul, but once again he refused to let her go.

'Not yet,' he answered as they reached the top of the stairs. 'This way.'

The walls of the wide corridor were hung with more portraits. They paused several doors opening off it before they finally reached a set of imposing double doors that blocked off the whole corridor.

When Saul produced a key to unlock the doors Giselle tried not to look surprised, but she recognised he was aware of her reaction when he turned to her as he unlocked and opened the door and told her succinctly, 'I consider this apartment to be just as much my private space as my London home, and as such I prefer it to remain exactly that—private. Ludmilla, the housekeeper, has been here for almost as long as I can remember, as have many of the staff. She has a key, and I know I can trust her with it.'

Meaning that there were those he could not? Natasha, for instance?

The room beyond the double doors had all the

elegance one would expect in such a building, with its baroque design and decor, but it was in a stripped-back way that was unexpectedly pleasing to both the eye and the senses. The wood-panelled walls were painted a soft grey, plain off-white curtains hung at the windows, and the mirror above the fireplace reflected the room's few pieces of what Giselle suspected must be very valuable antique furniture. The heavy Knole sofas, covered in a matt grey and cream damask velvet, had highly polished tables behind them, with lamps with dark grey shades, and the carpet was obviously old, with beautifully soft shades of creams and blues woven into a design that echoed the ornately plastered ceiling. The light from a chandelier filled the room, throwing softly delicate shadows.

It was a masculine room, but one in which a woman could enjoy and appreciate her surroundings, Giselle recognised, immediately clamping down on her thoughts as she realised where they might be leading.

'Your room is this way,' Saul told her.

Her room? So, despite what he had implied to Natasha, he had no real intention of them being lovers. But of course she had known that. Known it but wished it was otherwise? Of course not.

'I'm not going anywhere until you tell me what's going on,' she repeated, 'and why you let Natasha think...'

'Think what?'

'You know perfectly well what. You implied to her that we are lovers.'

'Yes, I did.'

His unexpected admission had Giselle momentarily

unable to think of any response other than a weak, protesting, 'Why?'

'Isn't it obvious?' Saul challenged with a small shrug.
'You've seen Natasha. You've heard her. She makes it
very obvious what she wants, I would have thought.'

What he meant was that Natasha had made it very
obvious that she wanted him, Giselle knew. An attack of
helpless, hopeless emotion gripped her by the throat and
shook her like a rabid dog shaking its prey. Surely she
wasn't feeling jealous and desperate because Natasha
wanted Saul and was so obviously much more his kind
of woman than she could ever be? Was this what wanting Saul had reduced her to? *Wanting* him? How could
such a mundane word possibly express the agony of what
had been happening to her since he had kissed her? The
savage aching pain of the need that had grown so intense
that it woke her from her sleep to possess her body and
undermine her defences?

Out of her despair, Giselle said the only thing she
could think of say to protect herself. 'You must have
given her some cause to believe that her...her feelings
would be reciprocated,' she accused. Just as he had done
to *her* when he had kissed her. With a man like Saul that
was all it took to turn a woman into an aching misery
of desire—one kiss. As she knew.

'No. Never,' Saul defended himself curtly.

'If that's true, why don't you simply tell her that you
aren't interested? Instead of...of taking refuge behind
a fake relationship with me.'

'Natasha is married to my cousin,' Saul responded.
'He loves her. He is besotted with her, in fact, and he
believes that she loves him in return. The truth is that

Natasha turned her attentions to Aldo and pursued him after I had made it plain that she was wasting her time pursuing me. Natasha does not like being refused what she wants. She's perfectly capable of blatantly breaking her marriage vows, and I wouldn't put it past her to lie in wait for me in my bed if she thought that would get her what she wants.'

'And would it?'

Giselle could see from Saul's expression that she had angered him—again. Would he punish her this time as he had done before? By kissing her? The rush of sick longing that burst through her left her feeling weak and distraught. She hated herself for what was happening to her even more than she resented Saul for causing it to happen.

Panicking, she accused him, 'You planned this all along, didn't you? You brought me here intending to use me, to sacrifice my professional status, by pretending that I'm just another silly fool who wants to crawl into your bed and can't think of anything else. You are every bit as immoral and devious as your cousin's wife. The two of you deserve one another. You probably really do want to sleep with her.'

Was that really what Giselle thought of him? That he was the kind of man who would betray his closest blood relative? It shocked Saul to realise just how much her opinion of him mattered to him. He took a step towards Giselle, and then stopped as she in turn stepped back from him.

'Yes, I did bring you with me partly in the hope that your presence would make it plain to Natasha that I am not interested in her—which I am not.'

'Only partly?' Giselle challenged him. 'So what are the other reasons?'

Hell, but he wanted her—right here, right now, her mouth under his, her body beneath his, his hands free to explore every centimetre of her. Saul's heart slammed into his ribs. He wanted her, and if he didn't get out of here and fast he wouldn't be responsible for what might happen.

So why, instead of taking her to her room and leaving her there, was he stepping up to her and deliberately taunting her. 'Are you hoping secretly that it's because I want to take *you* to bed?'

'No!'

She was saying no, but the look in her eyes, the convulsive movement of her throat, the rise and fall of her chest betrayed her, so that suddenly and searingly Saul knew that against all the odds she shared the unwanted need that was driving him. There could be no other explanation for that wild, frantic, helpless look of mingled rage and longing in her eyes that portrayed so exactly what he was feeling himself.

Saul had guessed how she felt and he was tormenting her, ready to humiliate her—again, Giselle decided, and was panicked into another fierce, 'No!' before adding for extra emphasis, 'You would be the *last* man I would want as my lover.'

That was enough—more than enough, Saul recognized—to breach the dam of his self-control.

'Liar,' he breathed against her lips as he took her in his arms. 'This is what you want, what we *both* want and need,' he told her.

Giselle was lost, helpless to protect herself, helpless

to resist the torrential flood of her own desire-laden reaction to his words and to him.

In his arms her body melted. Beneath his lips her own parted. She clung to him as pliable and responsive, as eager to meet and match his every need as though she had indeed been formed from one of his own ribs and was thus part of him—owned by him, given over to him. Everything that was not Saul ceased to matter. Everything other than her own need for him, which was now possessing her, driving her, consuming her.

Her own need... Just before her world of reality and logic spun off its axis, flinging her headlong into a new galaxy of previously unimagined and undreamed-of sensations and pleasures, her final shocked recognition was of just how much she wanted and needed what was happening. How much she wanted this and Saul himself, and how right he had been to mock her denials.

She tried to pull back, panicked by and afraid of her own vulnerability, recognising at a deep instinctive level her own danger, and yet at the same time filled with an equally intense longing to continue the kiss, to let it and Saul take her to that place her body now yearned to reach.

Beneath the possession of his mouth Saul felt her hesitation and looked down into her eyes, which like his own were open. In their smoky depths he could see confusion clouding the open heat of her arousal. He could see in those bewildered desire-clouded eyes everything that he was feeling himself.

He wanted, he recognized, to hold her, to wrap her in his arms and tell her that he too was confused and afraid, that he too did not understand how things had

sensation of Saul's more intimate touch, making her lean wantonly towards him.

In response Saul took hold of her hand with his own free hand and placed it against his erection. His other hand slid inside her briefs as he did so, to cup her soft eager flesh and then slide fingertips into the wet heat the aroused outer lips of her sex had opened so eagerly to offer him.

As he explored her Giselle's hand tightened on his erection and clung to it, caressing it with urgent, eager movements that reciprocated the rhythm with which he was arousing her. She longed for them both to be rid of their clothes so that she could be free to explore all of him—and not just with her hands. She wanted to breathe in the scent of him, to stroke her tongue-tip over the ridges of male muscle and flesh that made up his body, to arouse him up to and then past the point of madness as he was surely already doing to her.

He couldn't hold out much longer, Saul knew. Right now all he wanted to do was spread the soft willingness of her thighs and sink himself into her, over and over again, until she rose and fell against him with the song of her arousal filling his ears and the climax of her orgasm compelling from him the hot, wet exultation of his own satisfaction.

He bent his head and took her nipple into his mouth, licking and nipping erotically at the taut flesh, pressing his free hand flat against Giselle's upper back so that he could rock her with deliberate sexuality against both his mouth and his fingertips. He suckled deeply on her breast, stroking her clitoris.

Somehow, with a need born more of urgency than

skill, Giselle had managed to unzip Saul's trousers, and now her hand was enclosing the hot rigid tip of his sex. The male flesh moved erotically within her caress, eliciting a groan from Saul that was gasped against her breast. His response to her intimacy caused Giselle herself to shudder wildly at the raw sensuality of what Saul was doing to her. Hungry for him, she pressed closer to him, moving her body against his hand, moving her own hand against his flesh, her arousal increased by the mingled sounds of their shared sensuality, by the probing pleasure-giving fingers moving over eager, hot, wet flesh, the accelerated breathing and raw betraying groans of male desire-driven need.

She cried out when Saul's mouth abandoned her breast, but the sound was quickly stifled by the intimacy of the probing, thrusting kiss he gave her, and the knowledge that soon soon now the rhythmic movement of his tongue against her own would be mirrored by the possessive male thrusting of his body filling her own.

As though she had spoken her longing aloud, Saul's hand reached for the top of her briefs. A wave of heat and excitement engulfed her. She couldn't wait for the pleasure she knew there was going to be—and then it happened. The sharp, intrusive ring of Saul's mobile cutting through their shared intimacy like acid.

For a handful of seconds Saul tried to ignore the shrill demand, but the phone was in his jacket, which he had dropped on one of the chairs when they had first entered his private quarters, not close enough to hand for him to silence it without releasing Giselle.

'You'd better answer it. It might be something important.'

As she spoke Giselle felt as though she was breaking the protective bubble that had enclosed her, and
now—sharply and horribly—she was acutely aware of
her own nakedness and mortification. It was different
for Saul. All he had to do was discreetly zip himself up
as he reached for his phone. Giselle was thankful that
at least he had his back to her as he answered it, thus
giving her the chance to struggle awkwardly back into
her own clothes, whilst she heard him speaking.

'Yes, Aldo. Natasha did say that you were in the library. Yes, of course I can come down and talk to you
now. Just give me five minutes and I'll be with you.'

The cruel lash of reality had stripped the warmth
of sensuality and desire from Giselle as easily and no
doubt as uncaringly as Saul had all but stripped her
clothes from her, she acknowledged miserably, writhing
inwardly. How could she have behaved like that? How
could she have been so lost to everything she believed
in about herself and about the way she had to live her
life?

'I've got to go. But first I'll show you to your room.'
Saul didn't dare allow himself to look at Giselle as he
replaced his mobile in his jacket pocket. If he did then
he didn't know if he would be able to keep his promise
to his cousin—because if he looked at her with his body
aching for her in the way that it was he didn't think he'd
be able to walk away from her.

How had it happened? How had he come to allow a
woman to burn through his self-control and make him
want her so intensely that nothing else mattered? How
had he allowed it to happen? Saul grimaced. He hadn't
had any kind of control in the matter. He hadn't been

capable of allowing or not allowing anything. The truth was that he still wasn't. One word from Giselle—one look, one small sound—that was all it would take for him to reach for her. And that was why he couldn't trust himself to look at her.

Silently Giselle followed Saul until he opened a pair of double doors that led into another room—a library this time. Saul strode through it so quickly that she didn't have time to give it anything more than a cursory look. Saul was opening another set of double doors that led from the library into a rectangular hallway, with one flight of stairs going up from it, and another leading downwards. He hadn't looked at her once as they had traversed the large, elegantly furnished rooms with their stucco-plastered and painted ceilings and their antique furniture, and Giselle told herself that she was glad that he hadn't, ignoring the ache of unsatisfied desire eating into her that gave the lie to her mental claim.

'This apartment has its own entrance,' Saul was informing her, his voice clipped and formal, his manner towards her chillingly distant. 'The doors on the opposite side of this hallway lead to a dining room, and beyond them is a kitchen. Like me, my parents also valued their solitude and their privacy.'

Was that meant to be a warning to her not to read anything into the intimacy they had just shared? If so, there was no need for it. After all, she had her own reasons for knowing there could never be any true intimacy between them. No true intimacy, maybe—but, oh, how her body ached and, yes, screamed inwardly for the release and satisfaction it had been denied. A satisfaction that she would have had if only Saul's mobile had rung a handful of minutes later, Giselle was sure.

That she should have such thoughts was wrong, and surely shamed her, but her body was refusing to be shamed. It wanted her to close the distance between Saul and herself. It wanted— No. No, she must *not* let herself feel that way. Instead she should be relieved—glad that Saul had stopped when he had. Shouldn't she? She was on the pill, after all, prescribed for her a couple of years ago for her erratic periods, and she had continued to take it even though there was no contraceptive need for her to do so. There was no danger of her conceiving. No danger of either of them creating a situation they didn't want, since neither of them wanted any kind of commitment.

Why couldn't she have the appetite Saul had conjured up in her satisfied? Why shouldn't she know his possession?

Saul had started to climb the stairs, and was obviously waiting for her to do the same.

'On the next floor there are four bedrooms, each with its own bathroom. I've made arrangements for a guestroom to be prepared for you,' he was telling her, still in that same clipped and distant voice that told her quite clearly how little he wanted to return to the intimacy they had been sharing.

He was probably relieved and grateful that they had been interrupted, Giselle told herself as she reached the top of the stairs and a galleried landing with corridors running either side of it. Dutifully Giselle followed Saul down one of them to a door at the end which he opened for her.

Taking great care to avoid coming into contact with him, Giselle stepped into it, her private misery briefly eclipsed by the discovery that the bedroom looked like something out of one of the National Trust houses her great-aunt had so loved visiting.

A feminine-looking tester bed was draped with hangings in blue and cream patterned silk that echoed the colour of the patterned carpet and the painted panelled walls. Giltwood furniture decorated the room, and included a chaise longue at the bottom of the bed and a pretty desk and chair. Two rather more solidly comfortable-looking chairs were drawn up on either side of the fireplace, and either side of the bed was a pair of double doors.

'The doors lead to a bathroom and a dressing room,' Saul informed her, adding, 'Dinner won't be until ten, if you recall.'

Giselle nodded her head, and watched as Saul turned and left the room.

In London, even though he was the boss, the gulf between them hadn't seemed anything like as huge as it felt right now, as she recognised how very different their worlds were. Not that it mattered, of course. How could it? Just because of…of what had happened, the sensual intimacies they had shared, it didn't mean anything. Not to Saul. She already knew that. And the fact that she had enjoyed, even welcomed those intimacies did not mean anything either. It couldn't and it mustn't—not now and not ever.

Only now could she relax and allow herself to breathe properly, let her body tremble with the need that still ached through her. Giselle sank down onto the bed. How could this have happened to her? Why had it happened? Why should life be so cruel to her? Hadn't she already suffered enough? Hadn't she already been punished enough? Dark thoughts of hopelessness and despair swirled dangerously inside her head—thoughts of there being no point to anything, not even her own existence. But she must not think like that. That way lay terrible danger.

Panicking, Giselle got up from the bed. She must find something to do that would redirect and occupy her thoughts, restore them to…to… To what? To sanity? The sanity that had been denied her? But, no—she must not go down that route. Where was her laptop? She needed to work, to be professional, to think only about those things that did not involve her emotions.

An exploration of the bathroom and dressing room revealed two rooms both larger than the bedroom in her flat. The bath, she'd discovered, was huge and traditional, with claw-shaped feet, and stood in dignified solitude in the middle of the white tiled and gilt mirrored bathroom.

Someone had already unpacked for her, hanging the few clothes she had brought with her in one of the wardrobes that filled two walls of the dressing room. Her laptop case had been carefully placed on the dressing table stool, and Giselle seized on it with grateful relief, her hands trembling as she unzipped the case and removed her laptop.

Work—work was the panacea and the cure, the antidote for the disease that was threatening her. How could she have let things get so out of control? Things? By *things* did she mean her own desire, her longing, her aching, her need for Saul's touch, for his possession, for his…? Blindly pushing the laptop away from her, Giselle started to pace the dressing room.

He might be listening to Aldo, but his mind wasn't fully focused on what his cousin was saying to him, Saul knew. Instead his thoughts, like the ache that still tormented his body, belonged to Giselle.

How had it happened? How had a woman who had begun by irritating and infuriating him somehow developed the power to infiltrate his thoughts and his senses to such an extent that her presence there overwhelmed everything else? What was she doing? Was she aching as much as he was? Was she thinking about the pleasure they would have shared if they hadn't been interrupted?

'Natasha's father has offered me the opportunity to invest in a diamond mine he has recently added to his investments. If I can manage to get something back from this Ponzi scheme Natasha wants me to go ahead, but Ivan cannot confirm that the diamonds are being mined ethically,' Aldo was saying.

His comments caused Saul to grimace derisively to himself at the thought of Natasha's father being involved in *anything* that was remotely ethical. Not for the first time Saul wished that his cousin had not fallen under Natasha's spell.

'I'll provide you with enough money to cover all your outgoings,' Saul assured Aldo. 'I just wish you had consulted me before getting involved with the scheme.'

'I was going to, but Natasha said that there was no need. Now, of course, the poor darling feels absolutely dreadful and is convinced that you will blame *her*. You mustn't, Saul. If I was more of a man—more like you, more the kind of husband she deserves—then I would have realised the danger for myself. It isn't Natasha's fault that she is married to such a weakling and a failure.'

'You are neither of those things, Aldo. You are a good ruler, a good husband, and when you and Natasha have a child you will be a good father, the best of fathers, because you will be here for your children.'

When Aldo shook his head, Saul's heart ached for him. A woman like Giselle would *never* shame and humiliate the man to whom she had committed herself and her future in the way Natasha was doing to his cousin.

That knowledge, and just as shocking the thinking that lay behind it, froze Saul to his chair. What the hell was he doing, linking such thoughts together? The three words, Giselle, commitment and future, felt as though they were etched in fire inside him, producing an indigestible truth he didn't want to acknowledge. Against all the odds, against everything that he had always promised himself, somehow a link had been made between Giselle and his emotions.

That link must be dissolved and destroyed.

CHAPTER NINE

IT WAS no good her trying to work. She couldn't. Giselle sighed in defeat. What had happened couldn't be pushed out of her thoughts and under a carpet of other busy thoughts and actions, no matter how much she wished it could be.

She looked at her watch. Nine o'clock. What was Saul doing now? Was he with his cousin? With Natasha? Jealousy as swift and sharp as any serpent's fangs bit sharply into her heart. This was wrong, Giselle told herself. What she was feeling was wrong.

A sudden knock on her bedroom door had her stiffening and staring at it. Saul. He had come back. To finish off what they had started? The emotion that flamed through her wasn't denial or reluctance or any of the things it should have been. Instead it was yearning and delight and excitement.

She was halfway out of the chair when the door opened—only it wasn't Saul who had knocked on it, it was Natasha, and her appearance deflated Giselle's emotions as effectively as a pin piercing a child's balloon.

The other woman looked as though she was already dressed for dinner, the red dress she was wearing a perfect foil for her olive skin and dark colouring. It clung so tightly to her body that it left little to the imagination. Were her breasts real? Giselle found herself wondering. Or had they been surgically enhanced, as her Jessica Rabbit-shaped body seemed to suggest? She was wearing a collar of rubies and diamonds round her neck that must have cost a fortune, and matching bangles on both wrists. Her hair was swept up to fall in perfectly coiffured curls, her make-up was immaculate, and her nails were painted exactly the same shade of scarlet as her dress.

'I just thought I'd take the opportunity of having a word with you whilst Saul is talking to Aldo. You know, of course, that Saul will never commit to you and that you won't have a future with him?'

'Yes, I do know that,' Giselle agreed. It gave her a certain amount of unsisterly satisfaction to see that her response had not exactly pleased the other woman.

'And you don't mind? You don't care that he is only using you for sex, and that he will discard you once he grows bored with you? That he will never commit to you and most of all never, ever allow you to have his child? He wanted me for himself, but he felt obliged to step aside once he realised that Aldo wished to marry me.' Natasha continued, without giving Giselle the chance to say anything. 'Saul will never marry, you see. He will never marry and he will never have a child, especially a son, because he knows that his son will have to take second place to mine and Aldo's son...when we have one.'

She paused, a small hint of a frown marring her perfectly smooth face as though something displeased her, before continuing, 'Just as *he* has had to take second place to Aldo. Of course his pride cannot bear that thought. Saul has to come first in everything. As a child, the eldest born of a second son, he grew up resenting having to stand in Aldo's shadow. That is what drives him now. If I were you I would find myself someone else.'

She had turned away and was opening the door before Giselle could say anything to her. Had she herself been someone who hoped for commitment from Saul, someone who desperately craved the joy of bearing the child of the man she loved, then Natasha's cruelly calculated words would have destroyed her hopes and dreams. If she had been that someone. But she wasn't, and instead Natasha's assertion and the ring of truth it had held unleashed within her a potent mix of emotions and an intoxicating sense of being set free from the restrictions she had previously placed on herself.

Although Natasha didn't know it, what she had said to her about Saul made him the perfect man for Giselle. No. Not the perfect man, but the perfect lover. Now she could admit and accept the torrent of longing that was possessing her—now she could open the floodgates and let it surge and soar within her. Now, if Saul should approach her, she could surely allow herself to touch the fire and let it consume her without any fear for the future.

It was past nine. Time she got ready.

Once she had showered, Giselle went into the dressing room and opened the wardrobe, taking out the two evening dresses. Evening dresses provided and paid for by Saul. They weren't anything like as provocative as the dress Natasha had been wearing, but they were stylish.

They were dresses for a woman confident about herself, about her sensuality, and about the feelings of the man with whom she shared it. They were dresses that spoke clearly of personal pride and whispered of secret promises exchanged in private—which was initially why in Harvey Nichols she had wanted to reject them. And why she now wanted to wear them?

Giselle looked at them assessingly. One of them was a fluid handful of dark green jersey, with long sleeves and a boat-shaped neckline, and a floor-length skirt ruched slightly at the sides. The other was black, again with long sleeves, and had a scooped-out back that looked as though it dipped right down to the waist. The fabric was a sheer black silk, over a skintone underskirt.

Of the two, Giselle felt that she would be more comfortable in the green jersey. She looked at her watch. She hadn't got time to dither.

Twenty minutes later she was standing in front of the mirror in the dressing room staring at her own reflection. The dress fitted perfectly, and the colour was unexpectedly flattering for her skin tone, giving it a soft luminous sheen. Theoretically she was covered from her throat through to her wrists and her ankles by the jersey fabric, but somehow—unless she was deceiving herself because it was what she wanted to believe—the dress still managed to be extraordinary and very subtly sexy.

There was a knock at the door and this time it *was* Saul, wearing a dinner suit and looking so very male and handsome that her heart literally somersaulted inside her chest wall as she contrasted the formality of the way he looked now with the intimacy of how she had seen him earlier. And how she wanted to see him later? Her heart somersaulted again.

'I'm not quite ready, I'm afraid. I just need to brush my hair,' she told him, trying to sound calm as he stepped past her and into the room.

'Leave it. It suits you the way it is,' he told her.

Giselle looked at him with suspicion. She'd seen for herself that tendrils of hair had escaped from the clip she'd put in it, and were now curling softly onto her throat and the back of her neck.

'It's untidy,' she protested. 'It looks as though—' She stopped abruptly, realising that she had been about to say that it looked as though she had just got out of bed.

'It looks fine,' Saul insisted, adding, 'besides, we haven't got much time. Don't worry, though. I can promise you that Aldo won't notice. He won't have eyes for anyone other than Natasha, poor fool. Speaking of Natasha, though, I thought you might like to wear these.'

As he spoke Saul was reaching into his pocket and removing a dazzling diamond necklace and a pair of diamond stud earrings.

'They belonged to my mother,' Saul added.

'Your mother?' Giselle shook her head. 'Oh, no—I couldn't possibly wear them.'

'She'd want you to.' As he spoke, Saul recognised to his own surprise that it was the truth. His mother would have liked Giselle. 'You should wear them. Knowing Natasha, she'll be decked out like a Christmas tree.'

'She is,' Giselle agreed absently.

'You've seen her?' Saul queried.

'She came to see me. She wanted to warn me that

you would never commit to me or allow me to have your child. She said you couldn't bear the thought of your son taking second place to Aldo's.'

'It's true that I never intend to have children, but that decision doesn't have anything to do with them not inheriting the dukedom. Let me put this on for you— the catch is a bit awkward,' he told Giselle placing the diamond necklace round her neck before she could stop him.

In the mirror she could see the diamonds sparkling, and Saul standing behind her, his hands on the necklace's clasp. She didn't need to see him, though, to be aware of his presence. She could feel it with every cell of her body. She could feel too his breath on her skin, making her nerve-endings tingle, making her want to turn round and beg him to hold her and kiss her, making her ache to be back where they had been before Aldo's phone call had interrupted them.

Just thinking such thoughts was enough to have the female pulse buried deep inside her quickening into an aching urgency, her senses craving a renewal of that intimacy with him.

'So, if it isn't because they won't inherit the dukedom, then why don't you want children?' she asked, in an attempt to distract herself from her physical awareness of his proximity.

'It isn't a matter of not wanting them so much as a matter of knowing myself and knowing that my work means they would have to take second place in my life— just as my mother's work meant that I had to take second place in hers.'

Saul had finished fastening the necklace, but he didn't

move away from her. He was opening up to her in a way she had not expected, and his words touched her own emotions in a way that both made her ache with longing to comfort him and at the same time filled her with fear *because* she felt that way.

Giselle's silence, as opposed to more questions or a demand for further explanation, had Saul continuing grimly, 'What I learned from that experience taught me that a child deserves to be number one on its parents' list of priorities. My commitments and lifestyle mean that I can't guarantee I'll always be there for my child when he or she needs me. In my opinion it's kinder not to have children at all than to inflict that on them. And as for coveting the dukedom, if that is what Natasha tried to imply, Aldo's title and the responsibilities that go with it—such as the duty to provide an heir, as he must—are the very last thing I would want.'

He paused and then, as though the words were being dragged from him without him being able to control them, he told her, 'My parents could not be there for me when I needed them to be. I will not inflict that on a new generation. My mother used to say to me that I was very fortunate, and that I should not begrudge the time she gave to the children she was trying to help because I had so much. And I didn't begrudge it—I'm very proud of the work she did for those children who had nothing. But she couldn't understand that sometimes a child needs its parents, and I craved to see more of her. I will not father children who will—'

'Be hurt as you were hurt, because they have to come second?' Giselle finished for him.

She ached so much to hold him and be held by him

as she told him that she too knew that pain, that feeling of being pushed to one side, even if in her case it had been by only one child—her baby brother.

'Yes.' Saul's voice was terse. He had said too much, given away too much, and instinctively he wanted to pull back and distance himself both from his vulnerability and from Giselle herself

As a result he was short and sharp. 'Can you manage the earrings yourself?'

Giselle nodded her head.

She could sense that Saul was withdrawing from her, and she understood why. What he had told her had given her much to think about, though. She knew that Saul meant what he had said. She had heard it in his voice and seen it in his expression—and she, of course, understood why he felt the way he did as another woman might not have done. Because of her own experience. It formed a bond between them. But it was a bond that she suspected Saul did not want. And she did? How could she answer that question honestly when she knew the answer she ought to give was not the one that was in her heart.

'Ready?' Saul asked, after she had finished securing the earrings.

'Yes,' Giselle answered him.

'Ah, there you are, you two.'

Aldo might have his height, and something of his looks, but looking at Aldo was like comparing a pale shadow to the reality of all that Saul was, Giselle recognised as Saul introduced her to his cousin.

They were served pre-dinner drinks in the red drawing room, its decor a perfect backdrop for Natasha's gown and jewels, and then dinner in an even more formal dining room.

Giselle witnessed the genuine affection Saul felt for his cousin, and Aldo's reciprocal love and respect for Saul.

Eventually they were seated in the white drawing room, and Natasha, who had been drinking steadily all evening, became truculent as she complained about the lack of social life in Arezzio.

It was gone midnight, but Giselle wasn't tired. Instead she was strung up with nervous tension. All evening there had been only one thing on her mind. One thing. One end result. But oh, so many sensual diversions she might take to reach that end result if only Saul would let her.

She had made up her mind to stop fighting what she felt, to stop trying to deny herself the satisfaction she craved. Why shouldn't she for once taste the pleasures that other women her age took for granted? There could never be a more perfect man or a more perfect situation than there was here and now with Saul, who rejected the idea of commitment and children every bit as fiercely as she did herself—albeit for different reasons. If Saul wanted to satisfy the desire he had already aroused in her there was no reason for her to want to stop him. Maybe this was even meant to be. Her one chance to know what it truly meant to be a woman. Fate taking pity on her and giving her what she had denied herself. *If* Saul wanted it to happen.

How did a woman let a man know that she wanted him without risking humiliating herself if he did not want her? She had spent so long deliberately making sure that she did *not* encourage male advances that she did not know how to encourage them. Previously Saul had kissed her in anger. Did that mean that if she made him angry again it would lead to a resurgence of the passion he had shown her earlier?

Saul glanced discreetly at his watch.

'I think it's time Giselle and I called it a night,' he informed Aldo and Natasha, standing up and looking enquiringly at Giselle as he did so.

Obediently Giselle stood up as well, exchanging goodnights with her host and hostess before walking with Saul to the corridor that led to his apartment.

When they reached her bedroom door, Saul told her brusquely, 'I'll say goodnight here.'

Immediately Giselle's heart sank.

'But what about the necklace and the earrings?' she protested.

'You can give them to me in the morning.'

'I don't think I'll be able to unfasten the necklace.'

'Then sleep with it on.'

Saul's voice was sharp now as he stepped back from her. Another few seconds and he would be gone. Desperation filled her.

'I'd rather…' *I'd rather sleep with you.* She had been about to say it, driven to boldness by her need, but Saul didn't let her finish.

Shaking his head, he told her thickly, 'Giselle, just leave it, will you? Because if you don't…' He paused and then said grimly, 'If I go into that room with you, if I touch you, then I warn you that I won't stop touching you until you are lying naked underneath me and I've got you crying out to me in need.'

His voice became muffled as Giselle moved shakily towards him and put her hands on his shoulders. 'And in ecstasy,' he said, and Giselle shuddered wildly as he finished, 'And in the small death that comes from fulfilment.'

'Don't tell me,' she whispered boldly against his mouth. 'Show me.'

Opening the door, Saul swept her up into his arms, kissing her fiercely as he kicked the door shut behind them and carried her over to the bed.

Before he had placed her on it Giselle had slid her hands inside his jacket and started to unfasten his shirt, greedy for the sight and the scent and the feel of him.

As he kissed her, his tongue probing the soft welcome of her mouth, feeling her own tongue twining with his, Saul unzipped her dress, tugging it free of her body, deepening his kiss, passion surging through him as he cupped her breasts.

'The necklace,' Giselle reminded him, reaching behind her neck for the fastening.

'Leave it,' he answered her. 'It suits you.'

The glitter of the diamonds against her naked skin gave her a look of almost pagan sensuality, and made him feel— What? That he had claimed her and set his mark on her? Made her his just as she had made him a prisoner of his desire for her?

He sat up in the bed, intending to remove his jacket and shirt, but Giselle shook her head to stop him, insisting, 'No, let me. I want to do it.'

Saul supposed he must have been undressed by a woman before, but if so he couldn't remember it, and he certainly couldn't remember anything ever being as intoxicatingly erotic as the absorbed concentration of Giselle's gaze on his body, the increasingly rapid, shallow sounds of her breathing, which lifted her breasts as she removed his jacket and her fingers found the buttons on his shirt and unfastened them.

'I want you to lie down.'

Obediently he did as she commanded, caught on a savagely sweet surge of sensual delight when she straddled his hips, leaning over him as she placed her hands on his shoulders, cupping the ball joints of his shoulders, stroking her hands over them and then back again, and then down his arms, closing her eyes and shuddering in a mute delight that he could see reflected in her own flesh as her nipples flared into even more swollen arousal.

Automatically he gripped her hips and then slid his own hands up over her body, but she stopped him, her expression determined and serious as she told him, 'I can't concentrate if you do that, and I want to know every bit of you—how you feel, how you smell, how you taste. I want to know it all.'

There had never been a woman like this one, nor a feeling like the one she was arousing within him, a need like the need raging through him. He slid his hands up and reached for her.

When she bent over him to taste the flesh of his throat Saul wrapped her hair round his hand. He wanted all of her, right here, right now. He wanted to spread her legs and lift her over him and onto him and feel her taking him into her.

Her tongue flicked against his Adam's apple. Saul groaned and arched up against her mouth, begging, 'Stop tormenting me.'

'You're the one tormenting me.'

Her admission was no sooner made than Saul was drawing her down against him, sweeping the dress from her hips, holding her and kissing her and inflaming her senses so much that she didn't even realise that he had undressed himself until he brought her down against himself and she discovered that where there had been fabric there was now hard, bare male flesh.

Spread out on top of him, Giselle could feel the thick hardness of his erection pressing against her thigh. Saul's hands reached down to caress the inside of her parted legs, causing wet heat to explode inside her. His hands moved up and around, cupping her buttocks, then lifting her hips as he slid her up his torso until he could take the eager peak of her nipple into his mouth.

Was this pleasure or was it torture?

She was so wet and eager. Saul could feel her juices dampening his own flesh. His tongue flicked against her nipple, her sharp cry of longing feeding his own arousal. He rolled her over onto her back, his desire fed by her helpless arch towards him as she offered herself to him. He kissed her mouth, cupping her face so that he could take his fill of the sweet pleasure of kissing her, and feeling her body tremble helplessly beneath the lash of her need. Her sex was swollen, opening to the stroke of his hand and his fingers like a rare flower, spreading its petals for him, swelling and trembling wildly beneath his touch. Inside his head he could already taste her sweetness against his tongue, the softly musky scent of her invading his senses.

Giselle wanted to touch Saul as intimately as he was touching her. She wanted to know him and feel him and taste him. She wanted to caress the length and breadth of him with her hands and her lips.

She only knew that she had voiced those desires out loud in a sobbed litany of longing when she heard Saul groan that she was tormenting him beyond reason. And then her plea was answered, so that she could breathe in the most intimate scent of him and answer the aching female need within herself to know his scent and taste whilst he stroked and caressed her so intimately that she could scarcely bear the pleasure of it.

She was hot and wet, and the touch of her hand and her mouth against his sex was driving him to a frenzy of longing that demanded the ultimate satisfaction.

Momentarily bereft of Saul's touch and her contact with his body, Giselle cried out in protest. But it was a very different kind of cry that burst from her lips when he filled her with the firm, deliberate thrust of his body. Her legs wrapped round him, and she gasped out her pleasure in a delirious rush of breath.

Never had any woman held and caressed him so shockingly seductively, making him ache helplessly for the sweet, passionate movement of her muscles as she moved with him.

And then Saul felt it—the unfamiliar but instantly recognisable tightness, the swift tension in her body, the intake of breath. All of them relaying to him the unimaginable and unwanted truth of her virginity.

Saul knew. Giselle could tell. She could feel his attempt to withdraw from her but her body fought it, fiercely defending its need for the pleasure it had been promised. Her muscles wrapped protestingly around him as she gripped his shoulders and rose with him.

'No,' she told him. 'I can't bear it if you stop now. Please don't.'

It was her honesty that undermined him. That and the ache of her open need for him, the first and the only man to whom she had given herself. The full power of his own answering need for her was reignited within him. He hadn't expected or been prepared for the almost atavistic sense of male superiority that filled his body because he knew that hers had singled him out amongst all men to share this pleasure.

He hadn't intended to give in on a logical basis, even if she *had* told him so firmly, 'It's all right, I am on the pill.' There were still questions he needed and wanted to ask, after all. But she was moving against him, opening herself to him, Saul recognised on a shock of fiercely male arousal, taking him deeper, and his body took over from her, filling her, driving her pleasure and his own until they were moving as one, locked together, two bodies, maybe, but with one single goal that they were climbing towards together.

Giselle reached it first, crying out. He felt her body tighten and then expand around him in a succession of explosive movements that brought his own release in a series of hot, pulsing expulsions.

It had happened, Giselle thought gratefully, held in Saul's arms, her head resting on his still damp, thudding chest in weak post-orgasm euphoria and relief. She now knew all there was to know—had experienced the increasing intensity of each individual caress and pleasure there was to experience. She had crossed the barrier into true womanhood and was now complete, fulfilled, replete with the rich satisfaction to which Saul had taken her and then shared with her.

'I wanted it to happen.'

Saul could feel and hear her soft words, reverberating against his flesh, feel their echo striking into his heart and his emotions.

'I wanted it to happen and I wanted you.'

Giselle had no idea why she felt so impelled to say such words. They were not a defence, or even a justification, she needed neither of those. They were more a statement of reaffirmation, a proud simple declaration of her joy, and her belief in the rightness of what had happened. She had touched the heights and she would have that knowledge, that memory for ever to warm her through the cold darkness of the road that lay ahead. Somehow she had found the courage to take the gift fate had handed her in the shape of Saul a man who did not want either commitment from her or children. Yes she had touched the heights and now there was nowhere left for her to go other than to fall from them, but she must not think about that now.

It was later whilst they were showering together, Saul's knowing sensual touch on her body like hearing echoes of music from the most magnificent composer played by the world's best orchestra, singing in the most heavenly way inside her head, that Giselle touched him too. Quickly she lost herself in the delicious pleasure the freedom to touch him so intimately gave her, her concentration so absolute and intent, her gaze so filled with awed delight—like a child discovering that Father Christmas had appeared magically in the night and not only left every gift they could have wanted but also gifts they had never imagined wanting but which they now discovered were exactly what they would have wanted had they been able to think of them.

No woman had looked at him, touched him, wanted him as Giselle did, and watching her filled Saul with a sensation inside as if something hard and implacable in his chest had become a heavy, unwanted weight that was now cracking apart and dissolving, so that where there had been grimness and steel casing there was now lightness and the most ridiculous effervescent fountaining of happiness.

Hugging the towel which Saul had wrapped tenderly around her, Giselle sat on a stool in the ultra-modern grey, black and white kitchen of his royal apartment whilst Saul cooked Eggs Benedict for her. He had ruefully agreed to make her tea when she had shaken her head to the champagne he had originally offered her.

It was gone two o'clock in the morning, but Giselle had never felt more wide awake or more alive.

Sitting with Saul whilst he fed her forkfuls of delicious food, relishing every second of the equally delicious intimacy she was sharing with him, when he asked her the question she had been expecting she was ready for it, and relaxed enough to answer.

'You were a virgin,' he said quietly, followed by, even softer voiced, 'Why did you choose to lose your virginity with me?'

He had put the plate from which he had been feeding her down, and it gave Giselle a small pang of emotion that she hastily pushed away when Saul pulled her to him whilst he waited for her answer, settling her head comfortably against his shoulder. Thank goodness she already knew that this intimacy they were sharing now was no more than a sexually experienced man's way of showing his appreciation for the sex they had shared. It had nothing to do with anything deeply emotional that might have hinted at the development of a true relationship between them. That awareness helped her to focus on her answer to him, and she responded truthfully.

'You already know. Well, sort of.'

Saul's fingers beneath her chin lifted her face, so that he could look down into it.

'I do?' he questioned.

'Yes,' Giselle confirmed, nodding her head. 'I wanted you. That shocked and frightened me at first. It was relatively easy before I met you not to want anyone. I knew, of course, that I couldn't and mustn't, because I knew—well, I felt it would be wrong of me because of—'

'Because of your childhood?'

'Yes,' Giselle agreed, grateful to him for helping her over the stumbling block with which she had been struggling. 'Yes—exactly because of that. I knew I couldn't…I knew I *mustn't* have a child…children. I didn't want to be promiscuous and have a procession of men through my life and my bed, and besides I was afraid that I might start to care for one of them, or they for me, but with you it was different.'

'Because you knew that I would understand your childhood?'

'Yeees…'

Giselle hoped that Saul wouldn't hear the small hesitation in her confirmation and question her more deeply.

She couldn't tell him the deepest and darkest secret that separated her from the fulfilment and happiness other women were free to want—not now when she was so happy, when she felt so complete, and so...so normal. Telling him the truth would only spoil things, and there was no point. No point and no need for him to know, given that she knew this glorious, heavenly, wonderful gift from fate was simply a magical moment out of time, whose beauty, like a delicate soap bubble, could not exist for very long.

The truth was shocking, destructive and ugly. Were she to tell it to him he would look at her so very differently than he was doing now. It wasn't really wrong of her to want to keep these moments precious and safe, was it? Not when his knowing was so unnecessary, and when she already knew that the pleasure he had given her was quite literally all she could have of him.

Poor child. She must have suffered even more than *he* had because of the loss of her parents. And not just her parents, he remembered, there had been a small child involved as well—a baby sibling. Knowing that child had lost its life was bound to have created in her young mind an awareness of the fragility of human life and a fear of losing those she loved.

Saul drew her even closer, filled with tenderness for her and a desire to protect her—things he would once have repudiated with anger immediately had he thought he might experience them, but which now, instead of being his hated enemies, seemed natural and necessary accompaniments to the other emotions he was feeling. Emotions? He would question his own feelings later, Saul told himself. Right now his duty of care was for

Giselle. For the child she had once been when he had not been there to protect her, and for the woman she had become in his arms now that he was. Such a huge step could not be taken without the person taking it being deeply affected by it, even if Giselle herself was not aware of that fact yet. He was aware of it, and it was up to him to see to it that she made that transition safely.

'I was so afraid and angry when I realised that I wanted you, but then I kept hearing about your views on…on things.'

Saul knew she meant on his not wanting a child, and he bent to kiss the top of her head.

'Today—I mean yesterday, when we arrived,' Giselle corrected herself, squirming in heady pleasure as Saul kissed the side of her neck, his hand finding her willing breast beneath the wrappings of her towel and caressing it softly whilst she talked. 'When you kissed me and everything I wanted you so much.' She looked up at him. 'I'd wanted you before, and wanting you had kept me awake at night, thinking and imagining. I knew I couldn't bear not to know, to spend the rest of my life wishing. I felt at first that fate was tempting me and tormenting me—laughing at me because I couldn't be with you. But then I thought perhaps fate was really trying to *give* me something, to make it up to me, and that I should…if you wanted to. And then tonight, when you didn't want to come into my bedroom with me, I felt so desperate.'

'I didn't want to because I knew what would happen if I did,' Saul told her.

'And now that it has, do you regret it?' Giselle asked him anxiously.

'Do you?' Saul pushed the question back to her.

'No,' Giselle answered him, simply and truthfully.

'Good,' Saul told her, without answering her question himself, and pulling her to him he kissed her until nothing else mattered.

Somehow they made it back to the bedroom—his this time because, as he told her explicitly in between increasingly intimate caresses, it was closer than hers, and he was close to not making it as far as *any* bed, thanks to the way she was kissing him and touching him.

His bedroom, like the kitchen, was decorated in masculine shades of off-white, grey and black, with just a softening touch of dark cream.

Saul slammed the bedroom door and reached for her, leaning her back against it as he lifted her so that she could wrap her legs eagerly around him. His sex, almost of its own volition, was nudging its way between the lips of her sex, to rub eagerly against her slick readiness and then hotly and eagerly to move within her, filling her so wholly and completely that her body sang with joy.

This time there was no restriction and no hesitation. Her womanhood rejoiced in the full hard presence of him and embraced him, holding him, urging him to move ever deeper and faster.

Her orgasm was swift and intense, driving the breath from her lungs so that she couldn't even cry out her pleasure. Saul cried out his, though, in a deep shout of exultation as Giselle's body took the gift of his release from him and his body pumped its pleasure into her soft, warm readiness.

Another shower, with Giselle almost falling asleep

beneath it this time, and then they were back in bed. She was asleep as soon as her head touched the pillow.

Saul didn't sleep, though. Instead he propped his head up on his hand, his elbow on the pillow, and watched her, frowning as he did so.

What was happening to him? He didn't know. He only knew that tonight something profound and deep-rooted within him had been shaken to its core; beliefs he had thought set in stone had been revealed as shaky because the foundations had been split along a fault line that tonight had exposed.

He felt vulnerable, he recognised, like a creature robbed of its protective shell. It was only sex, he told himself. That was all. Just sex. And, no matter how fundamental its effect on him might be now, it did not and could not change anything about the way he intended to live his life. What had happened between them was just a one-off, an event out of time. It meant nothing to him other than that. And besides, it was Aldo he should be thinking about—not himself, and certainly not Giselle.

The discussions he had had with his cousin had shown him that the situation was even worse than he had first suspected. Aldo hadn't just invested his own money, or rather the money Saul had given him, in the fraudulent investment scheme with its far too high interest rates—which would have alerted anyone who understood the financial world better to the fact that it had to be a con—he had also invested the state's money in it. Money which was needed to pay for teachers and nurses and doctors, and to run public services and infrastructures.

When Saul had asked Aldo why he had said nothing to him prior to making these investments, why he had not sought his advice, Aldo had replied shamefacedly that he had been told not to discuss the scheme with anyone, because access to it was limited to only a few specially chosen investors.

'Natasha felt that if you knew you would want to invest in it as well. Please do not blame her,' Aldo had begged him. 'The fault is entirely mine. Natasha's only fault was that out of her love for me she wanted to prove to you that we could be independent of your generosity. She has far more pride than I do, Saul, and she feels that since I am Grand Duke, I should be...'

'Richer than me?' Saul had supplied wryly, but he had known that what his cousin did not want to say was that Natasha wanted her husband to take precedence over him in every single way—because she felt that that would punish him for not wanting her.

Right now, though, saving his cousin from the public embarrassment of being declared bankrupt, and the knock-on effect that would have on the country and its finances, was far more important to him than Natasha's spitefulness.

He mentally reviewed his own assets to assess which of them he could most readily and easily realise in order to refloat Aldo's finances.

It was perhaps a pity he had bought the island, but having done so he wasn't prepared to sell it at a loss. There were other assets he could sell, though, such as his share in a new office block in Singapore. Aldo was family, and sometimes family had to come first.

CHAPTER TEN

GISELLE had woken up once already, to find that she was pinned to the bed by the weight of Saul's leg lying across her lower body and his arm holding her against his side. It was a welcome imprisonment, though, and it enabled her to lie silently within its captivity and marvel at the magical events of the night and the happiness they had brought her. Now she was awake again—this time to find that she had the bed—his bed—to herself, and that she could stretch out languorously in it, entranced by the sweetly heavy ennui that possessed her body as intimately and intensely as Saul had possessed it during the night.

Saul *was* her perfect lover, in every single way. With him there was no need for her to feel guilt because of the pain she might ultimately cause him, or to fear her own emotions. She knew that this pleasure that filled her and surrounded her like a fluffy pink cloud of delight was only fleeting and could only be enjoyed very briefly. And if knowing that brought safety, perhaps it also heightened its sweetness—because she knew it could only be for now, for this short precious time beyond which she was not going to look until she had to.

Their time together, like the intimacy it had brought,

could not continue once they returned to London. That would be impossible. She knew that. There was no need for Saul to say so to her, and she hoped that he believed her and trusted her enough to know that. She didn't want a single second of this special time spoiled or marred by any kind of discord or distrust between them.

How she would deal with the realities of life once they were back in London she would figure out once she was back there. If Saul chose to end her secondment to him then so be it. It would be the sensible and practical action to take—and that sharp, agonised fluttering of anguish inside her chest was simply a knee-jerk reaction and didn't actually mean anything, she assured herself firmly. Nevertheless, it was enough to have her getting out of bed and making her way to her own bedroom, where she showered and dressed in one of the tee shirts and the skirt that her personal shopper had recommended to her.

It wasn't because last night Saul had stroked his hand along the length of her leg and said how long and slender her legs were that she was wearing a skirt instead of trousers or jeans. It was simply because she could see that outside the sun was shining. It was spring, the trees were in blossom, and a light skirt seemed more appropriate than something heavy.

Saul, already showered and dressed when he had kissed her awake earlier, had told her that they would have to stay in Arezzio for longer than he had originally planned because of the complexity of his cousin's financial affairs. Giselle had hugged that news to herself, gloating like a miser given a pure gold coin over the prospect of their intimacy being extended.

She was just brushing her hair when a messenger arrived in the form of a maid dressed in black, her brown hair coiled round her head in plaits. She looked young and nervous, Giselle could see, immediately feeling sorry for her as she bobbed a small curtsy and informed her that the Grand Duchess had sent her, to see if Giselle would like to accompany her on a shopping trip into the city.

Accompanying Natasha anywhere was the last thing Giselle felt like doing. But good manners compelled her to accept the other woman's invitation and to follow the maid back along the now more familiar corridors and down the flights of stairs until she was standing in a sunshine-filled room decorated in shades of lemon and powder-blue, where Natasha was seated on a gold-brocade-covered sofa.

'Ah, there you are,' she greeted Giselle, flicking a dismissive gaze over her before smoothing her hand over what Giselle knew must be an infinitely superior and far more expensive designer outfit of golden-yellow silk. The skirt of her dress was so short and tight that Giselle was surprised she was able to sit down in it—to sit down in it *and* then walk in the vertiginous strappy white leather metal-studded heels she was wearing.

Heavy diamond-encrusted bracelets circled her narrow wrists, and her make-up, if anything, was even more heavy than it had been the night before.

'A business associate of my father has opened a shop here in the city, and this morning he has telephoned me to say that he has in some clothes by a new designer that he knows I will love.'

* * *

It was late afternoon. The shopping trip had not been a success, at least as far as Giselle was concerned. Natasha had spent her time flirting with the odiously oily friend of her father, who had encouraged her to try on and then parade in front of him in a selection of increasingly short and tight-fitting outfits, each one of which had seemed to require that he tugged and pulled at the fabric, whilst leering at Natasha in a way that had turned Giselle's stomach and aroused her indignation and pity on Aldo's behalf. Poor Aldo. The outfits Natasha had tried on were surely more suited to a Page Three model desperate for attention than to a Grand Duchess, but of course it had not been Giselle's place to say so.

On their return to the palace Aldo had been so genuinely pleased that Natasha had had the chance to spend time with an old friend that Giselle had felt like asking Natasha if she *knew* how fortunate she was and what she was risking losing with her contempt for Aldo's adoration and love. But then Giselle had reminded herself that she was in no position to lecture anyone about their emotions, or allying sexual desire to those emotions, when she herself was so determined not to do so.

Now the four of them were sitting in the blue and yellow salon, and Aldo was telling her it had been his and Saul's grandmother's favourite room.

'Which is why we always take tea here—because it was her habit to do so.'

Natasha pulled a face when Aldo said this, and insisted that what *she* wanted was a vodka and champagne cocktail—the same cocktail she had been drinking at the dress shop, Giselle knew. And she felt even more sorry for Aldo when his kind face became slightly shadowed. Because Natasha threatened a fuss if she refused, Giselle was also obliged to drink a cocktail instead of the tea she would have preferred.

The alcohol did not seem to be improving Natasha's temper, which now flared up again as Aldo suggested very discreetly that perhaps she already had enough expensive clothes.

'What?' she challenged her husband, before gulping at her drink—her third since they had all sat down. 'So now you mean to deny me the only pleasure I've got left, do you? Since being good in bed isn't exactly your forte, is it, darling? You should perhaps ask Saul for some tips.'

Giselle could hear the sound of Saul's expelled breath as he stood behind her, and no wonder. Poor Aldo must feel mortified—although he was merely shaking his head and saying gently, 'I think you are embarrassing our guest a little, Natasha.'

'Is that possible?' Natasha retaliated. 'Can *anyone* embarrass one of Saul's women? I wouldn't have thought so.'

Giselle suspected that Natasha's drinking had brought her mood to that borderline where it could easily move from mere truculence to something more unpleasant. For Aldo's sake she didn't want to provoke her into crossing that line, even though her stomach muscles had tightened defensively with dislike for her.

Rather than retaliate, she decided to make her exit, and said quietly, avoiding looking at anyone, 'I'm feeling rather tired. If you will excuse me, I think I'll go to my room.'

'I'll come with you,' Saul said immediately. 'I've got some work to do myself.'

'I'm sorry about that,' Saul apologised the minute they were on their own. 'Natasha's behaviour was appalling. I don't know how Aldo puts up with her.

'He loves her, and he's afraid of losing her,' Giselle assessed as he unlocked the door that led to his private apartment and held it open for her.

'I feel desperately sorry for any child they end up having… I think that Natasha will be a very demanding mother, with exacting standards for any child they have, but especially a son. She's so competitive herself that a…a more sensitive child will find it hard to deal with.' He paused, mulling over the way she had behaved. 'If you were to ask me, I would say that there's a degree of instability within Natasha. I hadn't noticed it before, but today…'

Giselle's mouth had gone dry, and her heart was pounding. 'I think it was just the drink that made her behave the way she did.'

'You're defending her?' Saul's eyebrows rose. 'That's very charitable of you, but I thought her behaviour pointed quite plainly to some kind of emotional and perhaps even mental instability—and that can only lead to a great deal of unhappiness for those close to her.'

Giselle gave a small involuntary shiver, and Saul guessed why immediately.

'You're thinking of your own childhood?'

'Yes,' Giselle was forced to admit. 'I was just thinking how hard it will be for Aldo and Natasha's children.'

'Because Natasha will neglect them emotionally?''

'Yes. And…' She paused, and Saul prompted her.

'And?'

Her voice very low and sad, Giselle told him, 'And because they will have to bear the stigma of being tainted by their mother's emotional instability and the fear that she might have passed it down to them. They will be judged because of that. People always make judgements.'

'You sound as though you speak from personal experience?'

It was too late now to recognise that she had come perilously close to a very dangerous place and to wish she had stayed silent.

'I was judged because of the accident—because I lived and they…they didn't.' She forced herself to admit it. 'By my father and I dare say others.'

'Your father judged you?' Saul stopped walking and turned to her. 'Why should anyone judge you for something over which you had no control? You were a child.'

It was too late to hold back the roaring, rolling tide of her pain now. It was engulfing her and sweeping her up into its shuddering darkness, making her feel like a child again—alone, abandoned, unwanted, *guilty*…

They had reached the bedroom. Saul opened the door, surprising himself with his need to comfort her as he told her firmly, 'You were not to blame. It wasn't your fault.'

It wasn't your fault. She had hungered so much over the years to hear those words spoken to her, to feel that someone knew and understood her pain and wanted to help her. That they wouldn't blame her or turn away from her. That they wouldn't choose death rather than live with her. As her father had done.

She had heard the whispers after his death, murmured behind the hands of well-meaning adults too consumed by their own curiosity and shock to realise that a seven-year-old child was perfectly capable of translating what they were saying when they commented that her father had had a heart attack because he hadn't wanted to live after the deaths of her mother and her baby brother.

She had understood what they were saying. She had understood too why her father had sent her away to live with her great-aunt. It was because he had known the truth. He had always blamed her. He had recognised her guilt and he had left her alone with it and her fear of it.

Her father's desertion of her had hurt her dreadfully and left her feeling that she had been a burden to him that he hadn't wanted. A burden he had only been able to escape via death. She had known then that she must never burden anyone else with her love, just as she could never—

Her body shuddered again, but this time Saul's arms were around her. She didn't want to think about the past—she didn't walk to talk about it or be overshadowed by it. All she wanted was to be in this moment, in Saul's arms. She lifted her face for his kiss.

Saul kissed her, and kept on kissing her whilst he undressed her, and each slither of fabric sliding from her body made her feel as though she was shedding another unwanted layer of inhibition, in doing so setting free the passionate, sensual side of her nature that had for so long been repressed.

Only in Saul's arms, in Saul's bed, did she really feel that she became herself and truly alive, that she reached and touched the true essence of herself. But she knew that her pleasure and its intensity could only be hers for a very short span of time. That meant not wasting a second of it—which was why her hands were urgent in their determination to undress him, as his were to undress her. Their journey towards the pure flesh-on-flesh contact they both craved was broken and delayed by shared kisses and caresses that had soft crooning sounds of pleasure murmuring from Giselle's throat.

Eventually they were free to touch and enjoy one another as they both ached to do. Giselle ran her fingertips the length of Saul's erection and then tried to encircle it with her hand, lifting her awed and aroused gaze to meet the hot intensity of his when his width was too great for her to completely capture it in her hold. She could still caress him, and stroked the slick, hot, pliable flesh that covered the head of his erection with aching longing, feeling the moist heat swell within her own sex, already imagining the moment when his erection would stroke against her aroused and eager flesh, making it flower open for him whilst her muscles quivered in eager anticipation of his first longed-for thrust.

She wouldn't make it to the bed. She couldn't wait that long. But Saul had anticipated her need and they were already on the bed, and he was lying on his back and lifting her over him so that she could take control of her own pleasure.

She wanted desperately to rush and satisfy her hunger, but some age-old female instinct held her back, whispering to her that their shared pleasure would be all the greater for being taken slowly.

And that instinct was right. To look into Saul's eyes as she took him slowly into her, seeing how helpless he was in the face of his desire and her control of it, watching the longing and need he couldn't hide from her as she moved down a little on him, and then stopped to rise up again, brought her such a rush of pleasure that it was almost as though she had orgasmed already.

Her flesh quickened around Saul's, her own hunger overpowering her desire to draw out their shared pleasure and make it last. Saul's hands gripped her hips, holding her as he moved her up and down over his aroused flesh, slowly and deliberately, until the pleasure became a form of torment as she begged for more—deeper, harder.

'Like this, you mean?' he demanded, teasing her with a slower movement. 'Or like this?' He was holding her down on him now, thrusting fiercely and deeply into her, and the raw pleasure of it was making her cry out to him that she couldn't bear it, and not to stop.

And he didn't—not even when she orgasmed. He took her through it, carrying her on upwards whilst her body collapsed and clung, and she was wrung with orgasm after orgasm until finally he took the last of her pleasure from her and filled her with his own release.

Too exhausted to move, Giselle lay against his body as an unwanted realisation washed over her. She was in love with Saul. Panic exploded inside her. No. That mustn't happen. She mustn't love Saul. The most terrible pain was gripping her—the pain of having a protective veil ripped from her to reveal the edges of a wound that went so deep she knew she hadn't even begun to feel its real pain yet.

She loved Saul. *No!* Yes, she did. Of course she did. And he wanted her. Wanted her—that was all. This intimacy between them wouldn't and couldn't last, but for now he was here, and for now she could and would give thanks for that.

'I'm going to put on weight if we keep doing this,' Giselle mock-complained to Saul three hours later, as she sat up in bed greedily eating the smoked salmon and cream cheese bagels he had brought her when they'd realised they had well and truly missed dinner.

'Mmm? Then I'll have to come up with a way of making sure that you work it off,' Saul teased her.

He had been thinking about her all the time they'd been apart earlier in the day, longing impatiently to be with her—something he had never experienced before. That alone should have been enough to worry him, but strangely when he was with Giselle all he seemed able to think about was her. There'd be time enough when they returned to London for him to put things in their proper perspective and to end what should never really have begun.

But it *had* begun, and was he absolutely sure that he could end it? Of course he was. Commitment wasn't on his agenda. But then neither had Giselle herself been on his agenda when they had first met. That was different, Saul told himself impatiently. Commitment and Giselle went into different compartments in his life. So why was he thinking about them together?

Saul removed the plate from the bed, and then reached for Giselle's hand, drawing her close to him.

CHAPTER ELEVEN

THEY were returning to London this afternoon, Saul having cancelled their visit to the island because he needed to set up some meetings with regard to Aldo's financial affairs. Now, this morning, Giselle was exploring the old city in the May sunshine and trying to tell herself that she would be able to find the strength to live without Saul in her life. She knew she would have to.

She had it all planned. When he told her it was over, she was going to give in her notice and put her flat up for sale. She would buy a small house in Yorkshire and then she could look after her great-aunt herself. Far away from London and looking after her great-aunt she wouldn't be able to weaken and make a fool of herself by begging Saul to take her back to his bed. Because she had fallen in love with him. Despair shuddered through her. How easily she had given in to temptation and broken her self-imposed rules. But all was not lost. Saul did not love her. They would part. She could still keep the promise she had made to herself.

The narrow streets of the old town twisted and turned, the upper windows of the old medieval three- and four-storey houses almost touching one another across them. Some of them were built into the city walls, and others clung to a jumble of alleyways, their black and white façades stooping beneath the weight of their heavy slate roofs.

Saul couldn't concentrate on the complex financial data on the computer screen in front of him. He couldn't concentrate on anything other than Giselle, he recognised grimly. And that meant…? It meant nothing other than that for now he wanted her in his life and his bed. For now. Until they both agreed that whatever was currently burning in them was reduced to ashes and they were free to go their separate ways.

He tried to go back to his work, but the ache inside him refused to be ignored. He wanted to be with Giselle. He knew she was spending the morning exploring the old city. He wanted to be with her. Not just in bed with her, but *with* her. He wanted to see her expression as she explored his home city. He wanted to see it through her eyes. He wanted…

Cursing beneath his breath, he switched off his laptop and stood up. It shouldn't be hard to find her. The old city wasn't very large, and he knew every single winding inch of its narrow streets.

Once he was outside he started to walk briskly, and then more swiftly as the urgency within him grew.

When he finally saw her she was half the length of a street away from him, poised on the pavement of one of the busier streets, just where it opened out into the town square. She was standing completely still, her gaze apparently fixed on the opposite side of the road. At first Saul thought she must be waiting to cross it, and then he realised that she was watching a young mother who was trying to cope with a buggy with a baby in it and an impatient toddler, who was trying to push the buggy and refusing to take her hand.

Saul started to make his way towards her.

Giselle had seen the young mother with her two children as she herself was just about to cross the unexpectedly busy road, with traffic moving at speed, full-pelt towards the square.

The little boy had grabbed the handle of the buggy and was trying to push it, whilst his harassed mother remonstrated with him, insisting that he hold her hand. Giselle knew the words she would be saying—after all, they were engraved on her own heart, in her own mother's voice.

'Hold on to the pram. Hold my hand. Don't let go. Don't pull. Don't...'

The child was trying to pull free of his mother's hand. She turned away from the buggy to remonstrate with him for another minute, and...

Careless of her own safety, Giselle plunged into the seething traffic, oblivious to the sound of car horns and the warning shouts of drivers, only one thought in her mind as time swung backwards for her and she stepped through its open door into her own past.

She must save them. She must save all of them—not just herself.

What was Giselle doing, running blindly into the traffic like that? She was going to be killed.

Saul reacted automatically, driven by the greatest fear known to man—that of losing that which they loved above all things. He barely registered what his own reaction meant as he plunged after her, covering the distance with superhuman speed, snatching her almost from beneath the wheels of an oncoming car and dragging her to the safety of the pavement.

'What were you doing? Trying to kill yourself?'

Giselle could feel the angry thud of Saul's heart against her own chest. She could hear the voices of the concerned onlookers who had seen what had happened and were now pressing in on them to ask if she was all right. But those things were at a distance from her. All she could think of, all she could ask was, 'The buggy—the baby...is it all right?'

Saul looked down into her pale tense face, and then glanced across the road.

'All three of them are fine,' he told her truthfully.

All three of them. All three of them, but not all three of her family. Not all three of *them.* They had not been fine. She had saved herself, but she had let her mother and her baby brother die. She had sent them to their deaths. She had...

A terrible dry sob tore at her throat.

'I killed them. It was my fault. I shouldn't have let go of the pram. I should have saved them or died with them.' She was not looking at him, Saul saw, his heart turning over inside his chest, but past him.

'Giselle?'

Immediately she focused on him.

'I'm sorry,' she told him politely—as politely as though he was a stranger, he recognized.

Suddenly he was desperate to make her look at him and be with him—to make her... To make her what? Recognise what *he* had just recognised when he had feared that he might lose her, and to tell him as he wanted to tell her that she was his life and he never wanted to let her out of his sight again? Was this love? This feeling that a part of you lay open and bleeding with a wound that could only be healed by complete fusion with another person, a special person, one's perfect other half? If it was, no wonder he had feared it. It was so huge, so all-encompassing, so fearsome, that any human could be forgiven for trembling when confronted by its might. He wanted to tell Giselle what he had discovered, but now was not the time when she was so obviously suffering from shock.

'I'm taking you back to the palace,' he told her, 'and then I'm going to call a doctor.'

'No.' Giselle stopped him. 'No. I don't need a doctor. I'm perfectly all right.'

It wasn't true, of course, and she could see from Saul's grim expression that he didn't believe her.

Saul looked across at the bed where Giselle lay, fully dressed and fast asleep. She had been trembling violently and convulsively by the time he had got her back to the palace, and she had made no demur when he had insisted on pouring her a brandy and making her drink it, and had passively acquiesced when he'd suggested that she should lie down and rest.

Her near accident had obviously and naturally shocked her. It had shocked *him*. He could still hear the protesting squeal of the tyres and brakes on the cars that had thankfully managed to avoid hitting her.

On the bed, Giselle moved restlessly in her brandy-induced sleep, a protesting *'No!'* wrenched from her throat, followed by an almost violent movement of her limbs, as though she was trying to run, and then she screamed.

'Mummy, no!'

Her agonized cry was filled with such terror that the sound of it ripped at Saul's heart and took him to his feet. He reached the bed just as she opened her eyes and struggled to sit up.

She had had the nightmare again—the first time for years—and this time it had seemed so real, every detail so clear and sharp. She had even been able to smell the rain mingling with her mother's scent, and then the smell of the blood—blood everywhere—on her clothes and on her hands. She looked down at them and then closed her eyes, agonised tears seeping from them to burn her face in the same way that the acid of her guilt was burning into her soul.

'Giselle?' She felt Saul reach for her and take her in his arms. 'Talk to me,' he commanded. 'Tell me what's wrong.'

Giselle opened her eyes again. She was too weary to fight to protect herself and conceal her guilt any longer. She was going to lose Saul anyway, so what did it matter if she had to look at him and see the disgust in his eyes?

She exhaled in defeat.

'It was the mother—the mother with the buggy and the little boy. They reminded me... I thought...'

Her voice was so low that Saul had to strain to hear what she was saying.

'I should have stopped them. I shouldn't have let go of my mother's hand and the pram. If I hadn't...'

She was talking about her childhood, Saul realised, beginning to understand that in some way seeing that mother with her buggy and her young child must have reminded her of the terrible accident that had robbed her of her own mother and baby brother.

'I should have died with them. That's what my father thought. That's why he sent me away instead of letting me stay with him. He couldn't bear the sight of me because I didn't save them. He knew I should have died with them.'

Saul was appalled.

'No, Giselle,' he assured her, wrapping his arms round her. 'No. That's not true.'

'Yes, it is,' Giselle insisted. 'It was my fault. If I'd held on to them… But I didn't. I pulled away. I let go and they died. Mummy was angry with me because I hadn't wanted to go out. It was dark and raining, but she said we needed to go out because Thomas wouldn't stop crying. She told me to put Thomas in his pram, and then she said that we'd walk to the park and I could go on the swings. But then when we were nearly at the park she changed her mind and said that we were going to cross the road instead. She told me to hold her hand, but I didn't want to. I wanted to go to the park like she had promised. She grabbed hold of my arm, but I pulled free, and then she started to cross the road. I screamed at her to stop because there was a lorry coming, but she wouldn't, and then…and then it was too late. It was my fault they were killed.'

'No.' Saul immediately rejected her guilt, horrified to think of the mental pain and guilt she must have endured. 'No. It was not your fault. It was an accident and you were not to blame.' He smoothed her damp hair back off her face and commanded, 'Look at me.'

Silently Giselle did so.

'Do you really think that fate would have wanted or allowed you to die when she had already promised you to me?'

His words had Giselle's eyes widening.

'What…what do you mean?'

'When I saw you plunge into that traffic and thought that I might lose you I realised the truth. I love you, Giselle. I think I probably fell in love with you in that wretched car park when you stole my parking space and then defied me. Fate brought us together there that day because she meant us to be together.'

'No,' Giselle protested, immediately panicking. 'You can't love me. You mustn't. We mustn't love each other.'

'Because we might be hurt?' Saul leaned his forehead against hers and kissed the bridge of her nose. 'This is why you feel you shouldn't love anyone and why you don't want a child, isn't it? Because of what happened to your mother and baby brother?'

Giselle hesitated. Now was the time to tell him everything. She wanted to. She wanted to desperately. But somehow the words just would not come. She was too afraid to speak them, so instead she nodded her head.

It was after all the truth in its way—even if it was not the whole of that truth. Surely she could have this sweetest of precious times with him? Surely she could have just a little longer before she had to give him up to a woman who would be able to give him what she never could?

'I didn't want you to know. I didn't want you to blame me and look at me the way my father did. I could have saved them, Saul, but I didn't—I let them go,' she told him emotionally.

'No. You think that now, but you were a child—what could you have done?'

He could so easily picture the scene—the dark wet road, the tired mother impatient to get home, her mind on other things, stepping out into the road, expecting the child whose hand she had released to follow her. The thought of what all the years of carrying the guilt she should never have been allowed to carry must have done to her brought a huge lump to his throat and a vow to his heart that he would love her so much that she would never again feel any pain.

'I love you,' he told her, knowing as he said the words that he meant them, and surprised only that he had been foolish enough to fight against the truth for so long with his mind, when his body and his heart had already recognised and given themselves up to their love for Giselle. 'There is nothing you could ever do or be that could stop me loving you,' he said softly. 'Nothing. I want to marry you, Giselle.'

Immediately she stiffened in his hold.

'No. You can't. You can't want to marry me.'

Saul was amused, and teased her. 'Oh, I see—you've got a husband already, have you? Very well, then, that marriage will have to be annulled. After all, you were never properly his—not like you have become my woman, my love, my life,' he told her, his voice thickening as he bent his head to kiss her.

She couldn't resist him any more than she could resist her own need.

'Fate intended us to be together,' Saul insisted firmly. 'I am more sure of that than anything I have been sure of before. For us to meet, for us to love, for us to be together is our mutual and shared destiny.' Every cell within him, inherited from the generations that had gone before, told Saul that. 'Fate even gave us both a messed-up childhood, so that we could understand one another. Out of the cruelty of the loss we have known fate has forged a bond and a bridge for us which we can cross from our separate aloneness to a shared future.'

'Those are lovely words,' Giselle responded. 'But...'

'They are more than words,' Saul assured her. 'They are my promise to you for our future together—and we *will* have a future together, Giselle. What we have together is too special for us not to.'

Every word he spoke was like a knife being driven into her heart. She so much wanted what he was offering her—but how could she trust him to love her as she was, for always?

'Marriage usually means children,' she told him huskily, 'and I can never have your child, Saul. My feelings on that will never change.'

His hand closed round hers.

'Have I said that I want them to? The truth is, Giselle, that I am *glad* that you do not want children. My own feelings on that subject have not changed. You and I, we can travel together, be together, work together. Together we will construct buildings of great beauty, great power and passion wherever we are called upon to do so. We cannot do that, commit wholly to that and to one another, *and* have children. Our creations shall be our progeny, our gift.'

He spoke so eloquently, so believably and so enticingly, that Giselle felt dazzled by the breadth of his vision and the depth of his commitment to her and to their future together.

'Do you promise?' she asked him. 'Do you promise that you mean it, Saul?'

'We don't need children to prove our love for one another. I don't need anything or anyone other than you, Giselle.'

Such emotive, tender words—soothing her hurts, filling her with courage, feeding her own love for him.

'I love you, Giselle.'

'And I love you too.'

There it was—said. A promise asked for and given. A commitment made. A love shared.

Would it be wrong of her to take Saul's love and give him her own? If they didn't have children their love would be safe. He need never know about that... that other thing. He would surely turn away from her in revulsion if he did. But he didn't need to know, did he? she pleaded inwardly with her conscience. If they were destined to be together, as he had said, then she must be destined not to have a child and not to have to tell him.

The temptation was too much for her—especially when he was kissing her as he was right now...

EPILOGUE

THEY were married three months later, in the cathedral in Arezzio, in keeping with Parenti family tradition.

Giselle wore a white Chanel bridal gown. Saul had insisted on her wearing white. Her great-aunt attended the ceremony, and Giselle saw in the old lady's face how happy she was for her.

Natasha, wearing one of her favoured too-short, too-tight dresses, glared at her when she walked back down the aisle on Saul's arm as his wife, but Giselle didn't care. She was too happy, too filled with love and gratitude to feel anything other than pity for Natasha.

Saul had dealt with Aldo's debts and discreetly restored the country's finances to stability. Once they returned from their honeymoon work was going to start on the island, and the new resort was going to be Giselle's personal project—a wedding gift to her from Saul.

Now there was just time for a final few minutes with her great-aunt whilst Saul was with Aldo, before they left on their honeymoon.

'I wish your father was here today to see you so happy, Giselle. He loved you so much.'

'My father *loved* me?' She was too shocked to

hold back the words. 'How could he when he sent me away?'

'Oh, Giselle. He asked me to take you because he felt there were too many sad memories for you in being with him. He wanted you to have a fresh start. He felt so guilty about what had happened—and over your mother.'

'*He* felt guilty? I thought he blamed me.'

'Never.' Her great-aunt shook her head vigorously. 'He blamed himself. He worried that what you had witnessed would scar you, and that being with him would only make that worse. He would have been so proud to see you as you are today. You have married a good man, Giselle, a man who loves you as you deserve to be loved—and I can see that you love him in the same way. That is good. No one should marry for anything less than the very best love there is.' She paused, and then asked gently, 'You have told Saul everything, I expect?'

Giselle couldn't meet her great-aunt's probing look.

'I've told him everything he needs to know,' she replied.

Her great-aunt squeezed Giselle's hand.

'I'm so glad. There should not be secrets between a couple who love one another. Secrets can cause such dreadful damage.'

Saul was coming over. Giselle kissed her great-aunt's cheek, and felt the now familiar quiver of achingly sweet need possess her body as she looked up at her new husband. Surely nothing could spoil her happiness now. Surely now she could finally put the past behind her?

'It's time for us to leave,' Saul told her.

Nodding her head, Giselle gave him her hand—just as she had already given him her heart.

Now, finally, they were on their own—alone together in their bungalow on a luxurious and exclusive resort complex. Their butler had cleared away the remains of their evening meal, they had walked on their private beach and then swum naked together in the moonlight, and now they were celebrating their commitment to one another in the most intimate and private way possible.

Saul was anointing her body with kisses so tender they were almost reverential, and the love they shared was surely as he had told her—meant to be, and strong enough to hold at bay even the darkest of fears. And the guilt? Could that be held at bay too?

It must be. It must be consigned to the past. Because it had no place here in her life with Saul. Nothing could hurt her now that she had his love. Nothing could harm her. She was safe, their love was safe, and she had nothing to fear.

'You are all I want and all I will ever want,' Saul told her, as he had told her when she had committed herself to him. 'Just you, only you, and nothing else.'

She knew he meant it. Surely nothing could spoil things for her now? Surely fate had decided to relent and allow her to be happy? Could she be happy, knowing the secret she was keeping from Saul? *Yes*. Yes, because it couldn't harm either of them now.

'Love me,' she begged Saul, clinging to him with fierce passion. 'Love me, Saul.'

Beneath his answering kiss she offered up a mental

prayer for their happiness, before offering up herself on the altar of their shared love.

Nothing could part them now. Nothing could damage or destroy what they had. *Nothing.*

CHAPTER ONE

'I'M GOING TO have to go,' Meg said to her mother. 'They've finished boarding, so I'd better turn off my phone.'

'You'll be fine for a while yet.' Ruth Hamilton persisted with their conversation. 'Did you finish up the work for the Evans purchase?'

'Yes.' Meg tried to keep the edge from her voice. She really wanted just to turn off the phone and relax. Meg hated flying. Well, not all of it—just the take-off part. All she wanted to do was close her eyes and listen to music, take some nice calming breaths before the plane prepared for its departure from Sydney Airport—except, as usual, her mother wanted to talk about work. 'Like I said,' Meg said calmly, because if she so much as gave a hint that she was irritated her mum would want to know more, 'everything is up-to-date.'

'Good,' Ruth said, but still she did not leave things there.

Meg coiled a length of her very straight red hair around and around one finger, as she always did when either tense or concentrating.

'You need to make sure that you sleep on the plane, Meg, because you'll be straight into it once you land. You wouldn't believe how many people are here. There are so many opportunities...'

Meg closed her eyes and held on to a sigh of frustration as her mum chatted on about the conference and then moved to travel details. Meg already knew that a car would meet her at Los Angeles airport and take her straight to the hotel where the conference was being held. And, yes, she knew she would have about half an hour to wash and get changed.

Meg's parents were prominent in Sydney's real estate market and were now looking to branch into overseas investments for some of their clients. They had left for Los Angeles on Friday to network, while Meg caught up with the paperwork backlog at the office before joining them.

Meg knew that she should be far more excited at the prospect of a trip to Los Angeles. Usually she loved visiting new places, and deep down Meg knew that really she had nothing to complain about—she was flying business class and would be staying in the sumptuous hotel where the conference was being held. She would play the part of successful professional, as would her parents.

Even though, in truth, the family business wasn't doing particularly well at the moment.

Her parents were always very eager to jump on the latest get-rich-quick scheme. Meg, who could always be relied on for sensible advice, had suggested that rather than all of them flying over maybe just one of them should go, or perhaps they should give it a miss entirely and concentrate on the properties they already had on their books.

Of course her parents hadn't wanted to hear that. This, they had insisted, was the next big thing.

Meg doubted it.

It wasn't that, though, which caused her disquiet.

Really, when she had suggested that only one of them go—given that she dealt with the legal side of things—Meg had rather hoped they might have considered sending only her.

A week away wasn't just a luxury she required—it was fast becoming a necessity. And it wasn't about the nice hotel—she'd stay in a tent if she had to, just for the break, just for a pause so that she could think properly. Meg felt as if she were suffocating—that wherever she turned her parents were there, simply not giving her room to think. It had been like that for as long as she could remember, and sometimes she felt as if her whole life had been planned out in advance by her parents.

In truth, it probably had.

Meg had little to complain about. She had her own nice flat in Bondi—but, given that she worked twelve-hour days, she never really got to enjoy it, and there was always something at work that needed her attention at weekends: a signature to chase up, a contract to read through. It just never seemed to end.

'We're actually going to look at a couple of properties this afternoon…' Her mum carried on talking as there was a flurry of activity in the aisle beside Meg.

'Well, don't go agreeing to anything until I get there,' Meg warned. 'I mean it, Mum.'

She glanced over and saw that two flight attendants were assisting a gentleman. His face was blocked from Meg's vision by the overhead lockers, but certainly from his physique this man didn't look as if he required assistance.

He was clearly tall and extremely fit-looking, and from what Meg could see he appeared more than capable of putting his own laptop into the overhead locker, yet the attendants danced around him, taking his jacket and offering their apologies as he went to take the seat beside Meg.

As his face came into view Meg, who was already struggling, completely lost her place in the conversation with her mother. The man was absolutely stunning, with very thick, beautifully cut black hair worn just a little too long, so that it flopped over his forehead. He had a very straight Roman nose and high cheekbones. Really, he had all the markings of a *very* good-looking man, but it was his mouth that held her attention—perfectly shaped, like a dark bruise of red in the black of his unshaven jaw, and even though it was a scowling mouth, it was quite simply beautiful.

He threw a brief nod in Meg's direction as he took the seat beside her.

Clearly somebody wasn't very happy!

As he sat down Meg caught his scent—a mixture

of expensive cologne and man—and, though she was
trying to focus on what her mother was saying, Meg's
mind kept wandering to the rather terse conversation
that was taking place beside her as the flight attendants
did their best to appease a man whom, it would seem,
wasn't particularly easy to appease.

'No,' he said to the attendant. 'This will be sorted to
my satisfaction as soon as we have taken off.'

He had a deep, low voice that was rich with an accent Meg couldn't quite place. Perhaps Spanish, she
thought, but wasn't quite sure.

What she *was* sure of, though, was that he demanded
too much of her attention.

Not consciously, of course—she just about carried
on talking to her mother, her finger still twirling in her
hair—but she could not stop listening to the conversation that was none of her business.

'Once again,' the flight attendant said to him, 'we
apologise for any inconvenience, Mr Dos Santos.' Then
she turned her attention to Meg, and although friendly
and polite, the flight attendant was not quite so gushing
as she had so recently been to Meg's fellow passenger.
'You need to turn off your phone, Ms Hamilton. We are
about to prepare for take-off.'

'I really do have to go, Mum,' Meg said. 'I'll see you
there.' With a sigh of relief she turned off her phone.
'The best part of flying,' she said as she did so—not
necessarily to him.

'There is nothing good about flying' came his
brusque response as the plane started to taxi towards

the runway. Seeing her raised eyebrows, he tempered his words a little. 'At least not today.'

She gave him a small smile and offered a quick 'Sorry,' then looked ahead rather than out of the window. After all he could be in the middle of a family emergency and racing to get somewhere. There could be many reasons for his bad mood and it was none of her business after all.

She was actually quite surprised when he answered her, and when she turned she realised that he was still looking at her. 'Usually I do like flying—I do an awful lot of it—but today there are no seats in first class.'

Niklas Dos Santos watched as she blinked at his explanation. She had very green eyes that were staring right at him. He expected her to give a murmur of sympathy or a small tut tut as to the airline's inefficiency; those were the responses that he was used to, so he was somewhat taken aback at hers.

'Poor you!' She smiled. 'Having to slum it back here in business class.'

'As I said, I fly a lot, and as well as working while flying I need to sleep on the plane—something that is now going to be hard to do. Admittedly I only changed my plans this morning, but even so...' He didn't continue. Niklas thought that was the end of the conversation, that he had explained his dark mood well enough. He hoped that now they could sit in mutual silence, but before he could look away the woman in the seat next to him spoke again.

'Yes, it's *terribly* inconsiderate of them—not to keep

a spare seat for you just in case your plans happen to change.'

She smiled as she said it and he understood that she was joking—sort of. She was nothing like anyone he usually dealt with. Normally people revered him, or in the case of a good-looking woman—which she *possibly* was—they came on to him.

He was used to dark-haired, immaculately groomed women from his home town. Now and then he liked blondes—which she was, sort of. Her hair was a reddish blonde. But, unlike the women he usually went for, there was a complete lack of effort on her part. She was very neatly dressed, in three-quarter-length navy trousers and a cream blouse that was delicate and attractive. Yet the blouse was buttoned rather high and she wore absolutely no make-up. He glanced down to nails that were neat but neither painted nor manicured and, yes, he did check for a ring.

Had the engines not revved then she might have noticed that glance. Had she not looked away at that moment she might have been granted the pleasure of one of his very rare smiles. For she seemed refreshingly unimpressed by him, and Niklas had decided she was not a *possibly* good-looking woman in the least...

But she spoke too much.

He would set the tone now, Niklas decided. Just ignore her if she spoke again. He had a lot of work to get through during this flight and did not want to be interrupted every five minutes with one of her random thoughts.

Niklas was not the most talkative person—at least he did not waste words speaking about nothing—and he certainly wasn't interested in her assumptions. He just wanted to get to Los Angeles with as much work and sleep behind him as possible. He closed his eyes as the plane hurtled down the runway, yawned, and decided that he would doze till he could turn on his laptop.

And then he heard her breathing.

Loudly.

And it only got louder.

He gritted his teeth at her slight moan as the plane lifted off the runway and turned to shoot her an irritated look—but, given that her eyes were closed, instead he stared. She was actually fascinating to look at: her nose was snubbed, her lips were wide and her eyelashes were a reddish blonde too. But she was incredibly tense, and she was taking huge long breaths that made her possibly the most annoying woman in the world. He could not take it for the next twelve hours, and Niklas decided he would be speaking again to the flight attendant—someone would have to move out of first class.

Simply, this would not do.

Meg breathed in through her nose and then out through her mouth as she concentrated on using her stomach muscles to control her breathing as her 'fear of flying' exercises had told her to do. She twisted her hair over and over, and when that wasn't helping she gripped onto the handrests, worried by the terrible rattling noise above her as the plane continued its less than smooth climb. It really was an incredibly bumpy take-

off, and she loathed this part more than anything—
could not relax until the flight stewards stood up and
the seatbelt signs went off.

As the plane tilted a little to the left Meg's eyes
screwed more tightly closed. She moaned again and
Niklas, who had been watching her strange actions the
whole time, noted not just that her skin had turned white
but that there was no colour in her lips.

The minute the signs went off he would speak with
the flight attendant. He didn't care if it was a royal family they had tucked in first class; someone was going to
have to make room for him! Knowing that he always
got his way, and that soon he *would* be moving, Niklas decided that for a moment or two he could afford
to be nice.

She was clearly terrified after all.

'You do know that this is the safest mode of trans-
port, don't you?'

'Logically, yes,' she answered with her eyes still
closed. 'It just doesn't feel very safe right now.'

'Well, it is,' he said.

'You said that you fly a lot?' She wanted him to
tell her that he flew every single day, that the noise
overhead was completely normal and nothing to worry
about, preferably that he was in fact a pilot—then she
might possibly believe that everything was okay.

'All the time,' came his relaxed response, and it soothed
her.

'And that noise?'

'What noise?' He listened for a second or two. 'That's the wheels coming up.'

'No, that one.'

It all sounded completely normal to him, yet Niklas realised *she* probably wasn't quite normal, so he continued to speak to her. 'Today I am flying to Los Angeles, as are you, and in two days' time I will be heading to New York...'

'Then?' Meg asked, because his voice was certainly preferable to her thoughts right now.

'Then I will be flying home to Brazil, where I am hoping to take a couple of weeks off.'

'You're from Brazil?' Her eyes were open now, and as she turned to face him she met his properly for the first time. He had very black eyes that were, right now, simply heaven to look into. 'So you speak...?' Her mind was all scrambled; she could still hear that noise overhead...

'Portuguese,' he said and, as if he was there for her amusement—which for a moment or two longer he guessed he was—he smiled as he offered her a choice. 'Or I can speak French. Or Spanish too, if you prefer...'

'English is fine.'

There was no need to talk any more. He could see the colour coming back to her cheeks and saw her tongue run over pinkening lips. 'We're up,' Niklas said, and at the same time the bell pinged and the flight attendants stood. Meg's internal panic was thankfully over, and he watched as she let out a long breath.

'Sorry about that.' She gave him a rather embarrassed smile. 'I'm not usually that bad, but that really was bumpy.'

It hadn't been bumpy in the least, but he was not going to argue with her, nor get drawn into further conversation. And yet she offered her name.

'I'm Meg, by the way.'

He didn't really want to know her name.

'Meg Hamilton.'

'Niklas.' He gave up that detail reluctantly.

'I really am sorry about that. I'll be fine now. I don't have a problem with flying—it's just take-off that I absolutely loathe.'

'What about landing?'

'Oh, I'm fine with that.'

'Then you have never flown into São Paulo,' Niklas said.

'Is that where you are from?'

He nodded, and then pulled out the menu and started to read it—before remembering that he was going to be moving seats. He pushed his bell to summon the stewardess.

'Is it a busy airport, then?'

He looked over to where Meg sat as if he had forgotten that she was even there, let alone the conversation they had been having.

'Very.' He nodded, and then saw that the flight attendant was approaching with a bottle of champagne. Clearly she must have thought he had rung for a drink—after all, they knew his preferences—but as he opened his mouth to voice his complaint Niklas conceded that it might be a little rude to ask to be moved in front of Meg.

He would have this drink, Niklas decided, and then he would get up and go and have a quiet word with the attendant. Or an angry one if that did not work. He watched as his champagne was poured and then, perhaps aware that her eyes were trained on him, he turned, irritated.

'Did you want a drink as well?'

'Please.' She smiled.

'That is what your bell is for,' he retorted. She didn't seem to realise that he was being sarcastic, so he gave in and, rolling his eyes, ordered another glass. Meg was soon sipping on her beverage.

It tasted delicious, bubbly and icy-cold, and would hopefully halt her nervous chatter—except it didn't. It seemed that a mixture of nerves about flying and the fact that she had never been around someone so drop-dead gorgeous before resulted in her mouth simply not being able to stop.

'It seems wrong to be drinking at ten a.m.' She heard her own voice again and could happily have kicked herself—except then he would perhaps have her certified. Meg simply didn't know what was wrong with her.

Niklas didn't answer. His mind was already back to thinking about work, or rather thinking about all the things he needed to get finalised so that he could actually take some proper time off.

He *was* going to take some time off. He had not stopped for the last six months at the very least, and he was really looking forward to being back in Brazil, the country he loved, to the food he adored and the woman who adored him and who knew how it was...

He would take two or perhaps three weeks, and he was going to use every minute of them indulging in life's simple but expensively prepared pleasures—beautiful women and amazing food and then more of the same.

He let out a long breath as he thought about it—a long breath that sounded a lot like a sigh. A bored sigh, even—except how could that be? Niklas asked himself. He had everything a man could want and had worked hard to get it—worked hard to ensure he would never go back to where he had come from.

And he *had* ensured it, Niklas told himself; he could stop for a little while now. A decent stretch in Brazil would sort this restless feeling out. He thought of the flight home, of the plane landing in São Paulo, and as he did he surprised himself. His champagne was finished. He could get up now and have that word with the flight attendant. But instead Niklas turned and spoke with *her*.

With Meg.

CHAPTER TWO

'São Paulo is very densely populated.'

They were well over the water now, and she was gazing out at it, but she turned to the sound of his voice and Niklas tried to explain the land that he loved, the mile after mile after mile of never-ending city.

'It is something that is hard to explain unless you have seen it, but as the plane descends you fly over the city for very a long time. Congonhas Airport is located just a couple of miles from downtown...'

He told Meg about the short runway and the difficult approach and the physics of it as she looked at him slightly aghast.

'If the weather is bad I would imagine the captain and crew and most *paulistanos*...' He saw her frown and explained it a little differently. 'If you come from Sao Paulo or know about the airport then you are holding your breath just a little as the plane comes into land.' He smiled at her shocked expression. 'There have been many near-misses—accidents too...'

What a horrible thing to tell her! What a completely inappropriate thing for him to say at this moment! And she had thought him so nice—well, nice-looking at least. 'You're not helping at all!'

'But I am. I have flown in and out of Congonhas Airport more times than I can remember and I'm still here to tell the tale… You really have nothing to worry about.'

'Except that I'm scared of landing now too.'

'Don't waste time in fear,' Niklas said, and then stood to retrieve his computer. He did not usually indulge in idle chatter, and certainly not while flying, but she had been so visibly nervous during take-off, and it had been quite pleasant talking her around. Now she was sitting quietly, staring out of the window, and perhaps he did not have to think about moving seats after all.

The flight steward started to serve some appetizers, and Meg had an inkling that Mr Dos Santos was being treated with some tasty little selections from the first-class menu—because there were a few little treats that certainly weren't on the business class one—and, given that she was sitting next to him, by default Meg was offered them too.

'Wild Iranian caviar on buckwheat blinis, with sour cream and dill,' the flight attendant purred to him, but Niklas was too busy to notice the selection placed in front of him. Instead he was setting up a workstation, and Meg heard his hiss of frustration as he had to move his computer to the side. Clearly he was missing his first-class desk!

'There is no room—' He stopped himself, realising that he sounded like someone who complained all the time. He didn't usually—because he didn't have to. His PA, Carla, ensured that everything ran smoothly in his busy life. But Carla simply hadn't been able to work her magic today, and the fact was between here and LA Niklas had a lot to get done. 'I have a lot of work to do.' He didn't have to justify his dark mood, but he did. 'I have a meeting scheduled an hour after landing. I was hoping to use this time to prepare. It really is inconvenient.'

'You'll have to get your own plane!' Meg teased. 'Keep it on standby…'

'I did!' he said. Meg blinked. 'And for two months or so it was great. I really thought it was the best thing I had ever done. And then…' He shrugged and got back to his laptop, one hand crunching numbers, the other picking all the little pieces of dill off the top of the blinis before eating them.

'And then?' Meg asked, because this man really was intriguing. He was sort of aloof and then friendly, busy, yet calm, and very pedantic with his dill, Meg thought with a small smile as she watched him continue to pick the pieces off. When the food was to his satisfaction there was something very decadent about the way he ate, his eyes briefly closing as he savoured the delicious taste entering his mouth.

Everything he revealed about himself had Meg wanting to know more, and she was enthralled when he went on to tell her about the mistake of having his own plane.

'And then,' Niklas responded, while still tapping away on his computer, 'I got bored. Same pilot, same flight crew, same chef, same scent of soap in the bathroom. You understand?'

'Not really.'

'As annoying as your chatter may be...' he turned from his screen and gave her a very nice smile '...it is actually rather nice to meet you.'

'It's rather nice to meet you too.' Meg smiled back.

'And if I still had my own plane we would not have met.'

'Nor would we if you were lording it in first class.'

He thought for a moment. 'Correct.' He nodded. 'But now, if you will forgive me, I have to get on with some work.' He moved to do just that, but just before he did he explained further, just in case she had missed the point he was making. 'That is the reason I prefer to fly commercially—it is very easy to allow your world to become too small.'

Now, that part she *did* understand. 'Tell me about it.' Meg sighed.

His shoulders tensed. His fingers hesitated over the keyboard as he waited for her to start up again.

When she inevitably did, he would point out *again* that he was trying to work.

Niklas gritted his teeth and braced himself for her voice—was she going to talk all the way to Los Angeles?

Except she said nothing else.

When still she was quiet Niklas realised that he was actually *wanting* the sound of her voice to continue their conversation. It was at that point he gave up working for a while. He would return to the report later.

Closing his laptop, he turned. 'Tell *me* about it.'

She had no idea of the concession he was making— not a clue that a slice of his time was an expensive gift that very few could afford, no idea how many people would give anything for just ten minutes of his undivided attention.

'Oh, it's nothing…' Meg shrugged. 'Just me feeling sorry for myself.'

'Which must be a hard thing to do with a mouthful of wild Iranian caviar…'

He made her laugh—he really did. Niklas really wasn't at all chatty, but when he spoke, when he teased, when she met his eyes, there was a little flip in her stomach that she liked the feeling of. It was a thrill that was new to her, and there was more than just something about him…

It was *everything* about the man.

'Here's to slumming it,' Niklas said. They chinked their glasses and he looked into her eyes, and as he did so somehow—not that she would be aware of it— Niklas let her in.

He was a closed person, an extremely guarded man. He had grown up having to be that way—it had meant survival at the time—yet for the first time in far too long he chose to relax, to take some time, to forget about work, to stop for a moment and just be with her.

As they chatted he let the flight steward put his

laptop away. They were at the back of business class, tucked away and enjoying their own little world.

The food orders were taken and later served, and Meg thought how nice Niklas was to share a meal with. Food was a passion in waiting for Meg. She rarely had time to cook, and though she ate out often it was pretty much always at the same Italian restaurant where they took clients. They'd chosen different mains, and he smiled to himself at the droop of her face when they were served and she found out that steak tartare was in fact raw.

'It's delicious,' he assured her. 'Or you can have my steak?'

At the back of her mind she had known it was raw, if she'd stopped to think about it, but the menu had been incredibly hard to concentrate on with Niklas sitting beside her, and she had made a rather random selection when the flight steward had approached.

'No, it's fine,' Meg said, looking at the strange little piles of food on her plate. There was a big hill of raw minced steak in the middle, with a raw egg yolk in its shell on the top, surrounded by little hills of onions and capers and things. 'I've always wanted to try it. I just tend to stick to safe. It's good to try different things…'

'It is,' Niklas said. 'I like it like this.'

Something caught in her throat, because he'd made it sound like sex. He picked up her knife and fork, and she watched him pour in the egg, pile on the onions and capers, and then chop and chop again before sliding the mixture through Worcestershire sauce. For a fleeting moment she honestly thought that he might load the fork and feed her, but he put the utensils down and returned to his meal, and Meg found herself breathless and blushing at where her mind had just drifted.

'Good?' Niklas asked when she took her first taste.

'Fantastic,' Meg said. It was nice, not amazing, but made by his hands fantastic it was. 'How's *your* steak?'

He sliced a piece off and lifted the loaded fork and held it to her. This from a man who had reluctantly given her a drink, who had on many occasions turned his back. He was now giving her a taste of food from his plate. He was just being friendly, Meg told herself. She was reading far, far too much into this simple gesture. But as she went to take the fork he lifted it slightly. His black eyes met hers and he moved the fork to her mouth and watched as she opened it. Suddenly she began to wonder if she'd been right the first time.

Maybe he *was* talking about sex.

But if he had been flirting, by the time dessert was cleared it had ended. He read for a bit, and Meg gazed out of the window for a while, until the flight attendant came around and closed the shutters. The lights were lowered and the cabin was dimmed and Meg fiddled with her remote to turn the seat into a bed.

Niklas stood and she glanced up at him. 'Are you off to get your gold pyjamas?'

'And a massage,' Niklas teased back.

She was half asleep when he returned, and watched idly as he took off his tie. Of course the flight attendant rushed to hold it, while another readied his bed, and then he took off his shoes and climbed into the flight bed beside her.

His beautiful face was gone now from her vision, but it was there—right there—in her mind's eye. She was terribly aware of his movements and listened to him turn restlessly a few times. She conceded that maybe he did have a point—the flight bed was more than big enough for Meg to stretch out in, but Niklas was easily a foot taller than her and, as he had stated, he really needed this time to sleep, which must be proving difficult. For Niklas the bed was simply too small, and it was almost a sin that he sleep in those immaculate suit trousers.

She lay there trying not to think about him and made herself concentrate instead on work—on the Evans contract she had just completed—which was surely enough to send her to sleep. But just as she was closing her eyes, just as she was starting to think that she might be about to drift off even with Niklas beside her, she heard him move again. Her eyes opened and she blinked as his face appeared over hers. She met those black eyes, heard again his rich accent, and how could a woman not smile?

'You never did tell me…' Niklas said, smiling as he invited her to join him in after hours conversation. 'Why is your world too small?'

CHAPTER THREE

THEY PULLED BACK the divider that separated them and lay on their sides, facing each other. Meg knew that this was probably the only time in her life that she'd ever have a man so divine lying on the pillow next to hers, so she was more than happy to forgo sleep for such a glorious cause.

'I work in the family business,' Meg explained.

'Which is?'

'My parents are into real-estate investments. I'm a lawyer…'

He gave a suitably impressed nod, but then frowned, because she didn't seem like a lawyer to him.

'Though I hardly use my training. I do all the paper-work and contracts.'

He saw her roll her eyes.

'I cannot tell you how boring it is.'

'Then why do you do it?'

'Good question. I think it was decided at conception that I would be a lawyer.'

'You don't want to be one?'

It was actually rather hard to admit it. 'I don't think I do…'

He said nothing, just carried on watching her face, waiting for her to share more, and she did.

'I don't think I'm supposed to be one—I mean, I scraped to get the grades I needed at school, held on by my fingernails at university...' She paused as he interrupted.

'You are *never* to say this at an interview.'

'Of course not.' She smiled. 'We're just talking.'

'Good. I'm guessing you were not a little girl who dreamed of being a lawyer?' he checked. 'You did not play with wigs on?' His lips twitched as she smiled. 'You did not line up your dollies and cross-examine them?'

'No.'

'So how did you end up being one?'

'I really don't know where to start.'

He looked at his watch, realised then that perhaps the report simply wasn't going to get done. 'I've got nine hours.'

Niklas made the decision then—they would be entirely devoted to *her*.

'Okay...' Meg thought how best to explain her family to him and chose to start near the beginning. 'In my family you don't get much time to think—even as a little girl there were piano lessons, violin lessons, ballet lessons, tutors. My parents were constantly checking my homework—basically, everything was geared towards me getting into the best school, so that I could get the best grades and go to the best university. Which I did. Except when I got there it was more push, push, push.

I just put my head down and carried on working, but now suddenly I'm twenty-four years old and I'm not really sure that I'm where I want to be...' It was very hard to explain it, because from the outside she had a very nice life.

'They demand too much.'

'You don't know that.'

'They don't listen to you.'

'You don't know that either.'

'But I do.' He said. 'Five or six times on the telephone you said, "Mum, I've got to go." Or, "I really have to go now..."' He saw that she was smiling, but she was smiling not at his imitation of her words but because he had been listening to her conversation. While miserable and scowling and ignoring her, he had still been aware. 'You do this.' He held up an imaginary phone and turned it off.

'I can't.' she admitted. 'Is that what you do?'

'Of course.'

He made it sound so simple.

'You say, *I have to go*, and then you do.'

'It's not just that though,' she admitted. 'They want to know everything about my life...'

'Then tell them you don't want to discuss it,' he said. 'If a conversation moves where you don't want it to, you just say so.'

'How?'

'Say, *I don't want to talk about that*,' he suggested. He made it sound so easy. 'But I don't want to hurt them either—you know how difficult families can be at times.'

'No.' He shook his head. 'There are some advantages to being an orphan, and that is one of them. I get to make my own mistakes.' He said it in such a way that there was no invitation to sympathy—in fact he even gave a small smile, as if letting her know that she did not need to be uncomfortable at his revelation and he took no offence at her casual remark.

'I'm sorry.'

'You don't have to be.'

'But…'

'I don't want to talk about that.' And, far more easily than she, he told her what he was not prepared to discuss. He simply moved the conversation. 'What would you like to do if you could do anything?'

She thought for a moment. 'You're the first person who has ever asked me that.'

'The second,' Niklas corrected. 'I would imagine you have been asking yourself that question an awful lot.'

'Lately I have been,' Meg admitted.

'So, what would you be?'

'A chef.'

And he didn't laugh, didn't tell her that she should know about steak tartare by now, if that was what she wanted to be, and neither did he roll his eyes.

'Why?'

'Because I love cooking.'

'Why?' he asked—not as if he didn't understand how

it was possible to love cooking so much, more as if he really wanted her tell him why.

She just stared at him as their minds locked in a strange wrestle.

'When someone eats something I've cooked—I mean properly prepared and cooked…' She still stared at him as she spoke. 'When they close their eyes for a second…' She couldn't properly explain it. 'When you ate those blinis, when you first tasted them, there was a moment…' She watched that mouth move into a smile, just a brief smile of understanding. 'They tasted fantastic?'

'Yes.'

'I wanted to have cooked them.' It was perhaps the best way to describe it. 'I love shopping for food, planning a meal, preparing it, presenting it, serving it…'

'For that moment?'

'Yes.' Meg nodded. 'And I know that I'm good at it because, no matter how dissatisfied my parents were with my grades or my decisions, on a Sunday I'd cook a meal from scratch and it was the one thing I excelled at. Yet it was the one thing they discouraged.'

'Why?' This time he asked because he didn't understand.

'"Why would you want to work in a kitchen?"' It was Meg doing the imitating now. '"Why, after all the opportunities we've given you…?"' Her voice faded for a moment. 'Maybe I should have stood up to them, but it's hard at fourteen…' She gave him a smile. 'It's still hard at twenty-four.'

'If cooking is your passion then I'm sure you would be a brilliant chef. You should do it.'

'I don't know.' She knew she sounded weak, knew she should just say to hell with them, but there was one other thing she had perhaps not explained. 'I love them,' Meg said, and she saw his slight frown. 'They are impossible and overbearing but I do love them, and I don't want to hurt them—though I know that I'll probably have to.' She gave him a pale smile. 'I'm going to try and work out if I can just hurt them gently.'

After a second or two he smiled back, a pensive smile she did not want, for perhaps he felt sorry for her being weak—though she didn't think she was.

'Do you cook a lot now?'

'Hardly ever.' She shook her head. 'There just never seems to be enough time. But when I do…' She explained to him that on her next weekend off she would prepare the meal she had just eaten for herself and friends…that she would spend hours trying to get it just right. Even if she generally stuck with safer choices, there was so much about food that she wanted to explore.

They lay there, facing each other and talking about food, which to some might sound boring—but for Meg it was the best conversation she had had in her life.

He told her about a restaurant that he frequented in downtown São Paulo which was famed for its seafood, although he thought it wasn't actually their best dish. When he was there Niklas always ordered their *feijoada*, which was a meat and black bean stew that tasted, he told her, as if angels had prepared it and were feeding it to his soul.

In that moment Meg realised that she had not just one growing passion to contend with, but two, because his gaze was intense and his words were so interesting and she never wanted this journey to end. Didn't want to stop their whispers in the dark.

'How come you speak so many languages?'

'It is good that I do. It means I can take my business to many countries...' He was an international financier, Niklas told her, and then, very unusually for him, he told her a little bit more—which he never, ever did. Not with anyone. Not even, if he could help it, with himself. 'One of the nuns who cared for me when I was a baby spoke only Spanish. By the time I moved from that orphanage...'

'At how old?'

He thought for a moment. 'Three, maybe four. By that time I spoke two languages,' he explained. 'Later I taught myself English, and much later French.'

'How?'

'I had a friend who was English—I asked him to speak only English to me. And I—' He'd been about to say looked for, but he changed it. 'I read English newspapers.'

'What language do you dream in?'

He smiled at her question. 'That depends where I am—where my thoughts are.'

He spent a lot of time in France, he told Meg, especially in the South. Meg asked him where his favourite place in the world was. He was about to answer São Paulo—after all, he was looking forward to going back there, to the fast pace and the stunning women—but he paused for a moment and then gave an answer that surprised even him. He told her about the mountains away from the city, and the rainforests and the rivers and springs there, and that maybe he should think of getting a place there—somewhere private.

And then he thanked her.

'For what?'

'For making me think,' Niklas said. 'I have been thinking of taking some time off just to do more of the same...' He did not mention the clubs and the women and the press that were always chasing him for the latest scandal. 'Maybe I should take a proper break.'

She told him that she too preferred the mountains to the beach, even if she lived in Bondi, and they lay there together and rewrote a vision of her—no longer a chef in a busy international hotel, instead she would run a small bed and breakfast set high in the hills.

And she asked about him too.

Rarely, so rarely did he tell anyone, but for some reason this false night he did—just a little. For some reason he didn't hold back. He just said it. Not all of it, by any means, but he gave more of himself than usual. After all, he would never see her again.

He told her how he had taught himself to read and write, how he had educated himself from newspapers, how the business section had always fascinated him and how easily he had read the figures that seemed to daunt others. And he told her how he loved Brazil—for there you could both work hard and play hard too.

'Can I get you anything Mr Dos Santos…?' Worried that their esteemed passenger was being disturbed, the steward checked that he was okay.

'Nothing.' He did not look up. He just looked at Meg as he spoke. 'If you can leave us, please?'

'Dos Santos?' she repeated when the steward had gone, and he told her that it was a surname often given to orphans.

'It means "from the Saints" in Portuguese,' he explained.

'How were you orphaned?'

'I don't actually know,' Niklas admitted. 'Perhaps I was abandoned, just left at the orphanage. I really don't know.'

'Have you ever tried to find out about your family…?'

He opened his mouth to say that he would rather not discuss it, but instead he gave even more of himself. 'I have,' he admitted. 'It would be nice to know, but it proved impossible. I got Miguel, my lawyer, onto it, but he got nowhere.'

She asked him what it had been like, growing up like that, but she was getting too close and it was not something he chose to share.

He told her so. 'I don't want to speak about that.'

So they talked some more about her, and she could have talked to him for ever—except it was Niklas who got too close now, when he asked if she was in a relationship.

'No.'

'Have you ever been serious about anyone?'

'Not really,' she said, but that wasn't quite true. 'I was about to get engaged,' Meg said. 'I called it off.'

'Why?'

She just lay there.

'Why?' Niklas pushed.

'He got on a bit too well with my parents.' She swallowed. 'A colleague.' He could hear her hesitation to discuss it. 'What we said before about worlds being too small…' Meg said. 'I realised I would be making mine smaller still.'

'Was he upset?'

'Not really.' Meg was honest. 'It wasn't exactly a passionate…' She swallowed. She was *so* not going to discuss this with him.

She should have just said so, but instead she told him that she needed to sleep. The dimmed lights and champagne were starting to catch up with both of them, and almost reluctantly their conversation was closed and finally they slept.

For how long Meg wasn't sure. She just knew that when she woke up she regretted it.

Not the conversation, but ending it, falling asleep and wasting the little time that they had.

She'd woken to the scent of coffee and the hum of the engines and now she looked over to him. He was still asleep, and just as beautiful with his eyes closed. It was almost a privilege to examine such a stunning man more intently. His black hair was swept back, his beautiful mouth relaxed and loose. She looked at his dark spiky lashes and thought of the treasure behind them. She wondered what language he was dreaming in, then watched as his eyes were revealed.

For Niklas it was a pleasure to open his eyes to her.

He had felt the caress of her gaze and now he met it and held it.

'English.' He answered the question she had not voiced, but they both understood. He had been dreaming in English, perhaps about her. And then Niklas did what he always did when he woke to a woman he considered beautiful.

It was a touch more difficult to do so—given the gap between them, given that he could not gather her body and slip her towards him—but the result would certainly be worth the brief effort. He pulled himself up on his elbow and moved till his face was right over her, and looking down.

'You never did finish what you were saying.'

She looked back at him.

'When you said it wasn't passionate…'

She could have turned away from him, could have closed the conversation—his question was inappropriate, really—only nothing felt inappropriate with Niklas. There was nothing that couldn't be said with his breath on her cheek and that sulky, beautiful mouth just inches away.

'I was the one who wasn't passionate.'

'I can't imagine that.'

'Well, I wasn't.'

'Because you didn't want him in the way that you want me?'

Meg knew what he was about to do.

And she wanted, absolutely, for him to do it.

So he did.

It did not feel as if she was kissing a stranger as their lips met—all it felt was sublime.

His lips were surprisingly gentle and moved with hers for a moment, giving her a brief glimpse of false security—for his tongue, when it slipped in, was shockingly direct and intent.

This wasn't a kiss to test the water, and now Meg knew what had been wrong with her from the start, the reason she had been rambling. This thing between them was an attraction so instant that he could have kissed her like this the moment he'd sat down beside her. He could have taken his seat, had her turn off her phone and offered his mouth to her and she would have kissed him right back.

And so she kissed him back now.

There was more passion in his kiss than Meg had ever tasted in her life. She discovered that a kiss could be far more than a simple meeting of lips as his tongue told her exactly what else he would like to do, slipping in and out of her parted lips, soft one minute, rougher the next. Then his hand moved beneath the blanket and stroked her breast through her blouse, so expertly that she ached for more.

Meg's hands were in his hair and his jaw scratched at her skin and his tongue probed a little harder. As she concentrated on that, as she fought with her body not to arch into him, he moved his hand inside her top. Now Niklas became less than subtle with his silent instructions and moved his hand to her back, pulling her forward into his embrace. She swallowed the growl that vibrated from his throat as beneath the blanket he rolled her nipple between his fingers—hard at first, and then with his palm he stroked her more softly.

To the outside world they would appear simply as two lovers kissing, their passion indecent, but hidden. Then Niklas moved over her a little more, so all she could breathe was his scent, and his mouth and his hand worked harder, each subtle stroke making her want the next one even more. Suddenly Meg knew she had to stop this, had to pull back, because just her reaction to his kiss had her feeling as though she might come.

'Come.' His mouth was at her ear now, his word voicing her thought.

'Stop,' she told him, even if it was not what she wanted him to do, but she could hardly breathe.

'Why?'

'Because,' she answered with his mouth now back over hers, 'it's wrong.'

'But *so* nice.'

He continued to kiss her. Her mouth was wet from his but she closed her lips, because this feeling was too much and he was taking her to the edge. He parted her lips with his tongue and again she tried to close them, clamped her teeth, but he merely carried on until she gave in and opened again to him. He breathed harder, and his hand still worked at her breast, and she was fighting not to gasp, not to moan, to remember where they were as he suckled her tongue.

Meg forced herself not to push his hand far lower, as her body was begging her to do, not to pull him fully on top of her as Niklas made love to her with his mouth.

She hadn't a hope of winning.

He removed his hand from her breast and prised her knotted fingers from his hair. Then he moved her hand beneath his blanket, his body acting as a shield as he held her small hand over his thick, solid length. Her fingers ached to curl and stroke around him, but he did not allow it. Instead he just flattened her palm against him and held it there. His mouth still worked against hers, and she tried to grumble a protest as her hand fought not to stroke, not to feel, not to explore his arousal.

He won.

He smothered her moan with his mouth and sucked, as if swallowing her cry of pleasure, and then, most cruel of all, he loosened his grip on her hand and accepted the dig of her fingers into him. He lifted his head and watched her, a wicked smile on his face, as she struggled to breathe, watched her bite on her lip as he too fought not to come. And he wished the lights were on so he could watch her in colour, wished that they were in his vast bed so the second she'd finished they could resume.

And they would, he decided.

'That,' Niklas said as he crashed back not to earth but to ten thousand feet in the air, 'was the appetiser.'

She'd been right the first time.

He *had* been talking about sex.

She put on a cardigan and excused herself just as the lights came on.

As she stood in the tiny cubicle and examined her face in the mirror she fastened her bra. Her skin was pink from his prolonged attention, her lips swollen, and her eyes glittered with danger. The face that looked back at her was not a woman she knew.

And she was *so* not the woman Niklas had first met.

Not once in her life had she rebelled; never had she even jumped out of her bedroom window and headed out to parties. At university she had studied and worked part-time, getting the grades her parents had expected before following them into the family business. She had always done the right thing, even when it came to her personal relationships.

Niklas had been right. She hadn't wanted her boyfriend in the way she wanted Niklas, and had strung things out for as long as she could before realising she could not get engaged to someone she cared about but didn't actually fancy. She had told her boyfriend that she wouldn't have sex till she was sure they were serious, but the moment he'd started to talk about rings and a future Meg had known it was time to get out.

And *that* was the part that caused her disquiet.

She wasn't the passionate woman Niklas had just met and kissed—she was a virgin, absolutely clueless with men. A few hours off the leash from her parents and she was lying on her back, with a stranger above her and the throb of illicit pulses below. She closed her eyes in shame, and then opened them again and saw the glitter and the shame burned a little less. There was no going back now to the woman she had been, and even if there were she would not change a minute of the time she had spent with Niklas.

She heard a tap against the door and froze for a second. Then she told herself she was being ridiculous. She brushed her teeth and sorted her hair and washed in the tiny sink, trying to brace herself to head back out there.

As she walked down the aisle she noticed her bed had been put away and the seats were up. She attempted polite conversation with Niklas as breakfast was served. He didn't really return her conversation. It was as if what had passed between them simply hadn't happened. He continued to read his paper, dunking his croissant in strong black coffee as if he *hadn't* just rocked her world.

The dishes were cleared and still he kept reading. And as the plane started its descent Meg decided that she now hated landing too—because she didn't want to arrive back at her old life.

Except you couldn't fly for ever. Meg knew that. And a man like Niklas wasn't going to stick around on landing. She knew what happened with men like him, wasn't naïve enough to think it had been anything more than a nice diversion.

She accepted it was just about sex.

And yet it wasn't just the sex that had her hooked on him.

He stretched out his legs, his suit trousers still somehow unrumpled, and she turned away and stared out of the window, trying not to think about what was beneath the cloth, trying not to think about what she had felt beneath her fingers, about the taste of his kisses and the passion she had encountered. Maybe life would have been easier had she not sat next to him—because now everything would be a mere comparison, for even with the little she knew still she was aware that there were not many men like Niklas.

Niklas just continued reading his newspaper, or appeared to be. His busy mind was already at work, cancelling his day. He knew that she would have plans once they landed. That she probably had a car waiting to take her to her hotel and her parents. But he'd think of something to get around that obstacle.

He had no intention of waiting.

Or maybe he would wait. Maybe he'd arrange to meet up with her tonight.

He thought of her controlling parents and turned a page in the paper. He relished the thought of screwing her right under their nose.

She, Niklas decided, was amazing.

There was no *possibly* about it now.

He thought of her face as she came beneath him and shifted just a little in his seat.

'Ladies and gentlemen…' They both looked up as the captain's voice came over the intercom, 'Due to an incident at LAX all planes are now being re-routed. We will be landing in Las Vegas in just over an hour.'

The captain apologised for the inconvenience and they heard the moans and grumbles from other passengers. They felt the shift as the plane started to climb, and had she been sitting next to anyone else Meg might have been complaining too, or panicking about the prolonged flight, or stressing about the car that was waiting for her, or worried about what was going on…

Instead she was smiling when he turned to her.

'Viva Las Vegas,' Niklas said, and picked up her remote, laid her chair flat again and got back to where he had left off.

CHAPTER FOUR

'IT WAS A false alarm.'

They were still sitting on the plane on the tarmac. The second they had landed in Vegas Niklas had pulled out his phone, turned it on and called someone. He was speaking in Portuguese. He had briefly halted his conversation to inform Meg that whatever had happened in Los Angeles had been a false alarm and then carried on talking into his phone.

'Aguarde, por favour!' he said, and then turned again to Meg. 'I am speaking with my PA, Carla. I can ask her to reschedule your flight also. She will get it done quickly, I think.'

And make sure he'd sit next to her too, Niklas decided.

'So?' he asked. 'When do you want to get there?'

Of course the normal response would be as soon as possible, but there was nothing normal about her response to him. Niklas was looking right at her, and there was undoubtedly an invitation in his eyes, but there was something he needed to know—somehow she had to tell him that what had happened between them wasn't usual for her.

To put it mildly.

Except Niklas made her stomach fold into herself, and his eyes were waiting, and his mouth was so beautiful, and she did not want this to end with a kiss at an airport gate. She did not want to spend the rest of her life regretting what would surely be a far more exciting choice than the one she should be making.

He made it for her.

'It sounds as if there is a lot of backlog. The airport will be hell with so many people having to re-route. I could tell her to book our flights for tomorrow.' Niklas had already made the decision. He had not had twenty-four hours to himself in months, had not stopped working in weeks, and right now he could think of no one nicer to escape the world with.

'I'm supposed to be…' She thought of her parents, waiting for her at the conference, waiting for her to arrive, to perform, to work twelve-hour days and accept weekends constantly on call. Hers was a family that had every minute, every week, every year of her life accounted for, and for just for a little while Meg wanted to be able to breathe.

Or rather to struggle to breathe under him as he kissed her and took her breath.

He looked at her mouth as he awaited her answer, watched the finger that twirled in her hair finally pause as she reached her decision, saw her tongue moisten her lips just before she delivered her answer.

'Tomorrow,' Meg said. 'Tell her tomorrow.'

He spoke with Carla for a couple more moments, checked he had the right spelling of her surname and date of birth and passport number, and then clicked off his phone.

'Done.'

She didn't know what his life was like—didn't really understand what the word *done* meant in Niklas Dos Santos's world…

Yet.

They waited for their baggage and she got to kiss him for the first time standing up, got to feel his tall length pressed against her. He loaded their bags onto one trolley and then he did a nice thing, a very unexpected thing: he stopped at one of the shops and bought her flowers.

She smiled as he handed them to her.

'Dinner, breakfast, champagne, kisses, foreplay…' God, he didn't even lower his voice as he handed her the flowers. 'Have I covered everything?'

'You haven't taken me to the movies,' Meg said.

'No…' He shook his head. 'There was a movie on. You chose not to watch it. I cannot be held responsible for that…'

Oh, but he had been. She felt the thorns of the roses press in as he moved closer again and crushed the flowers.

'Consider yourself dated.'

There was no waiting in long queues for Niklas. Customs was a very different thing in his world, and as his hand was holding hers, she too was processed quickly. Suddenly they had cleared Customs and were walking out—and it was then she got her first glimpse of what *done* meant in a world like Niklas's.

Carla must have been busy, for there was already a driver waiting, holding a sign with 'Niklas Dos Santos' written on it. He relieved them of their bags and they followed him to a blacked-out limousine. She never got a glimpse of Vegas as they drove to the hotel, just felt the brief hit of hot desert sun.

No, she never saw Vegas at all.

She was sitting on his lap.

'I'm going to be the most terrible let-down...' She peeled her face from his.

'You're not,' he groaned.

'I am...' God, her head was splitting just at the attempt to be rational. 'Because I have to ring my mum...'

Her hands were shaking as she dialled the number, her mind reeling, because she *had* to tell him she was a virgin. Oh, God, she really was going to be a let-down! His fingers were working the buttons on her trousers now, his hand slipping in and cupping her bum. His mouth was sucking her breast through her blouse as she was connected to her mother, and she heard only smatters of her conversation.

'Yes, I know it was a false alarm...' She tried to sound normal as she spoke with a less than impressed Ruth. 'But all the flights are in chaos and tomorrow was the earliest I could get.' No, she insisted for a third time, there was simply nothing she could do that would get her there sooner. 'I'll call you when I've sorted out a hotel and things. I have to go, Mum, my battery's about to go flat.'

She clicked off the phone and he turned her so that she was sitting astride him. Holding her hips, he pushed her down, so she could feel what would soon be inside her, and for the first time she was just a little bit scared.

'Niklas…'

'Come on…' He did her blouse up. 'We are nearly there.'

She made herself decent, slipped her cardigan over her blouse to hide the wet patch his mouth had made, and found out once again what it was like in his world.

They breezed through check-in, and even their luggage beat them to their huge suite—not that she paid any attention to it, for finally they were alone. As soon as the door shut he kissed her, pushing her onto the bed. He removed his jacket and pulled condoms from his pocket, placing them within reach on the bedside table, and then he removed her trousers, taking her panties with them at the same time.

God, he was animal, and he moaned as he buried his face in her most private of places. Meg felt the purr of his moan, and this new experience coupled with her own arousal terrified her.

'Niklas…' she pleaded as his tongue started to probe. 'When I said my relationship wasn't passionate…'

'We've already proved it had nothing to do with you.' His words were muffled, but he felt her tense and as he looked up he met anxious eyes.

'I haven't done this before.' She saw him frown. 'I haven't done anything.'

There was a rather long pause. 'Good. I will look after you...'

'I know that.'

'I *will*.'

And then his mouth resumed, and she felt his breath in places she had never felt someone breathe before, but still the tension and fear remained. Niklas must have sensed it too, as he raised himself up on his elbows and looked down at her beneath him, her face flushed.

Niklas was a very uninhibited lover; it was the only piece of himself that he readily gave. Sex was both his rest and recreation, and with his usual lovers there was no need for long conversation and coaxing, no need for reticence or taking his time. But as he looked down at her flushed cheeks he recalled their long conversations on the plane, and the enjoyment of spending proper time with another person. He thought of all the things he had told her that he never usually shared with anyone, and he realised he liked not just the woman who lay beneath him but the words that had come from her mouth.

He kissed it now, as if doing so for the first time.

Not their first kiss. Just a gentle kiss—albeit with his erection pressing into her as he thought about what to do.

His first intention had been to push her on the bed and take her quickly, just so that they could start over again, but he really liked her, and he wanted to do this well.

Thoroughly.

Properly.

'I know…'

He sounded as if he'd had an idea, and he stopped kissing her, smiling down at her before rolling off and picking up the phone. He told Meg that a bath would relax her, and as they waited for a maid to come and run it he wrapped her in a vast white dressing gown. She lay on the bed, watching him as he went through his case, and then he joined her on the bed and showed her some documents, his fingers pointing to the pertinent lines, which she read, frowning.

'I don't get this.'

'I had to get a check-up when I was in Sydney, for my insurance…' he explained.

'So?'

'I wasn't worried about the results. I always use protection…' He was so completely matter-of-fact.

'I'm not on the pill,' Meg replied as she understood his meaning, and she saw his eyes widen just a little as she dampened his plans.

'But still…' He stopped himself, shook his head as if to clear it. What the hell had he been thinking? For a second a baby had seemed a minor inconvenience compared to what they might miss out on. He was, Niklas decided, starting to adore her, and that always came with strong warnings attached—that was always his signal to leave.

'Niklas…am I making a big mistake?'

He was as honest with Meg as he was with all women, because his was a heart that would remain closed. 'If you are looking for love, then yes,' Niklas said. 'Because I don't do that.'

'Never?'

'Ever,' Niklas said. He could not bear even the thought of someone depending on him, could not trust himself to provide for another person, just could not envisage sharing, yet alone caring—except already a part of him cared for *her*.

'Then I want as long as we've got,' Meg said.

When the maid left he took her by the hand and led her to the bathroom. The bath was sunken, and as she slid into the water he undressed, and she was looking up at his huge erection, her cheeks paling in colour. Niklas found himself assuring her that nothing would happen between them just yet—not until she was sure she was ready. The need to comfort her and reassure her was a new sensation for him, and as he looked down at her he decided that for the next twenty-four hours he would let himself care.

He climbed into the water with her and washed her slowly, sensually, smoothing the soap over her silky skin. He dunked her head in the water too, just so he could see the red darken.

'Your last boyfriend—did he try...?' Niklas asked as he soaped her arms, curious because he wondered how any man could resist the beautiful woman he held in his arms.

'A bit...' Meg said.

Even her arms blushed, he noted.

'I just...'

'What?' He loved her blushing, and found himself smiling just watching her skin pinken, feeling the warmth beneath his palms as she squirmed.

'I told him I didn't want to do anything like that till we were really serious. You know...'

His eyes widened. 'Married?'

'Engaged,' she corrected.

'Do people really say that?' He sounded incredulous, his soapy hands moving lower, past her breasts and down to her waist. 'How would you know if you wanted to marry someone if you hadn't—?'

'That had nothing to do with it. I wasn't demanding a ring. I realised I was just making up excuses...'

'Because?' He was sliding his soapy hands between her legs now, and she didn't know how to answer. 'Because?' he insisted.

'Because I didn't have any compulsion to sit in a bath with him and let him wash me *there*...' She couldn't believe he expected her to speak as he was doing what he did. 'And then he started talking rings.'

'I bet he did,' Niklas said, because, naked with her like this, what man wouldn't want his ring on her finger?

Suddenly his brain went to a place it should not, and Niklas tried hard to shut it down. This had to stay as just sex between them. He pulled her straight over to him, hooked her legs over his and kissed her shoulder.

'I loved flying with you...' He said it like a caress as he lifted her hair, and his mouth moved to the back of her neck and sucked hard.

She closed her eyes at the bruise he was making, and then felt his hand move up her thigh. It was his neck she was now kissing, licking away the fragrant water just to get to his skin. As they continued to nip and kiss each other Niklas moved his hand, his finger slipping inside, and when she felt a moment's pain she sucked harder on his neck. He pushed in another finger, stretching her, and again she bit down on his shoulder as pain flashed through her body. She knew he had to stretch her—she had seen that he was huge and this was her first time after all—but he did it with a gentleness that moved her.

He continued to slide his fingers in and out, and then kissed her breast, sucking on her wet nipple. She began to moan and lift herself to his fingers as pleasure washed over her. Niklas realised that things were moving rather faster than he had intended. He wanted her on the bed—or rather they needed to get back to the condoms.

'Come on…' He moved to stand, except her hand found him first and, yes, she deserved a little play too.

He liked being touched by a woman. He had just never expected to enjoy it as much as he did now. Had never expected the naked pleasure in her eyes and the tentative exploration of her hands, just her enjoyment of him, would make him feel as it did.

For enjoy him, Meg did. It was bliss to hold him, huge and slippery and magnificent in her hands, and she was still scared, but rather more excited at the prospect of him being inside her.

'Like this?' she checked, and he closed his eyes and leant his head back on the marble wall behind him.

'Like that,' he said, but then changed his mind. 'Harder.' And he put his hand over hers and showed her—showed her a little too well.

'Come here.' He pulled her up over him. He was seconds away, had to slow down, but he had to have her. He was rubbing himself around her and she was desperate for him to be inside her too.

'We need…' It was him saying it, and he knew he should take her to bed and slip on a condom, but he wanted her this moment, and for once in his life he was conflicted. He knew he could have her now, that he was the only one thinking, and he wanted the pleasure. But as he looked at her, hovering over him, Niklas knew he wouldn't have a hope of pulling out in time.

Her hands were on his shoulders and he was holding her buttocks, almost fighting not to press her down. He wanted to give in, to drive her down and at the same time lift his hips, and he would have—absolutely he would have, in fact—had her phone not rung.

He swore in Portuguese, and then French, and then Spanish at the intrusion.

'Leave it,' he said.

But it rang again, and for a brief moment common sense returned. He stood, taking her wet hand and helping her out as they headed for the bed. He turned off her phone, and checked that his was off too, for he was tired of a world that kept invading his time. Then he looked at the shiny foil packets and realised that the last thing he wanted was to be sheathed when he entered this woman.

'I want to feel you,' he said. 'I want you to feel me.'

And his mind went to a place he never allowed it to go.

He'd been told by plenty of people that he was damaged goods, that a man with his past was not capable of a stable relationship.

Yet he wanted to be stable for a while.

He was tired of the noise and the endless women. Not once had he considered commitment, and he didn't fully now, but surely for a while longer he could carry on caring? He had amassed enough that he could trust himself to take care of another person for a while at least, and if there were consequences to his reckless decision then he could take care of that too.

He could.

In that moment he fully believed that he could.

He would.

No, he did not want others around him today—did not want his thoughts clouded. Usually, to Niklas, rapid thoughts were right, and they were the ones that proved to be the best. He looked at her, pink and warm and a virgin on his bed, and decided he would do this right.

Thoroughly.

Properly.

'Marry me.'

She laughed.

'I'm serious,' he said. 'That's what people do when they come to Vegas.'

'I think they usually know each other first.'

'I know you.'

'You don't.'

'I know enough,' Niklas said. 'You just don't know me. I *want* to do this.'

And what Niklas Dos Santos wanted he usually got.

'I'm not talking about for ever—I could never settle with one person for very long, or stay in one place—but I can help you sort out the stuff with your family. I can step in so you can step back...'

'Why?' She didn't get it. 'Why would you do that?'

He looked at her for a long time before answering, because she was right. Why *would* he do that? Niklas had had many relationships, many less than emotional encounters, and there had been a couple of long high-maintenance ones. Yet not once in his life had he considered marriage before. Not once had he wanted another person close. He had actually feared that another person might depend on a man who had come from nothing, but as he looked at her for the first time he wasn't daunted by the prospect at all.

Around her—again for the first time—he trusted in himself.

'I like you.'

'But what would you get out of it?'

'You,' he replied, and suddenly it seemed imperative that he marry her—that he make her his even if just for a little while. 'I like sorting things out...and I like you. And...' He gestured to the condoms on the bedside table.

'And I don't like them. So,' he said, reaching for the hotel phone, 'will you marry me?'

There was nothing about him she understood, but more than that there was nothing about herself she understood any more, for in that moment his proposal seemed rather logical.

A solution, in fact.

'Yes.'

He spoke on the phone for just a few moments and then turned and smiled at his bride-to-be.

'Done.'

CHAPTER FIVE

IT WAS THE quickest of quick weddings.

Or maybe not.

They were in Vegas, after all.

Niklas rang down to the concierge and informed them of their plans, telling him how they wanted them executed.

'Do you want them to bring up a selection of dresses?' he asked Meg. 'It's your day; you can have whatever you want.'

'No dress.' Meg smiled.

But there were *some* traditional elements.

He ordered lots of flowers, and they arrived in the room along with champagne, and there was even a wedding cake. Meg sat at a table trying on rings as the celebrant went through the paperwork.

He'd arranged music too, but Niklas chose from a selection already on his phone, and Meg found herself walking at his side to music she didn't know and a man she badly wanted to.

The bride and groom wore white bathrobes, and she stood watching as the titanium ring dotted with diamonds she had chosen was slipped onto her finger. Perhaps bizarrely, there was not a flicker of doubt in her mind as she said yes.

And neither was there a flicker of doubt in Niklas's mind as he kissed his virgin bride and told her that he was happy to be married to a woman he had only met yesterday.

'Today,' Meg corrected and, yes, because of the time difference between Vegas and Australia it *was* still the day they'd first met.

'Sorry to rush you.' He grinned.

There was a mixture of nerves and heady relief when everyone had left.

He undid her robe and took off his, and then he pulled her onto the bed.

'Soon,' Niklas promised as his hands roamed over her, 'you will be wondering how you got through your life without this.'

'I'm wondering now,' Meg admitted, and she wasn't just talking about the sex. She was talking about him too. She had never opened up more fully with another person, had never felt more like herself.

Niklas's kiss was incredibly tender—a kiss she would never have expected from him. He kissed her till she almost relaxed, and then his mouth became more consuming. He needed to shave, but she liked the roughness, liked his naked body wrapped around hers.

She was on her back, and he was on top as he had so badly wanted to be on the plane. He could not wait—not for a moment longer. His knees nudged hers apart and he slipped his fingers briefly in, checking she was ready for him, finding that she was.

And now there was nothing between them.

And he was no longer patient.

He warned her it would hurt.

He watched her face as she blanched in pain, then kissed her hard on the mouth.

As he drove into her she screamed into his mouth, because that first thrust seemed to go on for ever, and every part of her felt as if it was tearing just to accommodate his long, thick length. He tried to be gentle, but he was too large for that. But once he had ripped off that Band-Aid he kept moving within her, kept on kissing her mouth, her face, giving her no choice but to grow accustomed to the new sensations she was feeling. He moved within her as his tongue had earlier described that he would, moving deep till he had driven her wild. He wasn't kissing her now, and she looked up to see his face etched with concentration, his eyes closed, his body moving rapidly as hers rose to meet him.

Now it was Meg's hands urging him on, digging her fingers into his tight buttocks, whimpering as she sought relief, and then he opened his eyes and let her have it, spilled every last drop deep into her. Her orgasm followed quickly after, and she was frenzied as she came, almost scared at the power of her body's response, at the things he had taught her to do.

And then he collapsed on top of her, his breathing heavy, and although it felt like a dream somehow it was real. Meg realised that he had been right—she had no idea how she'd got through her life without this.

Without him.

'Shouldn't we be regretting this by now?' Meg asked.

They were lying in a very rumpled bed and it was morning. Her body ached with the most delicious hurt, but Niklas had assured her for this morning's lesson she would need only her mouth.

'What's to regret?' He turned on the bed and looked over to her.

He didn't do happiness, but he felt the first rays of it today. He liked waking up to her, and the rest was mere detail that he would soon sort out.

'You live in Brazil and I live in Australia...'

'As we both know, there are planes...' He looked across the pillow. 'Do you worry about everything?'

'No.'

'I think you do.'

'I don't.'

'So how shall we tell your parents?'

He saw her slight grimace.

'They might be pleased for you.'

As the real world invaded so too did confusion. 'I doubt it. It will be a terrible shock.' She thought for a moment. 'I think once they get used to the idea they'll be pleased.' And then she swallowed nervously. 'I *think*.'

He smiled at her worried face. 'First of all *you* need to get used to the idea.'

'I don't know much about you.'

'There isn't much to know,' Niklas said.

She rather doubted that.

'I don't have family, as I said, so you have avoided having a mother-in-law. I hear from friends they can sometimes be a problem, so that's an unexpected bonus for you!'

He could be so flippant about things that were important, Meg thought, and there was so much she wanted to find out about him. She wondered how he had survived without a family, for a start, how he had made such a success of himself from nothing—because clearly he had. But unlike their wedding some things, Meg guessed, had to be taken more slowly—she couldn't just sit up and fire a thousand questions at him. Somehow she knew it wasn't something he would talk about easily, but she tried. 'What was it like, though?' Meg asked. 'Growing up in an orphanage?'

'There were many orphanages,' he said. 'I was moved around a lot.' Perhaps he realised he wasn't answering her question, because he added, 'I don't know, really. I try not to think about it.'

'But…'

He halted her. 'We're married Meg. But that doesn't mean we need every piece of each other. Let's just enjoy what we have, huh?'

So if he didn't want to talk about himself she'd start with the easier stuff instead. 'You live in São Paulo?'

'I have an apartment there,' Niklas said. 'If I am working in Europe I tend to stay at my house in Villefranche-sur-Mer. And now I guess I'll have to look for somewhere in Sydney...' His smile was wicked. 'If your father gets really cross, maybe I can ask if he knows any good houses—if he would be able to help...'

Meg started to laugh, because it sounded as if he did understand where she was coming from. Niklas was right—a nice big commission would certainly go a long way towards appeasing her father. She realised that the shock would wear off eventually, and that her rather shallow parents would be delighted to find somewhere for their rich new son-in-law to live.

As Meg lay there, and the sun started to work its way through the chink in the curtains, she started to realise that this was the happiest she had been in her life. But even with that knowledge there was one part about last night that had been unjustifiably reckless.

'I'll go on the pill...' she said. 'If it isn't already too late.'

He had said this wasn't for ever, and the wedding ring that had seemed a solution yesterday was less than one now.

'If last night brings far-reaching consequences you will both be taken care of.'

'For a while?'

He looked over and knew that, unlike most women, Meg wasn't talking about money. But his bank account was the only thing not tainted by his past.

'For a while,' Niklas said. 'I promise you—we'll be arguing within weeks, we'll be driving each other insane—and not with lust...' He smiled in all the wrong

places, but he made her smile back. 'You'll be glad to
see the back of me.'

She doubted it.

'I'm hard work,' he warned.

But worth it.

Though she *was* going on the pill.

And then he looked over to her again, and for as long
as it was like this she could adore him.

'I am going to write to the airline tomorrow and
thank them for not having a first-class seat,' he said.

'I might write and thank them too.'

'It will be okay,' he told her. 'Soon I will ring Carla
and I will have her re-schedule things. Then we will
meet with your parents and I will tell them.' He grinned
at her horrified expression.

'*I'll* speak to my parents.'

'No,' Niklas said. 'Because you will start apologis-
ing and doubting and I am a better negotiator.'

'Negotiator?'

'How long do you want off for our honeymoon?' Niklas said. 'Of course you will want to give them notice—
you don't want to just walk out—but for now we should
have some time together. Maybe I'll take you to the
mountains...' There was no gap between them now, so
he pulled her across. 'And I will also tell them that we
will have a big wedding in a few weeks.'

'I'm happy with the wedding we had.'

'Don't you want a big one?'

Her hand slid down beneath the sheet and she loved
it that he laughed, not understanding that laughter was

actually rare for him. Then her mouth followed her hands, and he lay there as she inexpertly woke another part of him.

'Don't you want a proper wedding, with family and dancing?'

'I hate dancing…' She kissed all the way down his length and she felt his hand in her hair, gently lifting her to where he wanted more attention.

'I do too.'

'I thought all Brazilians could dance?'

'Stop talking,' Niklas said. 'And I never said I couldn't. I just don't.'

She looked up at the most stunning, complicated man who had ever graced her vision and thought of his prowess and the movement of his body. All of it had been for her, and she shivered at the thought of the days and nights to come, of getting to know more and more of him. Already she knew that she was starting to want for ever, but that wasn't what this was about.

And then she tasted him again.

His hands moved her head as he promised she would not hurt him and told her exactly what to do with her mouth. She was lost in his scent, the feel of him in her mouth, and the shock of his rapid come was a most pleasant surprise. It was a surprise for Niklas too, but this was how she moved him.

He did not want to get out of bed—did not want to get back to the world. Except no doubt it was screaming for him by now—he had never had his phone turned off for so long.

He climbed out of bed and she lay there, just staring at the ceiling, lost in thoughts of him and the time they would take to get to know the other properly.

And Niklas was thinking the same. He had been looking forward to some time off, had been aware that he needed some, now he could not wait to take it.

He showered quickly and considered shaving, and then he picked up his phone, impatient to speak to Carla, to change his plans yet again. He grimaced when he saw how many missed calls he'd had, how many texts, and then he frowned—because there were hundreds. From Carla, from Miguel, from just about everyone he knew...

It was his first inkling that something was wrong.

Niklas had no family, and the only person he had ever really cared about was in bed in the next room, so he didn't have any flare of panic, but there was clearly a problem. Problems he was used to, and was very good at sorting them out.

It just might take a little time, that was all, when really he would far rather be heading back to bed. He dialled Carla's number, wondering if he should tell Meg to order some breakfast. He would just as soon as he made this call.

She could hear him in the lounge, speaking in his own language into his phone. She lay there for ages, twisting her new ring around her finger. Then, as he still spoke on the phone, she realised she wasn't actually terrified at the prospect of telling her parents, and even if this wasn't the most conventional of marriages, even if he had warned her it would end some day, she was completely at peace with what had occurred.

The only thing she was right now, Meg realised, was starving.

'I'm going to ring for breakfast,' she said as he walked back into the room, and then she looked over and frowned, because even though he had been gone ages she was surprised to see that he was dressed.

'I have to return to Brazil.'

'Oh.' She sat up in the bed. 'Now?'

'Now.'

He was not looking at her, Meg realised. What she did not realise was that precisely two seconds from now he was going to break her heart.

'We made a mistake.'

As easily as that he did it.

'Sorry?'

'The party's over.'

'Hold on…' She was completely sideswiped. 'What happened between there and here?' She pointed to the lounge he had come from. 'Who changed your mind?'

'I did.'

'What? Did you suddenly remember you had a fiancée?' Meg shouted. 'Or a girlfriend…?' She was starting to cry. 'Or five kids and a wife…?' It was starting to hit home how little she knew about him.

'There's no wife…' he shrugged '…except you. I will speak with my legal team as soon as I return to Brazil, see if we can get it annulled. But I doubt it…'

He didn't even sit on the bed to tell her it was over,

and she realised what a fool she had been, how easily he had taken her in.

'If it cannot be annulled they will contact you for a divorce. I'll make a one-off settlement,' he said.

'Settlement?'

'My people will sort it. You can fight me for more if you choose, but I strongly suggest that you quickly accept. Of course if you are pregnant...'

He stood there with the sun streaming through the curtains behind him, and all she could see was the dark outline of a man she didn't know.

'It might be a good idea to think about the morning-after pill.'

And then there was a knock on the door and it was a bellboy to take his case.

'I've asked for a late check-out for you, if you want to reschedule your flight. Have breakfast...' he offered, as if this was normal, and then he tipped the bellboy, who left with his luggage.

'I don't understand...' She was turning into some hysterical female, sitting screaming on a bed as her one-night stand walked off.

'This is the type of thing people do in Vegas. We had fun...'

'Fun!' She couldn't believe what she was hearing.

'It's no big deal.'

'But it is for me.'

'It's about time that you grew up, then.'

She had never expected him to be cruel, but she had

no idea what she was dealing with. Niklas could be cruel when necessary, and today it was.

Very necessary.

He could not look at her. She was sitting on the bed in tears, pleading with him, and also, he noted, growing increasingly angry. Her voice rose as she told him that *he* was the one who needed to grow up, that *he* was the one who needed to sort out his life, and her hands were waving. Any minute now he thought she would rise and attack him. He wanted to catch her wrists and kiss the fear away, wanted to feel just for a moment her body writhing in anger and to reassure her—except he had nothing he could reassure her with. He knew how bad things would be shortly, so he had to be cruel to be kind.

'What did you have to marry me for?' she shouted. 'I was clearly already going to sleep with you...'

She was about to lunge at him, Niklas knew. She was kneeling on the bed, still grabbing the sheet around her for now, but in a moment it would be off. Her green eyes were flashing, her teeth bared and with his next words he knew he would end this.

'I told you yesterday.' He went to the bedside and flicked a few foil packets to the floor. 'I don't like condoms.'

He took the clawing to his cheek, stood there as she sprang towards him, then caught and held her naked fury by the arms for a moment. And then he pushed her back on the bed.

And as simply as that he was gone.

* * *

A minute ago the only things on her mind had been breakfast and making love with her new husband.

Now they were talking annulments and settlements.

Or rather they weren't talking.

He was gone.

He had left with cruel words and livid scratches on his cheek and she just lay there, reeling, her anger like a weight that did not propel her, but instead seemed to pin her down to the bed. It was actually an achievement to breathe.

A few minutes later Meg realised she was breathing in through her nose and out through her mouth, as she had done on the plane during take-off. Her own body was rallying to bring her out from the panic she now found herself in. Still she lay there and tried to make sense of something there was no sense to be made of.

He had played her.

Right from the start it had all been just a game to him.

Except this was her life.

Maybe he was right. Maybe she did need to grow up. If a man like Niklas could so easily manipulate her, could have her believing in love at first sight, then maybe she *did* need to sort herself out. She curled into herself for a moment, breathed for a bit, cried for a bit, and then, because she had to, Meg stood.

She didn't have breakfast.

She ordered coffee instead, and gulped on the hot

sweet liquid in the hope that it would warm her, would wean her brain out of its shock. It did not.

She showered, blasting her bruised, tender body with water, for she could not bear to step into the bath where they had kissed and so nearly made love.

Sex, Meg reminded herself. Because as it turned out love at first sight had had nothing to do with it.

She dressed quickly, unable to bear being in a room that smelt of them, and then she looked at the rumpled and bloodstained sheet on the bed where he had taken her and thought she might throw up.

Within an hour she was at the airport.

And just a little while later she was sitting on a plane and trying to work out how to get her life back to where it had been yesterday.

Except her heart felt as bruised and aching as the most intimate parts of her body, and her eyes, swollen from crying, felt the same.

Meg ordered a cool eye mask from the attendant. Before putting it on she slid off her wedding ring and put it on a chain around her neck, trying to fathom what had happened.

She couldn't.

She did her best with make-up in the toilet cubicle just before they came in for landing. She lifted her hair and saw the bruise his mouth had left on her neck and felt a scream building that somehow she had to contain. She covered her eyes with sunglasses and wondered how she would ever get through the next few hours, days, weeks.

'Thank God...' Her mum met her at the baggage carousel. 'The car's waiting. I'll bring you up to speed on the way.' She peered at her daughter. 'Are you okay?'

'Just tired,' Meg answered, and then she looked at her mum and knew she could never, ever tell her, so instead she forced a smile. 'But I'm fine.'

'Good,' said her mum as they grabbed her case and headed for the car. 'How was Vegas?'

CHAPTER SIX

MEG STOOD IN her office, looking out of the window, her fingers, as they so often did, idly turning the ring that still, almost a year later, lived on a chain around her neck.

She wasn't looking forward to tonight, given what she had to tell her parents.

It had nothing to do with Niklas. There had been eleven months of no contact now. Eleven months for Meg to start healing. Yet still she didn't know how to start.

She couldn't bear to think about him, let alone tell anyone what had happened.

And even though she could not bear to think about him, even though it actually hurt to do so, of course all too often Meg did.

It hurt to remember the good bits.

The bad bits almost killed her.

Surprisingly, she couldn't quite work out if she regretted it.

Niklas Dos Santos, for the brief time he had appeared in it, had actually changed her life. Meeting him had changed her. Hell *did* make you stronger. This was her life and she must live it, and Meg had decided that she was finally going to follow her dreams and study to be a chef. Now she just had to tell her parents. So in a way tonight did in fact have something to do with him.

The strange thing was, she wanted to tell Niklas about her decision too—was fighting with herself not to contact him.

As painful as it was to remember, as brutal as his departure had been, still a part of her was grateful for the biggest mistake of her life and, fiddling with his ring as she so often did, Meg felt tears sting her eyes.

That was the only thing that was different today.

She hadn't cried for him since that morning. Actually, she had, but it had only been the once—the morning a couple of weeks later when she had got her period. Meg had sunk to her knees and wept on the toilet floor, not with relief, but because there was nothing left of them.

Nothing to tell him.

No reason for contact.

Apart from the paperwork it was as over as it could be.

So for the best part of a year she had completely avoided it. Had tried not to think of him while finding it impossible not to.

Every day had her waiting for a thick legal letter with a Brazilian postmark and yet it had never arrived.

Every night was just a fight not to think.

Sometimes Meg was tempted to look him up on the

internet and find out more about the man who she could not forget—yet she was scared to, scared that even a glimpse of his face on her computer screen would have her picking up the phone to beg.

That was how much she still missed him.

Sometimes she grew angry, and wanted to contact him so that they could initiate the divorce, but that would be just an excuse to ring him. Meg knew she didn't need to speak with him to divorce him, yet she had not even started the simple process, because once she started down that path it would stop being a dream—which sometimes she thought it must have been...

Then her fingers would move to the cool metal of his ring and she'd find out again it was real.

She looked up at the clock and saw that it was time for lunch. Grateful for the chance of some fresh air while she worked out exactly how to tell her parents she was leaving the family business, Meg was tempted to ignore the ringing phone.

She wished she had when she answered it, because some new clients had arrived and were insisting that they be seen immediately.

'Not without an appointment.' Meg shook her head. She was fed up with pushy clients and the continual access she was expected to provide. 'I'm going to lunch.'

'I've told them that you're about to go for lunch.' Helen sounded flustered. 'But they said that they would wait till you get back. They are adamant that they see you today.'

Meg was sick of that word—everyone was *adamant* these days, and because there wasn't much work around her parents insisted more and more that they must jump to potential clients' unreasonable demands.

'Just tell them that they need to book,' Meg said, but as she went to end the call she froze when she heard a certain name.

A name that had her blood running simultaneously hot and cold.

Cold because she had dreaded this day—dreaded their worlds colliding, dreaded the one mistake in her crafted life coming back to haunt her—but at the same time hot for the memories the name Dos Santos triggered.

'He's here?' Meg croaked. 'Niklas is here?'

'No,' Helen answered, and Meg was frustrated at her own disappointment when she heard that it wasn't him. 'It's *regarding* a Mr Dos Santos, apparently, and these people really are insistent...'

'Tell them to give me a moment.'

She needed that moment. Meg really did.

She sank into her chair and poured a drink of water, willed herself to calm down, and then she checked her appearance in the mirror that she kept in her drawer. Her hair was neatly tied back and though her face was a touch pale she looked fairly composed—except Meg could see her own eyes were darting with fear.

There was nothing to fear, Meg told herself. It wasn't trouble that had arrived. It had been almost a year after all. No doubt his legal team were here to get her signature on divorce papers. She closed her eyes and tried to calm herself, but it didn't help because all she could see was herself and Niklas, a tangle of legs and arms on a bed, and the man who had taken her heart with him when he left. Now it really was coming to an end.

She stood as Helen brought her visitors in and sorted out chairs for them. Then Helen offered water or coffee, which all three politely declined, and finally, when Helen had left and the door was closed, Meg addressed them.

'You wanted to see me?'

'First we should introduce ourselves.'

A well-spoken gentleman started things off. He introduced himself and his colleague and then Rosa, a woman whom Meg thought might be around forty, took over. It was terribly difficult to tell her age. She was incredibly elegant, her make-up and hair completely immaculate, her voice as richly accented as Niklas's had been, and it hurt to hear the familiar tone—familiar because it played over and over each night in her dreams. But she tried not to think of that, tried to concentrate on Rosa as she told Meg that they worked at the legal firm Mr Dos Santos used. She went through their qualifications and their business structure, and as she did so Meg felt her own qualifications dissolve beneath her—these were high-end lawyers and clearly here to do business. But Meg still didn't understand why Niklas had felt it necessary to fly three of his most powerful lawyers all the way to Australia, simply to oversee their divorce.

A letter would have sufficed.

'First and foremost,' Rosa started, 'before we go any further, we ask for discretion.'

They were possibly the sweetest words that Meg could hope to hear in this situation.

'Of course' was her response, but that wasn't enough for Rosa.

'We *insist* on your absolute discretion,' Rosa reiterated, and for the first time Meg felt her hackles rise.

'I would need to know what you're here in regard to before I can make an assurance like that.'

'You are married to Niklas Dos Santos?'

'I think we all know that,' Meg said carefully.

'And do you know that your husband is facing serious charges of embezzlement and fraud?'

Ice slid down her spine. Her hackles were definitely up now, and Meg thought for a moment before answering, 'I had no idea.'

'If he is found guilty he will probably never be released.'

Meg ran her tongue over her lips and tasted the wax of the lipstick she had applied earlier. She could feel beads of sweat breaking out on her forehead and felt nauseous at the very thought of a man like Niklas confined and constricted. She felt sick, too, at the thought of what he must have done to face serving life behind bars.

'He is innocent.' The man who had first introduced them spoke then, and Meg couldn't help raising one of her eyebrows, but she made no comment.

Of course his own people would say that he was innocent.

They were his lawyers after all.

She didn't look at Rosa when she spoke. Instead she examined her nails, tried incredibly hard to stop her fingers from reaching for her hair. She did not want to give them any hint that she was nervous.

'We believe that Niklas is being set up.'

What else would they say? Meg thought.

'I really don't see what this has to do with me.' Meg looked in turn at each of the unmoved faces and was impressed by her own voice when she spoke. She possibly sounded like a lawyer, or a woman in control, though of course inside she was not. 'We were married for less than twenty-four hours and then Niklas decided that it was a mistake. Clearly he was right. We hardly knew each other. I had no idea about any of his business affairs. Nothing like that was ever discussed…'

Rosa spoke over her. 'We believe that Niklas is being set up by the head of our firm.'

It was then that Meg started to realise the gravity of the situation. These people were not just defending their client, they were implicating their own principal.

'We have had little access to the case, which in something as big as this is unusual, and without access to the evidence we cannot supply a rigorous defence. For reasons we cannot yet work out, we believe Miguel is intending to misrepresent Niklas. Of course we cannot let our boss know that we suspect him. He is the only one who has access to Niklas while he is being held awaiting a trial date.'

'He's in prison now?'

'He has been for months.'

Meg reached for her water but her glass was empty. Her hands were shaking as she refilled it from the jug. She could not stand the thought of him locked up, could not bear to think of him in prison, did not want those thoughts haunting her. She didn't like the new nightmares these people had brought, and she wanted them gone now.

'It really is appalling, but...' She didn't know how she could help them—didn't know the Brazilian legal system, just didn't know why they were here. 'I don't see how it has anything to do with me. As I said, I'm not involved in his business...' And then she started to panic, because maybe as his wife she had a different involvement with Niklas that they were here to discuss.

'We have made an application of behalf of Niklas for him to exercise his conjugal rights...'

Meg could hear her own pulse pounding in her ears as Rosa continued speaking and she drained her second glass of water. Her throat was still impossibly dry. Her fingers moved to her hair and she twirled the strand around one finger, over and over.

'Niklas is entitled to one phone call a week and a two-hour conjugal visit once every three weeks. He is being brought before the judge in a fortnight for the trial date to be set and we need you to fly there. At your visit with him on Thursday you are to tell him that only when he is in front of the judge he is to fire his lawyer. Before that he is to give no hint. Once he has fired Miguel we will step in for him.'

'No.' Meg shook her head and pulled her finger out of her hair. She was certain of her answer, did not need to think about this for a moment. She just wanted them gone.

'The only way we can get in contact with him is through his wife.'

'I'll phone him.' It was the most she would do. 'You said that he was entitled to a weekly phone call...' And then she shook her head again, because of course the calls would be monitored. 'I can't see him.' She could not. 'We were married for twenty-four hours.'

'Correct me if I am wrong...' Rosa was as tough with the truth as she was direct. 'According to the records we have found you have been married for almost a year.'

'Yes, but we—'

'There has been no divorce?'

'No.'

'And if Niklas was dead and I was here bringing you a cheque would you hand it back and say, *No, we were only married for twenty-four hours?* Would you say, *No, give this to someone else. He had nothing to do with me...?*'

Meg's face was red as she fought for an answer, but she did not know that truth—not that it stopped Rosa.

'And because you have not screamed annulment I am assuming consensual sex occurred.'

Meg felt her face grow redder, because sex had been the only thing they had had between them.

'If you had found yourself pregnant, would you not have contacted him? Would you have told yourself it did not count as you were only married for twenty-four hours? Would you have told your child the same…?'

'You're not being fair.'

'Neither is the system being fair to my client,' Rosa said. 'Your husband will be convicted of a crime he did not commit if you do not get this message to him.'

'So I'm supposed to fly to Brazil and sit in some trailer or cell and pretend that we're…?'

'There will be no pretending—you *will* have sex with him,' Rosa said. 'I don't think you understand what is at stake here, and I don't think you understand the risks to Niklas and his case if it is discovered that we are trying to get information in. There will be suspicions if the bed and the bin…'

Thankfully she did not go into further detail, but it was enough to have Meg shake her head.

'I've heard enough, thank you. I will start preparing the paperwork for divorce today.' She stood.

They did not.

'Marrying Niklas was the biggest mistake of my life,' Meg stated. 'I have no intention of revisiting it and I'm certainly not…' She shook her head. 'No. We were a mistake.'

'Niklas never makes mistakes,' Rosa countered. 'That is why we know he is innocent. That is why we have been working behind our own principal's back to ensure justice for him.' She looked to Meg. 'You are his only chance, and whether or not it is pleasant, whether or not you feel it is beneath you, this *must* happen.'

She handed her an envelope and Meg opened it to find an itinerary and airline tickets.

'There is a flight booked for you tomorrow night.'

'I have a life,' Meg flared. 'A job, commitments...'

'A visit has been approved for Thursday. It is the only chance to make contact with him before the pre-trial hearing in two weeks' time. After you have seen him you can go to Hawaii—though we might need you to go back for another visit in three weeks, if things don't go well.'

'No.' How else could she say it? 'I won't do it.'

Rosa remained unmoved. 'You may want this all to go away, but it cannot. Niklas deserves this chance and he will get it. You will see, when you check your bank account, that you are being well compensated for your time.'

'Excuse me?' Meg was furious. 'How dare you? How on earth did you...?' But it wasn't about how they had found out her bank details. It wasn't that that was the problem right now. 'It's not about money...'

'So it's the morality of it, then?' Rosa questioned. 'You're too precious to sleep with your own husband even it means he has to spend the rest of his life behind bars?'

Rosa made it sound so simple.

'For the biggest mistake of your life, you chose rather well, did you not?' Rosa sneered. 'You are being paid to sleep with Niklas—it's hardly a hardship.'

Meg met her eyes and was positive that he and Rosa had slept together. They both stared for a moment, lost in their own private thoughts. Then Rosa stood, a curl on her lip, and another sassy Brazilian gave her opinion of Meg as she upended her life.

'You need to get over yourself.'

CHAPTER SEVEN

WHEN THEY HAD GONE, Meg did what she had spent a year avoiding.

She looked up the man she had married and found out just how powerful he was—or had been before he had been charged. She understood now that the Niklas Dos Santos she was reading about would be less than impressed to find himself in business class. And then she read about the shock his arrest had caused. Niklas might have a reputation in business as being ruthless, but he had always seemed honest—which was apparently why it had made it so easy for him to con some high-flying people into parting with millions. They had believed the lies that had been told to them. His business peers' trust in him had made them gullible, and despite Rosa's and her colleagues' protestations of his innocence, for Meg the articles cast doubt.

She knew, after all, how effortlessly he had read *her*, how easily he had played *her*. Meg had seen another side to Niklas and it wasn't one she liked.

And yet, as Rosa had pointed out, he was her husband, and she was apparently his one hope of receiving a fair trial.

And then Meg clicked on images and wished she had not.

The first one she saw was of him handcuffed and being bundled into a police car.

There were many more of Niklas, but they were not of the man she knew. The suit was on and the tie was beautifully knotted, the hair was as she remembered, but not in one single image did she see him smiling or laughing. Not one single picture captured the Niklas she had so briefly known.

And then she found another image—one that proved the most painful of all to see.

His arrogant face was scowling, there were three scratches on his cheek that her nails had left there, and a deep bruise on his neck that her mouth had made. Meg read the headline: *Dos Santos vira outra mulher!* Meg clicked for a translation. She wanted to know if he had returned that morning and been arrested—wanted to know if that was the reason he had been so cruel to her. Had he known he was about to be arrested and ended it to protect her? She waited for the translation to confirm it, held her breath as it appeared: *Dos Santos upsets another woman!*

And even in prison, even locked up and a world away, somehow he broke her heart again.

There was a knock at the door. Her mother didn't wait for an answer, just opened it and came in. 'Helen said you had visitors?'

'I did.'

'Who were they?'

'Friends.'

She saw her mum purse her lips and knew she would not leave until she found out who her friends were and what they wanted. Even without the arrival of her visitors Meg remembered she had been due for a difficult conversation with her parents today, and now seemed like a good time to get it over with.

'Can you get Dad...?' Meg gave her mum a pale smile. 'I need to speak to you both.'

It didn't go well.

'After all we've done for you' was the running theme, and the words Meg had expected to hear when she told them that she had chosen not to continue working in the family firm.

She didn't mention Niklas. It was enough for them to take in without giving them the added bonus of a son-in-law! And one in prison too.

It should have been a far harder conversation to have, yet she felt as if all her emotions and fears were reserved for the decision that was still to come, and Meg sat through the difficult conversation with her parents pale and upset, but somehow detached.

'Why would you want to be a chef?' Her mother simply didn't get it—didn't get that her daughter could possibly want something that had not been chosen for her. 'You're a lawyer, for God's sake, and you want to go and work in some kitchen—?'

'I don't know exactly what I want to do,' Meg broke in. 'I don't even know if I'll be accepted...'

'Then why would you give it all up?'

And she didn't know how to answer—didn't know how to tell them that she didn't feel as if she was actually giving up *anything*, that she was instead taking back her life.

Just not yet.

She told them she was taking a holiday, though she still wasn't sure that she was, but even without Niklas looming large in her thoughts taking a few weeks off while her parents calmed down seemed sensible.

'And then I'll come back and work for a couple of months,' Meg said. 'I'm not going to just up and leave...'

But according to her parents she already had.

Later, as she sat on the balcony of her small flat and looked at the stunning view, Meg thought about her day. What should have been a difficult conversation with her parents, what should have her sitting at home racked with guilt and wondering if she'd handled things right, barely entered her thoughts now. Instead she focused on the more pressing problem looming ahead.

Quietly she sat and examined the three things she had that proved her relationship with Niklas had actually existed.

She took the ring from the chain around her neck and remembered the certainty she had felt when he had slipped it on—even though he had told her it could never be for ever, somehow she had felt it was right.

And then she picked up the marriage certificate she

had retrieved from her bedside table and examined the
dark scrawl of his signature. *Niklas Dos Santos*. She
saw the full stop at the end of his name and could even
hear the sound his pen had made as he'd dotted the
document.

Finalised it.

And then she examined the third thing, the most
painful thing—a heart that even eleven months on was
still exquisitely tender.

There had been no one since, no thought of another
man since that time. She felt dizzy as she peered into
her feelings, scared as to what she might find. The truth
was there waiting and she hadn't wanted to see it. It hurt
too much to admit it.

She loved him.

Or rather she had.

Absolutely she had, or she would never have married
him. Meg knew that deep down. And, whether or not
he had wanted it, still that love had existed. Her very
brief marriage with him had for Meg been the real thing.

And, as Rosa had pointed out, they *were* still married.

It was getting cool, so Meg went inside and read
the itinerary Rosa had handed her. Then she looked up
the prison he was being held at and could not believe
that he was even there, let alone that on Thursday she
might be too.

Would be.

Meg slid the ring back on her finger.

A difficult decision, but somehow easily made. Yes, Rosa was right. In legal terms he was still her husband.

But it wasn't in legal terms only that she made her choice. There was a part of herself that she must soon sort out, must work out how to get over, but for now at least, in every sense, Niklas was still her husband.

Though her hotel and flights had been arranged, any problems had to be dealt with by the travel agent, Rosa had told her. Meg must not, under any circumstance, make contact with them. She must not be linked to them in any way—not just to protect them, or even Niklas, they had warned her, but to protect herself.

And she registered the danger but tried not to dwell on it, just tried to deal with a life that had changed all over again.

There was another row with her parents—a huge one this time. They had no comprehension as to why their usually sensible daughter might suddenly up and take off to Brazil.

'Brazil!' Her mother had just gaped. 'Why the hell do you want to go to Brazil?'

They didn't come to the airport to say goodbye. Still, there was one teeny positive to the whole situation: Meg barely noticed the plane taking off. Her thoughts were too taken up with the fact that she was on her way to see Niklas.

And she barely noticed it a second time, when she transferred at Santiago and knew she was on the last leg of her journey to see him. Shortly after take-off the stewards stood, and after a little while she was offered a drink.

'Tonic water…' Meg said, and then changed her mind and added gin.

'Off on holiday?'

She turned to her friendly fellow passenger, an elderly lady who had cousins in São Paulo, she told Meg.

'Yes…' Meg said. 'Sort of.'

'Visiting family?'

'My husband.' How strange it felt to say it, but she was, after all, wearing his ring, and her documents were in her bag, and she might have to say the same thing at Customs, so maybe she'd better start practising.

'Brazil first and then three weeks in Hawaii…'

'Lovely.' The old lady smiled and Meg returned it. Just as Niklas had that first day, she wished her neighbour would just keep quiet.

She could hardly tell her the real purpose for her visit!

Instead she ordered another gin.

It didn't help.

She cried as they descended over São Paulo—she had never seen anything like it. Stretched below her was a sea of city, endless miles of buildings and skyscrapers. The population of this city alone was almost equivalent to the entire population of Australia, and never had Meg felt more small and lost.

The final approach was terrifying—more so because of all he had told her about it, more so now that she could see just how closely the cars and the planes and the city co-existed, more so because she was actually here.

Bizarrely, her eyes searched for him after she'd cleared Customs—a stupid flare of hope that this was a strange joke, that he was testing her, that he might be waiting with flowers and a kiss. Perhaps she might once more feel the thorns press into her skin as he teased her about the lengths she'd go to for just a couple of hours with him.

It wasn't a joke, though. It wasn't a game. There was no one here to greet her.

Meg exited the airport and tried to hire a taxi, but she had never seen a taxi queue like this one. She was exhausted and overwhelmed as once again Niklas pushed her out of her comfort zone.

The driver's music was loud, his windows were down, and he drove her through darkening streets into Jardins. Everything was loud there too. The city pulsed with life. There were food stalls on the streets—unfamiliar scents came in through the windows of the car whenever they stopped at traffic lights—and it was more city than she could deal with. Which made sense, Meg thought with a pale smile. After all it was the city Niklas was from.

All Meg wanted to do was to get to her room.

Dishevelled, confused, *tired*, after they pulled up at a very tall hotel Meg paid the taxi driver. The second she stepped inside she knew she was back in his world.

Modern, cosmopolitan, with staff exquisite and beautiful.

It was a relief to get to her room and look out of the

window at the bewildering streets below, to fathom that she was actually here—that tomorrow she would be taking another taxi to visit Niklas in prison.

Meg scanned the confusing horizon, wondered as to his direction, wondered if he had any inkling at all that she was even here.

Wondered all night how she could stand to face him tomorrow.

'Hi, Mum…' She rang not because they had insisted she did—they were hardly talking, after all—she rang because, despite their problems, Meg loved her parents and wanted the sound of normality tonight.

'How's Brazil?' Her mother's voice was terse, but at least she spoke.

'Amazing,' Meg said. 'Though I haven't seen much of it…'

'Have you booked any trips?'

'Not yet,' Meg said, and was quiet for a moment. She didn't like lying, especially to her parents, but she found herself doing it at every turn. Tomorrow she would be ringing her parents again to tell them that she had changed her mind about Brazil and was going to spend the rest of her vacation in Hawaii—how would they react to that?

More than anything Meg just wanted tomorrow over with, so that she could lie on a beach and hopefully heal once and for all. She hadn't dared risk putting her divorce application in her luggage in case it caused questions at Customs, but the second she landed home it would be posted.

Her heart couldn't take any more of him.

'How's Dad?'

'Worried,' her mum said, and Meg felt her heart sink—because she hated that they were worried about her. 'It's going to cost an arm and a leg to hire a new lawyer...'

Meg knew her mum didn't mean to hurt her, but unintentionally she had. The business was always the biggest thing on their minds.

'I've told you that I'll work for a couple of months when I get back. You don't have to rush into anything. And you don't need a full-time lawyer; you can contract out. We'll go through it all properly when I get back.'

'You *are* coming back?'

And Meg gave a small unseen smile, because maybe it wasn't just about the business. As difficult as they could be at times, they did want what they thought was best for her, and they did love her—that much Meg knew.

'Of course I am. I'm just taking a few weeks to sort out my head—I'll be back before you know it.'

It was impossible to sleep. She was dreading tomorrow and seeing him again, dreading the impact of seeing him face to face. It was emotionally draining just thinking about him, let alone seeing him.

Let alone having sex with him.

If Meg slept, she didn't sleep much, and she was up long before her alarm call. She ordered breakfast, but her stomach was doing somersaults and she could hardly manage to hold down a small piece of bread and grilled cheese.

The coffee she was more grateful for.

Had she not loved him, she doubted she could do this.

But had she not loved him she would not have married him in the first place and wouldn't be in this mess.

Except she remembered his cruel words from that morning long ago and knew that love had no place in this.

She gave up on breakfast and lay in the bath, tried to prepare herself for what lay ahead, but had no idea how. As she picked up a razor and shaved her legs she did not know if her actions were for his pleasure or for her pride. It was the same with the body oil she rubbed in. She wore simple flesh-coloured underwear and an olive green shift dress with flat leather sandals. Her hand was shaking too much to bother with make-up so she gave in.

Rosa had given her the name of a good car company to use, rather than getting a taxi, and the desk rang to tell her that her driver was here. As she left the room she glanced around and wondered how she would feel when she returned. This time tomorrow she would be on a plane on her way to Hawaii. This time tomorrow it would be done—for despite what Rosa had said she would not be returning to him.

Once was enough.

Twice might kill her.

So she looked at her room and tried not to think too much about what had to happen before she returned.

They drove through the most diverse of cities, passed the Court of Justice, where in two weeks Niklas would be, and in daylight Meg saw more of this stunning city. There was beauty and wealth, and such poverty too. She thought of Niklas growing up on the streets, and of how much he had made of himself only to fall. She didn't know enough to believe in his innocence. She might be a fool for love, but she wasn't a blind fool. Still, he deserved a fair trial.

Meg had never known such fear in her life as they approached the jail. The sight of the watchtower, the sounds when she entered, the shame of the examination... Her papers were examined and her photograph taken and she was told her rights—or rather her husband's rights. She could return in three weeks; she could ring him once a week at a designated time and speak for ten minutes. And although Meg took the paper with the telephone number on it, she knew that she would never use it.

Then a female guard examined her for contraband and Meg closed her eyes, thinking she would spit at her if she ever faced Rosa again, before being allowed to pull her knickers back up. Maybe she did need to get over herself, but as she was led through to an area where two guards chatted she heard the Dos Santos name said a few times, and even if Meg didn't understand precisely what they were saying she got their lewd drift. As she stood waiting for Niklas to arrive Meg knew that, yes, she might have to get over herself—but right about now she was completely over *him*.

CHAPTER EIGHT

THE SLOT ON the door opened and lunch was delivered. Niklas ate beans and rice. It was tepid and bland and there were no herbs to pick out, but he was hungry and cleared his plate in silence.

His cellmate did the same.

It was how they both survived.

He refused to let the constant noise and shouts from other inmates rile him. He made no comment or complaint about the bland food and the filth. From the first day he had arrived here, apart from the odd necessary word, he had been silent, had conformed to the system though some of the guards had tried to goad him.

As he had entered the jail they had told him of the cellmate they had for him, of the beatings he could expect. They'd told the rich boy just how bad things would be in there for him as he'd removed his suit and shoes and then his watch and jewellry before they searched him and then hosed him.

Niklas had said nothing.

He had been hosed many times before.

There was no mirror to look in, so after his hair was

shaved he'd just run a hand over his head. He wore the rough denim without real thought. He had worn harsher clothes and been filthier and hungrier than this on many occasion.

Niklas was streetwise. He had grown up in the toughest place and survived it. He had come from nothing and he'd returned to nothing—as he had always silently feared that he would. This anonymous, brutal world was one that he belonged in, and the one he truly deserved. Perhaps this was actually his home, Niklas had realised—not ten thousand feet in the air, swigging champagne as caviar popped in his mouth; not considering a home in the mountains and a family to take care of. He had been a fool to glimpse it, a fool to let down his guard, for those things were not his to know.

Assets frozen, friends and colleagues doubting him… The eventual snap of cuffs on his wrists had provided temporary relief as Niklas went back to the harsh world he had known one day would reclaim him. He'd returned to another system and navigated it seemingly with ease. But the temporary relief had soon faded and a sense of injustice had started to creep in. His head felt as if it would explode at times, and his body was so wired that he was sure he could rip the bars from the cell window with his bare hands or catch bullets with his teeth—but then, as he had long ago taught himself to, he simply turned those thoughts off.

Not for a second did he show his anger, and rarely did he speak.

His cellmate was one the most feared men in the

prison. He ran the place and had contacts both inside and out. The guards had thought it would be like two bulls put in the same paddock. The motto of São Paulo was *I am not led. I lead.* So they had put the rich boy who led the business world in with the man who led the inmates and had waited for sobs from Dos Santos. But Niklas had held Fernando's eyes and nodded when he had been placed in his cell. He had said good evening and got no answer, and from that point on Niklas had said nothing more to him. He had ignored his cellmate—as suited Fernando, as suited him—and over the months the tension had dissipated. The silence between the two inmates was now amicable; both men respected the other's privacy, in a friendship of no words.

Niklas finished his lunch. He would exercise soon.

They had not been let out to the yard in over a week, so in a moment he would use the floor to exercise. He paced himself, sticking to routines to hold onto his mind. For while he slotted in with the system, while he followed the prison rules, more and more he was starting to reject them. Inside a slow anger had long been building and it was one that must not explode, because he wanted to be here when his trial date was set—did not want solitary till then.

He lay on his bunk and tried not to build up too much hope that he might be bailed in a fortnight, when he appeared for the pre-trial hearing. Miguel had told him that he thought bail was unlikely—there were too many high-profile people involved who did not want him to have freedom.

'But there is no one involved,' Niklas had pointed out at their last meeting. 'Because I did not do anything. That is what you are supposed to prove.'

'And we will,' Miguel said.

'Where's Rosa?' Niklas had asked to see Rosa at this visit. He liked her straight talking, wanted to hear her take on things, but yet again it was Miguel who had come to meet with him.

'She…' Miguel looked uncomfortable. 'She wants to see you,' he said. 'I asked her to come in, but…'

'But what?'

'Silvio,' Miguel said. 'He does not want her in here with you.'

And Niklas got that.

Rosa's husband, Silvio, had complained about Rosa working for him. Niklas and Rosa had once been an item for a few weeks, just before she had met Silvio, and though there was nothing between them now, her working for Niklas still caused a few problems.

As he lay there replaying conversations, because that was all he was able to do in this place, Niklas conceded that Silvio was right not to want Rosa to visit him here.

Nothing would happen between them, but it was not just Rosa's sharp insight he wanted. The place stank of testosterone, of confined angry male, and Rosa was open enough to understand that his eyes would roam. She would let them, and he knew that she would dress well for him.

He tried not to think of Meg—did not want even an

image of her in this place—but of course it was impossible not to think of her.

As his mind started to drift he turned those thoughts off and hauled them back to his pre-trial hearing. His frustration at the lack of progress was building—his frustration at everything was nearing breaking point.

He climbed down from his bunk and started doing sit-ups, counting in his head. And then he changed to push-ups, and for those he did not bother to count. He would just work till his body ached. But anger was still building. He wanted to be on the outside—not just for freedom but because there he could control things, and he could control nothing here except his small routines. So he kept on doing his sit-ups and as a guard came to the door Niklas carried on, ignoring the jeering, just kept on with his workout.

'Lucky man, Dos Santos.'

He did not miss a beat, just continued his exercise.

'Who did you pay?'

Still Niklas did not answer.

'You have a beautiful wife.'

Only then did he pause, just for a second, mid-push-up, before carrying on. The guard didn't know what he was talking about. No one knew of Meg—they were winding him up, messing with his head, and he chose not to respond.

'She's here waiting to see you.'

And then the slot in the door opened and he was told to get up. There was no choice now but to do as he was told. So Niklas stood, met Fernando's eyes for just a second, which was rare. The change in routine was notable for both of them.

Niklas put his hands through the slot and handcuffs were applied, then he pulled his cuffed wrists back as the cell door was opened. He walked along the corridor and down metal steps, heard the jeers and taunts and crude remarks as he walked past. There were a couple of shoves from the guard but Niklas did not react, just kept on walking while trying to work things out.

Miguel must have arranged a hooker, finally pulled a few strings.

Thank God.

Maybe now his mind would hold till the trial date.

Not that he showed any emotion as they walked. He'd learnt that many years ago.

Show weakness and you lose—he'd learnt that at eight.

He had walked through the new orphanage he'd been sent to—he had been on his third orphanage by then—and this one was by far the worst. Still, there was good news, he had been told—his new family were waiting to meet him. A beautiful family, the worker had told him. They were rich, well fed and well dressed and had everything they wanted in the world except children. More than anything they wanted a son and had chosen Niklas.

His heart had leapt in hope. He'd hated the orphanage, a rough home for boys where the staff were often cruel, and he had been grinning and excited as the door had been pushed open and he had prepared himself to meet his new family.

How the workers waiting for him in there had laughed at his tears—how they had jeered him, enjoying their little joke long into the night. How could he have been so bold as to think that a family might want him?

It was the very last time that Niklas had cried.

His last display of true emotion.

Now he kept it all inside.

He would not give the prison guards the same pleasure. Whatever their plan, he would not give them the satisfaction of reading his face.

But then he saw her.

It had not properly entered his head that it might actually be Meg.

He had not allowed it to.

She did not belong in here. That was his first thought as he saw her dressed in a linin shift dress. Her hair burned gold and copper, the colour of the sun at night through his cell window, and then he saw the anxiety in her eyes turn to horror as she took in the shaved head and the rough clothing. A lash of shame tore through him that he should be seen by her like this, and his expression slipped for just a second. He stared ahead as his cuffs were removed, and though he remained silent his mind raced. To the left was Andros, the guard he trusted the least, and he thought again how Meg did not belong here. He wanted to know who the hell had arranged this, who had approved this visit, for even though he was confined and locked up he still had a system in place, and he had told Miguel that everything was to be run by him.

He could feel Andros watching as she walked towards him, heard the fear and anxiety in her voice as she spoke.

'I've missed you so much.'

She was playing a part. Niklas got that. But as her lips met his cheek it did not matter. Her touch was the first reprieve for his senses in months. Her skin on his cheek was so soft that the contact actually shocked him. He wanted to know the hows and whys of her visit here, wanted to know exactly what was going on, yet his first instinct was not to kiss her, but to protect her— and that meant that he too must play a part, for Andros was watching.

It was a kiss for others, and his mind tried to keep it at that—except her breath tasted of the outside and he drank her in. The feel of her in his arms allowed temporary escape and it was Meg who pulled back.

Meg stood with her cheeks burning red, tears of shame and hurt and anger in her eyes, and her lips pressed closed as one guard said something that made the other laugh. Then a door opened and they walked into a small, simply furnished room. The guard shouted something to them, and whatever language you spoke it was crude, before closing the door behind them. Meg stood and then realised that she couldn't stand for very much longer, so she sat on a chair for a moment, honestly shaken.

It wasn't just shock at the sight of him—seeing Niklas with his hair cropped almost as short as the dark stubble on his chin, dressed in rough prison denim. Even like this he was still the most beautiful man she had ever seen. It was not just the shock that she had again tasted his mouth, felt his skin against hers, relighting all those memories from their one night together. It was everything: the whole journey here, the poverty in the streets she had driven through, the sight of the prison as she had approached, the watchtower and the guns on the guards and the shame of the strip-search. Surely all of those things had severed any feelings she had for him?

But, no, for then she'd had to deal with the impact of seeing him again, of tasting him. For a moment she just sat there and wondered how, after all she had been through, she could still hear her heart hammer in relief to be back at his side. She wanted to be over him—had to be for sanity's sake—so she tried not to look at him, just drank from the glass of water he offered her.

He stood and watched her and saw her shock, saw what just a little while in this place had done to her, and thought again how she did not belong here.

'Why?' He knelt down beside her and spoke in a rough whisper. 'Why would you come here?'

She didn't answer him—Meg couldn't open her mouth to speak.

'Why?' he demanded, and then she looked at him and he was reminded of the last time he had seen her. Because even with the absence of her bared teeth he could feel her anger, could see her green eyes flash with suppressed rage and hear the spit of her words when finally she answered him.

'You're *entitled* to me, apparently.'

Niklas remembered the first time he had met her. She had been anxious, but happy, and he knew that it was he who had reduced her to this. He could see the pain and the disgust in her eyes as she looked at the man she had married, as she saw the nothing he really was.

And he did not want her charity.

'Thanks, but no thanks.'

He moved to the door, preparing to call for the guards. He might regret it later, but he did not want a minute more in this room.

As he moved to go he heard her voice.

'Niklas.' She halted him. This was not about what had happened between them, not about scoring points, she was here for one reason only. 'Your people told me…' He turned to face her. 'I'm to tell you…'

He silenced her by pressing his finger to his lips and nodded to the door. He trusted no one—never had in his life, and wasn't about to start in here. But then he closed his eyes for a second, for that was wrong. Because for a while he had trusted *her*, and did still. He came over to her, knelt down again and moved his head to her mouth, so she could quietly tell him the little she knew.

'Miguel is working against you. You are to ask for a change of representation at your trial…'

His head pulled back and she watched as he took in the news. Quietly she told him the little she knew. His face was grey and his eyes shone black. He swallowed as if tasting bile and she heard his rapid angry breathing. His whisper was harsh when it came.

'*No.*'

It had to be a lie, because if his own lawyer was working against him he was here for life.

She *had* to be lying.

'How?' he demanded. 'Why?'

'I don't know anything more than that,' Meg said. 'It's all I've been told.'

'When?' he insisted, his voice an angry whisper. 'When were you told?'

And she told him about the visit—how on Monday morning Rosa and her colleagues had arrived at her place of work. He thought of her momentarily in Sydney, getting on with her life without him, and now here she was in Brazil.

'They should never have sent you…' He was livid. 'It's too dangerous…'

'It's fine…'

It was so *not* fine.

'Niklas…' She told him *all* they had told her—that they had to have sex, about the bed and the bin, and that the guards could not know she was here for any other reason.

He saw her face burn in shame, and she saw his disgust at what he had put her through.

'It's fine, Niklas,' she whispered. 'I know what I'm doing…' She could feel his fury; it was there in the room with them.

'You should not be here.'

'It's my decision.'

'Then it's the wrong one.'

'I'm very good at making those around you, it would seem. Anyway,' she whispered harshly, 'you don't have to worry—you're paying me well…'

'How much?'

She told him.

And he knew then the gravity of his situation, understood just how serious this was—because he had no money any more. Everything had been frozen. He thought of his legal team paying her with money of their own and it tempered the bitterness that sometimes consumed him a little. Then he looked at the woman he might even have loved and tasted bitterness one again, for he hated what the world had done to him.

'So you're not here out of the goodness of your heart?'

'You've already had that part,' Meg said. 'So can we just get it over with?'

She looked over to the bed and he saw the swallowing in her throat, knew that she was drenched in fear. He looked to the door again, knowing there was a guard outside, one he did not trust, who must never get so much as a hint as to the real reason she was here.

Paid to be here, Niklas reminded himself.

He trusted no one again.

He stood and ripped the sheet from the bed, and she sat there as he twisted it in his hands before throwing it back. She heard his anger as he took the bedhead in angry hands and rocked the bed against the wall. He felt his anger building as he slammed the bed faster and faster. He had never paid for sex in his life. Yes, he'd have been grateful for a hooker, but he'd never taken Meg as one and his head was pounding as the bed hit the wall again and again. He did not know who to believe any more, and as the bed slammed faster he shouted out.

Meg sobbed as he shouted, but it did nothing to dissipate the fury still building, and then he picked up the condoms by the bedside and went to the small wash area and got to work to make sure evidence of their coupling was in place. Meg sat there, listening and crying. She understood his anger but she did not understand her own self, for even here, amidst this filth and shame, she wanted him. So badly she wanted to be with the man she had so sorely missed. Not just the sex, but the comfort he somehow gave.

'Niklas…' She walked into the washroom and ignored him when he told her, less than politely, to go away. His back was to her. She moved to his side and saw his fury, saw his hand working fast. He repeated his demand for her to leave him, and when it was clear that she didn't understand just how much he meant the words he told her in French and then Spanish.

'How many ways do you need to hear it…?'

How deep was his shame to be seen like this, to be reduced to this? His back had been to Meg, for he could not face her, yet she'd slipped into the space between him and the wall and her mouth was on his. One of her hands joined his now.

'Leave me.'

'No.' She stroked him too.

'Leave me,' he said as her other hand slipped off her panties.

'No.'

And she put her hands around his neck and pressed herself against him, tried to kiss him. He spat her out.

'You don't know the fire you are playing with.'

'I want to, though.'

She wanted every piece of him—wanted a little more of what she could never fully have. Because a man like Niklas could only ever be on loan to her. She had flown to him not because she had to, not for the money, and not for the morality of doing the right thing by her husband. Purely because of him, and not once did his anger scare her.

Not once, as rough hands pulled her dress up, did she fear him.

He lifted her up and onto him and positioned her, pulling her roughly down to him. The most basic sex was their only release and she wrapped her legs tight around him, locked her arms around his neck. His kiss was violent now, and she felt the clash of their teeth and tongues and the rapid angry stabs of him. The rough feel of denim on her thighs was nothing compared to the roughness deep inside, and her back was hard against the wall. Meg could feel his anger, it blasted deep inside her, and it let Meg be angry too—angry at so many things: that she was here, that she still wanted him, even that this man still moved her so.

Her moans and shouts that he blocked with his mouth

shocked Meg even more—scared her, almost—but she was not scared of him as he pulled her down on him, as she felt the bruise of his fingers in her hips. She could feel her orgasm building rapidly, as if she had waited eleven months just to come to him, as if her body had been waiting for him to set it free.

There was a flash of confusion for Niklas too, for her cries and the grip of intimate muscles, the arch of her back and the spasm of her thighs, could never be faked. He had thought this was charity, a paid act at best, a sympathy screw at worst, but she was craving him again, the way she once had, and as he shot into her he remembered all the good again—the way they had been. He never cried, but he was as close to it now as he had ever been. They were both drenched in brief release and escape and his kisses turned softer now, to bring her back to him. Then he heard the drizzle of the tap and his eyes opened to his surroundings, to the reality they faced. There were no more kisses to be had and he lifted her off.

Stood her down.

But she would not lose him to his pride and she carried on kissing him, opened his shirt and put her palms to his chest. He felt as if her hands seared him, for there had been no contact, no touch of another on his skin for many months, and he loathed the exposure, the prying of her hands. It was just sex he wanted, not her, but her hands were still moving, exploring the defined muscles. Her fingers were a pleasure and he did not want her to be here—yet he wanted her for every second that they had.

There would be hours later for thinking, for working out what to do about Miguel. For now he wanted every minute he had left with her.

He took her to the bed and undressed her, took his clothes off too, and she looked at all the changes to his body. He was thinner, but more muscled, and his face wasn't the one she had turned to on the plane—it was closed and angry, and yet she had felt his pain back there, felt him slip into affection, and for a small moment had glimpsed the man she had once met.

'Is that why you ended things?' She looked over to him as he joined her on the bed, but he just lay and looked up at the ceiling. 'Did you find out the trouble you were in?'

'I didn't know then.' It would be easier for her if he lied.

'So what happened that morning to change things?'

'I spoke to my people at work, realised how much I had on…'

'I don't believe you.'

'Believe in your fairytale if you want.' Niklas shrugged.

'Are you going to tell me to grow up again?' she asked. 'Because I grew up a long time ago—long before you met me. I've realised that I wasn't being weak staying in my job—I simply won't ride roughshod over the people I care about. And I don't believe that you would either and,' she finished, 'I *do* believe that you cared about me.'

'Believe what you want to.'

'I will,' Meg said. 'And I care about you.'

'It makes no difference to me.'

She had been paid plenty to be here with him so he should turn and start things. She had told him what she had came to say and the clock was counting down. He should use every minute wisely. They should not bother with talking—there were more basic things to be getting on with. Except this was Meg, and she didn't know how to separate the two.

'How are you dealing with being in here? How—?' she started, but he soon interrupted.

'I was right the first time.' He turned to look at her face—the face he had first seen on a plane. 'You talk too much. And I don't want to talk about me.' But before he moved to kiss her he allowed himself the luxury of just one question. 'Are you still working for your parents?'

'I resigned…' Meg said. 'I'm trying to choose my course at the moment…'

'Good,' Niklas said. He should push her hand down to where he was hardening again, but first there was something else he wanted to know. 'Are you okay?'

'Of course.'

'Are you happy?'

'Working on it.'

'Do your parents know you are here?'

'They know that I am in Brazil…' he saw tears pool in her eyes '…they don't know I have a husband that I'm visiting in prison.'

'You need to get away from here,' Niklas said. 'As soon as this visit is over.'

'I fly to Hawaii tomorrow.'

'Okay.' Tomorrow should be okay, he told himself, but he wasn't sure. 'Maybe change it to tonight…'

'I fly out at six a.m.'

He saw her grimace at the thought, remembered the first time they had met and the conversation they had had.

'How was your landing?' And for the first time he smiled. He didn't care how much they'd paid her, that she'd flown into Congonhas was enough for him to know that this had nothing to do with money.

'It wasn't so bad…' she attempted, and then told him the truth. 'I was petrified. I thought I was going to throw up. Although,' she added, 'that might have been the gin!'

He laughed, and so did she. He hadn't laughed for almost a year, but this afternoon he did. She kicked him and they fought for a bit—a nice fight, a friendly fight—and he took her back to when they'd been lovers so easily, far, far too easily. But, given this was the last time she would be here, she let him. No one could kiss like he did. It was quite simply perfect, and the feel of him hard in her hands was perfect too.

This time he would be gentle, Niklas decided, worried that he had been too rough before. He didn't just kiss her mouth, he kissed her everywhere—her hair and her ears and down to her neck, breathing in her scent. He kissed down to her waist and then further, to

where he wanted to be. He had been too rough, for she
was hot and swollen, but Meg lay there and felt his soft
kiss and was lost to it.

When he couldn't hold on any more he reached for
the condom that was a requirement in here. Her hands
reached for it too, and he let her put it on, but before she
did she kissed him there, and he closed his eyes as she
did so. Two hours could never be enough for all they
wanted to do. She slid it on. He should roll her over and
take her, but he let her climb on top of him, because if
he looked up to her hair and her body for a little while
he could forget where he was.

And she looked down as she moved on him and knew
exactly why she was here. She loved him. Still. Her real
fear at coming here had nothing to do with the flight
or the prison or the danger, it was *him*—because she'd
known all along that this was the only way she would
ever be over him.

She should be grilling him about his involvement in
the charges, insisting she find out, or just lying on her
back martyred as he took her, ready to get the hell out
once he'd finished. Instead she'd told him she cared
about him. Instead she was riding him, and his hands
were busy elsewhere, roaming her body. He was watching her. She was moaning, and he told her to hush, for
he would not give the guards the turn-on of the sounds
that she made. He put his hand over her mouth and she
licked it, bit it, and he pushed his fingers into her mouth.
He was coming, and so was she, and when the moment
finally came she folded on top of him, buried his face

with her hair, and he felt the silent scream inside her as she clutched him tightly over and over till it ended.

That was when she told him she loved him.

'You don't know me,' he said.

'I want to, though.'

'Divorce me,' he said, still inside her, and pulled her close. 'Send the papers to Rosa and I'll sign them.'

'I don't want to.'

'You do.'

She didn't.

'I can see you again in three weeks...' She was drunk on him. 'I can come to the trial.'

'You are to *leave*!'

'I can ring you on Wednesday each week...'

He was scared now as to what he'd unleashed. Scared not of her passion, but that she might stay.

'No.'

'I can. I'm allowed one phone call a week.'

He looked up at her and all he knew was that she was not coming back here. With his own lawyer working against him he was probably done. Here was where he would always be and he would not do this to her. Even with new lawyers, trials took for ever in Brazil. Even with the best legal team he would be here for years at best. He lifted her off him and swore in three languages when he saw the condom was shredded. 'Get the morning-after pill and when I speak with my new lawyers I will have them file for divorce...'

'No...'

'You are to go to Hawaii.'

'Niklas—'

The guards were knocking at the door. Their time was up. He stood and threw her clothes at her, telling her to dress quickly for he did not want them getting one single glimpse of her. She continued to argue with him as he picked up her bra and clipped it on her, before lifting each leg into her panties, followed by her dress, and even as he zipped it up still she argued.

'We're finished,' he told her.

And he wasted time telling her that they *had* to be over when he should have told her how dangerous this was, just how little he knew about what was going on, and that he was scared for her life. But the guards were here now and he could not say.

He gave her a brief kiss, his eyes urging her. 'Have a safe flight.'

CHAPTER NINE

SHE DIDN'T WANT to lie on a beach in Hawaii.

There could be no healing from him.

She wanted to be close to him, wanted to be there for his trial hearing at least. She hoped for a miracle.

He would not want her there. Meg knew that.

But he was her husband, and she could at least be here in the city for him. Could watch it on the news, could be close even if he didn't know it.

And then she could visit him again before she left. She did not want a divorce from him now, and she wanted one more visit to argue her case.

She was probably going insane, Meg realised as she cancelled Hawaii and stayed on in Brazil, but that was how he made her feel.

She ventured out onto the busy streets and toured the amazing city. The sights, the smells, the food, the noise—there was everything to meet her moods.

And without Niklas she might never have seen any of this—might never have visited the Pinacoteca, a stunning art museum, nor seen the sculptured garden beside it.

At first Meg did guided tours with lots of other tourists around her, but gradually she tuned in to the energy of the place, to the smiles and the thumbs-up from the locals and ventured out more alone. She was glad to be here—glad for everything she got to see, to hear, to feel. Every little thing. She could have lived her whole life and never tasted *pamonah*, and there were vendors selling them everywhere—from the streets, from cars, ringing triangles to alert they were here. The first time Meg had bought one and had sunk her teeth into the new taste of mashed and boiled corn she had been unable to finish it. But the next day she had been back, drawn by the strange sweet taste—inadvertently she'd bought savoury, and found that was the one she liked best.

There were so many things to learn.

So badly she wanted to visit the mountains, to take a trip to the rainforests Niklas had told her about, yet it felt too painful to visit the mountains without him.

She didn't dare ring him that first week. Instead when six p.m. on Wednesday neared she sat in a restaurant the concierge had told her was famed for its seafood and ordered *feijoada*. Maybe it wasn't the same restaurant Niklas had told her about, but she felt as if angels were feeding her soul and that she was right to be there.

As the days passed she fell more and more in love with the city—the contrasts of it, the feel of it and the sound of it. The people were the most beautiful and elegant she had seen, yet the poverty was confrontational. It was a world that changed at every turn and she loved the anonymity of being somewhere so huge, loved being lost in it, and for two weeks she was.

As instructed, she did not contact Rosa. The only people she spoke to were her parents, and she gave Niklas no indication that she was there until the night before his trial date.

His face was on the TV screen, a reporter was already outside the court, and Meg had worked out that *amanhã* meant tomorrow. Until *amanhã* she simply could not wait. She just had to hear his voice. She had fallen in love with a man who was in prison and she should be signing paperwork, should be happily divorced, should be grateful for the chance to resume her life—but instead she sat in her hotel room, staring at the phone...

Confused was all she was without him. The passion and love she felt for him only made real sense when he was near her and she had an overwhelming desire to talk to him. She counted down the moments until she could make that call.

He knew that she would call.

Niklas could feel it.

Andros came and got him from his cell and he sat by the phone at the allotted time. The need for her to be safe overrode any desire to hear her voice.

His teeth gritted when he heard the phone ring, and he wondered if he should let it remain unanswered, but he needed her to get the message—to get out of his life and leave him the hell alone.

And then he heard her voice and realised just how much he craved it, closed his eyes in unexpected relief just to hear the sound of her.

'I told you not to ring.'

'I just wanted to wish you good luck for tomorrow.'

'It is just to arrange a trial date…' He did not trust the phones. He did not trust himself. For now he wanted her to visit him again. He wanted her living in a house in the mountains right behind the prison and wanted her to ring him every Wednesday, to come in to see him every three weeks. What scared him the most was that she might do it. 'You did not need to ring for that. It will all be over in ten minutes.'

She understood the need to be careful. 'Even so, I hope they give you a date soon.'

'What are you doing now?'

'Talking to you.'

'Is everything okay?'

She knew what he was referring to—had seen his face when he'd removed the condom.

'It's fine.'

'Did you go to a *pharmacia*?'

He closed his eyes when she didn't answer, thought again of her in a home in the mountains, but this time he pictured her with his baby at her side and selfish hope glimmered.

'How's Hawaii?'

He heard her pause, heard that her voice was a little too high as she answered him. 'You know…' She attempted. 'Nice.'

'I *don't* know,' Niklas said, and it was not about what he wanted, it was not about him, it was about keeping her safe. His words were harsh now. 'I've never been and I want a postcard,' he said. 'I want you, *tonight*, to write me a postcard from Hawaii.'

He was telling her what to do and she knew it.

'Niklas,' she attempted, 'I still have some holidays left. I thought maybe next week…'

'You want to be paid again?'

'Niklas, please—' She hated that he'd mentioned money. 'I just want to see you.'

'You've already earned your keep…go spend your money on holiday.'

'Niklas…I know you don't mean that.'

'*What* do you know?' His voice was black. 'We were married for one day; we screwed an awful lot. You know nothing about me.'

'I know that you care. I know when you saw me—'

'Care?' he sneered down the phone. 'The only way I can get sex in here is if they bring in my wife—that's it. I am sick of conversations, and you seem to want just as many of those as you give of the other.'

'Niklas, please…'

But he would not let her speak. He had to get her away from here. Did she not get that she could be in danger? He had no idea what was happening on the outside, had no idea what was going on, and he wanted her safely away—had to make sure she was safe.

So again he drowned her with words.

'Meg, if you want to come back and suck me, then do. But just so long as you know you mean nothing to me.'

He slammed down the phone—not in fury but in fear. He put his hands through the door and felt the cool of the cuffs. His mind was racing. Since her visit, since getting the information that Miguel was working against him, his mind had been spinning, trying to work out what the hell was going on, trying to figure things out. But now he had a head full of *her*, and he had more to be concerned with than that she was still here in Brazil.

He needed to speak with Rosa—had to work out what the hell was going on.

As he was walked back to his cell his face was expressionless, but his mind was pounding like a jackhammer and he cursed under his breath in Portuguese as Andros made some reference to his wife, about his nice little family, and asked how scum from the streets had managed that. Then Andros pushed him up the stairs and Niklas cursed again, but in French this time.

'Watch it, Dos Santos…' Andros told him, sensing his prisoner's rising anger and slamming him up against the wall.

The move was not meant to overpower him, Niklas realised, simply to provoke him, because Dos Santos was an orphan's name. Niklas went to swear again, in Spanish, but his brain was working quickly, far more quickly than his mouth, and in that second he knew what was happening.

Dos Santos meant something different in Spanish.

And it was a Spanish nun who had named him.

Dos Santos in Spanish meant two saints.

He had a twin.

In that very second it was as if a bomb had exploded in his brain and he worked it all out. He knew instantly how he had got to be here. Knew that his double was out there and had been working with Miguel against him. And with a lurch of fear that was violent to his soul he knew that Meg was in serious danger.

Niklas said nothing when Andros jeered again, just stood silent against the wall as Andros spoke filth about his wife. He stood still and refused to react as another guard came over. A decent guard this time, because there were plenty of them around.

'Trouble?' the guard asked.

'No trouble,' Niklas said, because he did not want to go to solitary tonight. He really needed to get to his cell.

He stood compliant as his cuffs were removed and went quietly into his cell. There he met the eyes of Fernando, and for the first time since his arrival he spoke with the other man.

'I need your help,' Niklas said, for he had worked out what was happening and urgent help was required. 'I need you to make contact on the outside.'

CHAPTER TEN

ANOTHER NIGHT CRYING over Niklas Dos Santos and Meg swore it would be the last.

Part of her could almost convince herself that he was just trying to get her to leave, that that was the reason behind his cruel words, but the more sensible part of Meg soon talked herself round. Her sensible side reminded her that this was a man she knew nothing about—a man who had caused her nothing but heartache and trouble since the day that they had met.

Hawaii sounded pretty good to Meg right now.

A week lying on the beach concentrating on nothing but how best to forget him.

It was well after lunchtime now, and Meg was *still* waiting for the travel agent to return her call. When she did, Meg would ask to be booked onto the earliest flight that could be arranged, and she packed her suitcase in preparation. Very deliberately she did not turn on the vast television to see how his trial was going, or to catch a glimpse of him on the news, because one glimpse of Niklas and she was lost to him—that much she knew.

She wanted her divorce now, wanted to be the hell

away from him, would not waste even one more single
minute on him.

But as she packed up her toiletries Meg threw tam-
pons into her make-up bag and suddenly realised that
it might be rather more complicated than that.

She looked at the unopened packet, an Australian
brand because she hadn't bought any since she had arrived here, and tried to remember when she'd last had
a period.

She tried to remember the days in Australia before
her life had been changed so dramatically by the visit
from Niklas's lawyers. No, she hadn't had her period
for a while.

There should be the reassurance that they'd used
condoms, but the last one hadn't held.

Could she be pregnant?

Would she tell him if she was?

Meg looked in the mirror and decided that, no, she
could not deny him that. Even if his life was to be spent
on the inside, he would have to know the truth, and it
wasn't the kind of news she could reveal in a letter—
maybe she would have to visit him again.

Maybe not.

A letter was probably more than he deserved.

But first she had to know for sure.

She was probably overreacting, Meg told herself as
she headed out of her hotel room and to the elevators.
Worrying too much, she tried to convince herself as
she headed onto the street. With all that she'd been

through these past weeks it was no wonder that her period was late.

The streets were busy, as always—the cars jammed together, horns blaring, and sirens blazing as police tried to thread their way through the impossible madness that was downtown São Paulo. She found a *pharmacia* and inside it was the same as the world over, with numerous pregnancy testing kits sitting on the shelves. Meg didn't need to speak the language to know she was making the right purchase.

What was different from Australia, though, was that instead of being pounced on by an assistant the second she entered the store, here Meg was pretty much ignored. Even when she tried to pay the pharmacist and his checkout assistants were all taking an impromptu break and watching the television, and Meg could feel mounting impatience. She really had to know now if she was pregnant. Had to make the decision of facing Niklas and telling him while she was still here.

Finally someone came over to serve her, still talking to her colleagues, and Meg froze when she heard one of them shout the name Dos Santos. She felt sweat bead on her forehead as she paid, because despite herself—despite all this—she wanted to turn the television on, wanted to know how he was.

She almost ran back to the hotel, terrified of her feelings for him, that even a mention of his name could reduce her to this petrified state.

It was blissfully cool and quiet in her room—such a contrast to the chaos down below. She fought not to turn on the television, picked up the remote and hurled it, tried not to look where it landed. The light on the phone said she had a new message. She hoped it was the travel agent and played it back, but heard her mum's voice instead. Meg honestly didn't know how she could ever begin tell her parents all that had happened. She had always hoped she would never have to, but if this test proved positive…

She could feel the tears starting again but refused to give in to them—just bit them back and headed to the bathroom, put her purchase in its bag on the bench, ready to find out. Then there was a knock on the door and Meg assumed it was the cleaner. She didn't want her coming in now. She wanted privacy for this at least.

So she went to tell them. She didn't even look through the peephole, just opened the door, and what was left of the sensible part of her mind struggled to remain calm because standing at her door was Niklas. She froze for a moment, unable to respond to seeing him in such an ordinary setting. She wanted to sob at him, to rage at him, to ask him how on earth he was here—except she just stood there.

'It's okay…' He stepped in. 'I know it must be a shock to see me here.'

'I don't understand…'

'The judge understood,' he said. 'Didn't you see it all on the news?'

'I haven't been watching it.'

'That is good.' He gave her a smile. 'I get to tell you the good news myself.'

'I don't want to hear it.' She was so very angry with him, and now finally she could tell him. 'I haven't been watching it because I'm sick of this, Niklas. I'm sick of how you make me feel at times. I can't do this any more.'

'You're upset.'

'Do you blame me?' She looked at him. She could smell his cologne—the same cologne he had worn the day they had met. He was dressed in a stunning suit now, just as beautiful as the day they had met, just as cruel as the day he had ended things between them, but she wanted to know. 'You've been let off?'

'I've been bailed while they take some time to review new evidence.'

'Well, after the way you spoke to me last night I need some time for a review too,' Meg answered. She refused just to go back to loving him. He had hurt her too much. And she could not find out if she was pregnant while he was near. She needed to do that part alone.

'Come here…' He moved to pull her into his arms.

'Just leave.' It took everything she had to shake her head. 'Just go, Niklas. I'm doing as you told me. I'm going to Hawaii…'

'You're upset.'

'Why do you keep saying that? Of *course* I'm upset!' she flared. 'Did you think I wouldn't be? How the hell do you justify speaking to me like that?'

'Meg…'

He walked over and she did *not* want him to take her in his arms, did not want him to melt her all over again.

'I say stupid things at times. You know that...'

'Stupid things?' There were so many other ways she could describe his words. 'It was more than stupid, it was foul...' She would not be fobbed off. 'Why?' she demanded. 'Why did you speak to me like that?'

'I've said I'm sorry.'

'No, you haven't, and you're clearly not as sorry as I was to hear it.' She went to open the door, to tell him to get out of here, but he stopped her and wrapped his arms around her shoulders. Meg just stood there, tears rising, remembering the love they had made and all the ways he made her feel. But she could not go back there. 'Get out!' She pushed him off her. 'I mean it, Niklas...'

'Meg...' His mouth was on her cheek and she pulled her head away. His hands were in her hair but she brushed them off.

'Please,' she said, 'can you just leave me? I'll call you later. I'll—'

His phone rang then, and it annoyed her that he took the call. Yes, of course he was busy, she knew that, and maybe she should be flattered that he had come straight to her, but it annoyed her that in the middle of a row he could just stop and take a call. It made her even more angry, and she was tired of making excuses for him. She wanted him gone and she told him so when he ended his call.

'You are cross...' He smiled at her. 'You look beautiful when you are cross...'

He aimed his phone at her and she blinked at the flash. 'What the hell are you doing?'

'I've missed things like this. I want to capture everything…'

'I just you want you to leave.'

But he simply refused to listen. 'Let's go for a walk.'

'A walk?'

The last thing she wanted was a walk. She wanted him to leave. She looked at his lips and not even his beautiful mouth could silence her doubts now. She just wanted him gone.

'A walk to clear the air…' Niklas said.

'No.' She shook her head. 'I'm waiting for the travel agent to ring me back.'

'She'll call back if you're not here.' He shrugged. 'Come,' he said. 'I want to taste the fresh air. I want to feel the rain…'

She looked out of the window. Yes, it was raining, and she realised that he wouldn't have felt the rain in a long time. She was relieved that he wasn't all over her, trying to kiss her back to confusion as he so often did, but she didn't feel she knew him at all.

'Meg, after all we have been through will you at least come for a walk with me?'

'You hurt me last night.'

'I apologise.' His black eyes met hers. 'Meg, I truly apologise. We can start again, without all this hanging over us…'

But she was stronger than she'd thought she could be.

She looked into his eyes and quite simply no longer wanted him—didn't want to get back on the roller-coaster ride beside him. It was then that she made a decision that was surprisingly easy; she looked at the man who had broken her heart and knew that he would break it all over again. She simply refused to let him.

It was over.

Whatever the pregnancy test told her, Meg knew it was far better that she find out well away from him. She would fly to Hawaii today, search for the clarity he so easily clouded and make better decisions alone.

'Come...' he said. 'I want to taste my freedom.'

Maybe it would be easier to tell him that they were finished while they were walking. Maybe it would prove easier out there. Because she knew his kisses made her weak. So she nodded and she went to get her jacket, to comb her hair.

'Don't worry about that...' he said. 'Your hair is fine...'

Niklas was right. Her hair really didn't matter right now—it was her heart Meg had to worry about. They rode down in the lift together and Meg looked at him more closely. She hated her swollen eyes. Even more she hated that she had let him cause them.

They headed out through the foyer and into the street and she felt the warm rain that was so regular here. His hand reached for her, but she pulled hers back, refusing to give this man any more chances. He'd already used his last one with his filthy words to her the previous night and now his pathetic attempt at an apology.

'I'm ending it, Niklas.' He kept on walking. 'I'm going to file for divorce.'

'We'll go to a bar and talk about it.'

'There's nothing to discuss.' Meg stopped—which wasn't the most sensible thing to do on such a busy street.

There were moans from a few pedestrians and he took her hand and they kept walking. She really was sure that she was making the right choice, because she did not know him, and he did not know her, and a walk would not clear the air. Only his kiss could possibly have given them a chance, because sex was the only thing they had going for them. Maybe she was mad for thinking it, but shouldn't that be the way a man cele-brated his freedom? If he loved her, if he wanted her, wouldn't the first thing he wanted be taking her to bed, not out for a walk?

'There's a bar up here that I know,' Niklas said. 'It's not far—just a couple of blocks away...'

'I don't want to go to a bar...'

'The street is too noisy. Come on, we can talk prop-erly there.'

'I don't want to talk.'

Meg was starting to panic now, and she didn't really know why. His hand was too tight on her wrist, and he was walking her faster, and she had the most appalling thought then that he hadn't been bailed at all. There was an urgency in the steps he was taking. She looked over to him and his head was down, and it dawned on Meg that maybe he had escaped from jail. She recalled the screams of the police cars and bikes. They were scream-ing in the streets even louder now. She remembered too the pharmacy staff all huddled around the television, saying his name. Maybe it was because Niklas Dos Santos had escaped. Still he walked her ever faster.

'Niklas…'

She could hear the thud of music as they turned into a side street, could hear the clang of triangles and the smell of *pamonah*. There were so many people around; surely she was safe. She pulled her hand from his and stopped walking, but he turned and put a hand to her cheek. She shivered, but not with pleasure. There was something dark and menacing in his eyes. She was a fool to have got involved with this man, a fool to follow her heart, for look where it had led her—to a dingy side street in Brazil with a man she was now terrified of.

'Come,' he said. 'We will talk about where our relationship is going later. Right now I want to celebrate my freedom and I want you to celebrate it with me.' His hand was tight on her arm. 'You wouldn't deny me that?'

'I do,' she said. 'And I want you to let me go.'

'Don't spoil this day for me, Meg—it's been a hell of a long year for both of us. Now we can drink *cachaca*, unwind, dance. Later we can talk, but first…'

He lowered his head to kiss her, but it was too late for that and she moved her head back from his, suddenly confused. Because Niklas didn't dance. It was one of the few things that she *did* know about him—or had that been just another of his lies? Suddenly she was scared, and with real reason now.

Meg turned to go but he pulled her roughly back and

pushed her against the wall. Then he opened his jacket and she saw that he had a gun.

'Try to run and it will be the last thing you do...'

'Niklas...' she begged, and when Meg heard her own voice she heard the way she sounded when she pleaded for her life. She was trying to show him that she wasn't panicked, trying to reason with a man she absolutely didn't know, trying to get away. 'Why do you need me?' she said. 'If you've escaped...'

People were turning to look at them, maybe alerted by the panic in her voice even though she wasn't screaming. Or perhaps it was that if he had just escaped then his picture would be everywhere, being flashed over the news. Perhaps that was why he lowered his face to her.

'Why do you need me with you?'

'Because you're my last chance.'

And his mouth came down on hers.

She could hear a car pulling up beside them and Meg knew this was *her* last chance to get away. She knew instinctively that when the car doors opened she would be shoved in, that that was why he had taken the call—to arrange all this. Terrified, Meg did the only thing she could think of to survive. She bit hard on his lip with all she had—took that beautiful mouth and bit it as hard as she could. In the second when he recoiled, as he cursed her in Portuguese and reached for his gun, Meg ran—ran as she never had—ran and ran faster as she heard gunshots.

She kept running till rough arms grabbed her and pulled her down, slamming her to the ground. She felt her cheek hit the pavement and the skin leave her leg as she rose to run again, heard another volley of gunshots and looked behind her. She saw police cars screeching up. Whoever had shielded her from him had gone. Then she stared at the body on the ground and it was the only thing she could see.

'Niklas!' she screamed, and tried to run back to him, for she hated the man but it was agony to see him lying dead and riddled with bullets.

She could not stop screaming. Not even when other arms wrapped around her and her face was buried in rough prison denim and she smelt him again—not his cologne, but the scent of Niklas, her drug of choice, a scent that till now had been missing. She heard him saying over and over that she was safe, that he was here, that now it would all be okay, but she still did not believe it was him—until he lifted her face and she met his eyes, saw that the beautiful mouth had not been bitten and knew that somehow it was him.

That she was safe.

It was just her heart that was in danger again.

CHAPTER ELEVEN

MEG DID NOT get to see him again. Instead she was taken to a police station. There were press clamouring outside as she was taken in to give a statement, and while she was waiting for a translator Rosa arrived.

Meg gave her statement as best she could. They kept talking about twins, and although she had already worked that out when she was being held in Niklas's arms, her brain was so scrambled and confused that even with a translator she could hardly understand the questions, let alone answer them.

Every time she closed her eyes she saw Niklas—or rather the man she had thought was Niklas—lying there dead. The raw grief and panic, the *knowing* in that moment that she would never see him again, that the man she had fallen so heavily in love with was now dead, was not a memory or a feeling she could simply erase.

Fortunately Rosa had told the police she would return with Meg tomorrow, but that for now she needed peace, and thankfully they accepted that.

'We will return at ten tomorrow,' Rosa told her.

They stepped out into the foyer and she saw him

standing there, still dressed in prison denim. He took her in his arms and she knew then that she had to be careful, because the one thing she had worked out before this embrace was that she wasn't strong around him—that she'd only been able to break up with Niklas when it hadn't actually been him.

'I'm still angry with you.'

'I thought you might be.' He kissed her bruised cheek and didn't let her go as he spoke. 'We can row in bed.'

Which sounded a lot more like the Niklas she knew. He held her tight and pressed his face into her hair and she could feel his ragged breathing. For a moment she thought he was crying, but he just held her a moment longer and spoke into her hair.

'The press are outside so we have to go out the back. I am taking you far away from here. I need to stay in the city, but—'

'*Não,*' Rosa said.

Meg heard the word *amanhã* again, and realised Rosa was telling him that Meg must return to the police tomorrow.

'I'll ring Carla, then.'

With his arm still around Meg he took Rosa's phone and started to dial the number. Whilst he was occupied Meg stepped out of his embrace, and a little later, when they climbed into a waiting car, she sat on the back seat far away from him, needing some time alone.

Even though they went out the back way the press still got some photos and it was horrible. They scrambled over to the car and blocked their exit, but the driver shook them off. Niklas told her it might be like this for a while, and that he was taking her to a hotel. He saw the start in her eyes.

'We're not going back *there*—I've asked Carla to book us into a different one.'

Us.

So easily he assumed.

They entered the new hotel the back way too, and were ushered straight to a waiting lift where Niklas pressed a high number. They stood in silence till Meg broke it.

'Did you get off?'

'I've been released on bail.'

'So why are you still wearing...?' And then she shook her head, because she was simply too tired for explanations right now.

They stepped out of the lift and there was hotel security in the corridor—'For the press,' Niklas said, but it felt a lot like prison to her, and no doubt to him too, but he said nothing, just swiped open a door, leading her into a plush suite.

Meg stood there for a moment, only knowing for certain the city she was in and that Niklas was alive. She remembered her feeling at seeing him dead, and the fear that had gripped her in the moments before, and started shaking.

'I wanted to take you away from the city tonight, but because we need to go back to the police station tomorrow it is better that we stay here. I've had your stuff packed up, but it is in the other place…you'll have to make do for now…'

It was hardly 'make do'; there was food and soon she would take a bath, and then she sat and had a strong coffee. Niklas offered her *cachaca*—the same drink she had been offered a little while ago—and she shuddered as she remembered. He opened the fridge and opened a bottle of champagne instead.

Which seemed a strange choice and was a drink she hadn't had it in almost a year.

Not since their wedding.

It was the drink they had shared on the day they had met, and he poured her a glass now, kissing her forehead as they chinked glasses and celebrated that somehow they were both here. It was a muted celebration, and there was still so much to be said, but Niklas dealt with the essentials first.

'You need to ring your parents.'

'I don't know what to say to them,' Meg admitted. She felt like crying just at the thought of them, was dreading the conversation that had to be had—and how much worse it was going to be now, after not telling them anything.

'Tell them the truth,' Niklas said. 'A bit diluted.' He nudged her. 'You need to speak to them now in case they hear anything on the news, or the consulate might contact them. Have they tried to ring *you*?'

'I didn't even bring my phone with me,' Meg said.

'It will be at the other hotel,' Niklas said. 'For now

they just need to know you are safe. I will speak to them if it gets too much.'

'No.' She shook her head—not at phoning them, but at the thought of him talking to them. She knew how badly things were going to go. 'I'll do it…'

'Now.'

'I still don't really know what happened.' But she took the phone, because he was right. They needed to know she was safe. 'Leave me,' she said, and was glad that he didn't argue.

Niklas headed into the bedroom and she dialled the number, then looked out of the window to a very beautiful, but very complicated city. She held her breath when she heard the very normal sound of her mum.

'How's Brazil?' Ruth asked. 'Or is it Hawaii this week?'

'Still Brazil,' Meg said, and because Ruth was her mum straight away she knew.

'What's wrong?'

It was the most difficult of conversations. First she had to tell her how Vegas had been and how she had married a man she had only just met. She diluted the story a lot, of course—an awful lot—but she still had to tell them how, the morning after their wedding, Niklas had upset her, how she had been trying to psyche herself up to divorce him.

And her mum kept interrupting her with questions that her father was shouting—questions that weren't really relevant because they still didn't know half of the story. So she told them she was here to visit him, that he had been arrested a while ago, but was innocent of all charges. Her mother was shouting and sobbing now, and her dad was demanding the phone, and they were simply getting nowhere, and then Niklas was back and she was so glad to hand the phone over to him.

She found out for certain then just how brilliant he was, how clever he was with people, for somehow he calmed her father down.

'My intention when I married your daughter was to take proper care of her. I was on my way to tell you the same when I found out that I was being investigated.'

He said a few more things, and she could hear the shouts receding as he calmly spoke his truth.

'I was deliberately nasty to her in the hope she would divorce me—of course she was confused, of course she was ashamed and did not feel that she could tell you. I wanted to keep her away from the trouble that was coming—in that I failed, and I apologise.'

They didn't need to know all the details, but he told them some pertinent ones, because as soon as they hung up they would be racing to find out the news for themselves. So he told them about the shooting, but he was brief and matter-of-fact and reiterated that Meg was safe. He told them that they could ring any time with more questions, no matter the time of day or night, and that he would do his best to answer them. Then he handed the phone back to Meg.

'You're safe,' her mum said.

'I am.'

'We need to talk…'

'We will.'

When she hung up the phone she looked at him. 'You could have told me the truth that day.' She was angry that he hadn't.

'What? Walk back in and tell you that I am being investigated for fraud and embezzlement? That the man you met twenty-four hours ago is facing thirty-five years to life in jail…?' He looked at her. 'What would you have said?'

'I might have suggested you didn't go back till you found out the case against you…' she flared. 'I might not be the best one in the world, but I *am* a lawyer…'

'My own lawyer was telling me to get straight back.' He kicked himself then, because had he confided in her—had he been able to tell her—he might not have raced back, might have found out some more information before taking a first-class flight to hell.

'I had to return to face it,' Niklas said. 'Would you have stood by me?'

'You never gave me that chance.'

'Because that was what I was most afraid of.' He was kneeling beside her and she could hear him breathing. 'You never asked if I did it.'

'No.'

'Even when you visited…even when you rang…'

'No, I didn't.'

'Did you believe I was innocent?'

'I hoped that you were.'

'There was too much love for common sense,' Niklas said.

She sat there for ages and was glad when he left her
alone and headed to the bathroom. She heard his sigh
of relief as he slipped into the bath water and thought
about his words—because while she had hoped he was
innocent, it hadn't changed her feelings towards him
and that scared her. After a little while she wandered
in to him.

'I am so sorry.' He looked at her. 'For everything I
have put you and your family through.'

'It wasn't your fault.'

'No,' he said. 'But still, I have scared you, and nearly
cost you your life…'

And then he looked at her and asked the question the
police had asked her earlier.

'Did he do anything to you?'

'Apart from hold a gun at me…' she knew what he
meant '…no.'

She watched him close his eyes in relief and knew
then that he *had* cried.

'He wanted to walk,' Meg said. 'That was when I
started to worry.' She gave him a pale smile. 'Not quite
the Niklas I know.' And then there wasn't a pale smile.
'I'm still cross about what you said on the phone.'

'I wanted you to leave,' he said. 'I wanted you to be
so angry, so upset, that you got on the next plane you
could…'

'I nearly did.'

'Do you want me tell you what happened?'

She wanted to hear it now, and he held his hand out to
her. Yes, he assumed she would join him—and for now

he was right. Her clothes and her body were filthy, and she wanted to feel clean again, to hear what had happened, and she wanted to hear it as she lay beside him. So she took off her clothes and slid into the water, with her back to his chest, resting on him, and he held her close and washed all her bruises and slowly he told her.

'There was bedlam in court,' Niklas said as he washed her gently. 'The place erupted when I asked for a new lawyer, and then Rosa presented the evidence implicating Miguel. He was arrested immediately, but of course I had to go back to prison…I knew they were never going to release me just like that. I told them that you were in danger, but they would not listen, and then, as they were taking me back, *he* made contact with Carla, asking for money. He said that he had my wife and texted a photo. The police only believed me then that I had a twin.'

She frowned and looked up to him. 'You *knew* you had a twin?'

'I guessed that I did last night, after I spoke to you.'

'How?'

'It made sense. I knew I was innocent.'

'But how did you work it out?'

'I swear in several languages…' She smiled, because that *was* what he did. 'I was angry after speaking to you—worried that you would not leave—and I swore in Portuguese. The guard warned me to be careful, he called me Dos Santos and I heard the derision in his voice, in his tone. I thought he was referring to me having no one, and I swore again, and then he said something about you. I went to curse again, but in Spanish…'

He was soaping her arms and his mouth was at her neck—not kissing, just breathing.

'The first nun who looked after me, till I was three, she taught me Spanish…'

Still Meg frowned.

'Dos Santos means something different in Spanish,' Niklas explained. 'In Portuguese it means "from the saints", in Spanish it means…'

'Two.' She turned and looked to him. '"Two saints".'

'There were two of us… That is why the Spanish nun chose our surname. It made sense. Apparently in the month before I was arrested I was having meals and meetings with very powerful people, persuading them to invest….'

'My God!'

'He and Miguel were rorting every contact I have made. A couple of months before it happened I thought I had lost my phone, but of course they had it and were diverting numbers. Both of them knew that they didn't have long before I found out, or the banks or the police did, so they were busy getting a lot of money based on my reputation. My lawyer had every reason to want me to be convicted and spend life in jail—every reason not to tell me about the evidence that would convict me. Because as soon as I saw it, I would know the truth. It was not me.'

She felt him breathe in deeply.

'I can see how people were fooled. When I saw him

lying there I felt as if I was looking at me.' He elaborated on his feelings no more than that, and told her the little he knew. 'His name was Emilios Dos Santos. The police said he had lived on the streets all his life but had no criminal record—just a few warnings for begging. I guess he was tired of having nothing. When he found out Miguel had been arrested he must have seen you as his last chance to get money from me…'

'How did he know I was here? How did he know what hotel…?'

'The prison guards, maybe.' He shrugged. 'Miguel would have been paying someone to keep an eye on me. You would have had to give your address for the prison visitors' list.'

She knew then how dangerous it had been not to listen to him, not to leave when he had told her to.

'I should have gone to Hawaii.'

'Yes,' he said, 'you should have.' But then he thought for a moment. Because without her here, without his fear that she was in danger, he might not have worked things out.

'It doesn't matter anyway,' Meg said. 'It's over now.' He didn't answer, and she turned and saw the exhaustion and agony still in his face. She could have kicked herself, for at the end of the day he had lost his twin, and Meg knew that despite all that had happened it had to hurt.

'Maybe he did want to talk to you when he found out he had a twin—perhaps Miguel dissuaded him, saw the chance to make some serious money and told him it was the only way.'

'I don't want to speak about that.'

So quickly he locked her out.

And then the phone rang—trust the hotel bathroom to have one.

Niklas answered it.

'It's your father.' He handed it to Meg, and she spoke with her parents. Neither shouted this time, just asked more questions—and, more than that, they told her how much they loved her, and how badly they wanted her to come home as quickly as possible.

She was glad she was facing away from him, but glad to be leaning on him as they spoke and he held her. Later her father asked to speak with him, and he held out his wet hand for the phone and listened to what her father was saying.

'We have to give some more statements to the police, so Meg needs to be here for a few more days,' he said, 'but I will take her somewhere quiet.' He listened for a moment and then spoke again. 'She's tired now, but I will see what she wants to do in the morning, once she has spoken to the police.'

And then he said goodbye, and she frowned because they almost sounded a little bit friendly.

'He's coming around to me.'

It was, as Meg knew only too well, terribly easy to do so.

'They want you home, Meg.'

'I know that, but I want to be here with you.'

'Well, they need to see you,' Niklas said. 'They need to see for themselves that you are not hurt.'

'I know that...' She wanted him to say he'd come with her, wanted him to say he would never let her go, but he didn't. She wanted more from him, wanted to be fully in his life, but still he would not let her in.

She turned her head and looked at him—looked at this man who'd told her from the start that they'd never last.

'This doesn't change things, does it?'

He didn't answer.

She surprised herself by not crying.

'You'll never find another love like this.' She meant it—and not in an arrogant way—because even if he didn't accept it, even if he refused to believe it, whether he wanted it or not, this really *was* love.

'I told you on the first day that it would not be for ever.'

'We didn't love each other as much then.'

'I have never said that I love you.'

'You did earlier.'

'I said there was too much love for common sense,' Niklas said. 'Too much love for you to think straight...'

'I don't believe you.'

'Believe in fairytales if you want to.' He said it much more nicely than last time, but the message was the same. 'Meg, I told you I could never settle in one place, that I could not commit to one person for ever. I *told* you that.'

He had.

'And I told you that I don't do love.'

He had.

'You said you wanted this for as long as it lasted.'

His voice was the gentlest and kindest she had heard it.

'In a few days, once all the questioning is over, you need to go home to your family.'

And even if she'd promised herself not to cry she did a bit, and he caught her tear with his thumb before lowering his head and tasting it. She could hear the clock ticking, knew that every kiss they shared now might be their last, that soon it would be a kiss goodbye.

'It could last...' She pulled her head away and opened her mouth to argue, but he spoke over her.

'I don't want to wait for the rows and the disenchantment to kick in. I don't want to do that to us because what we have now is so good. But, no, it cannot last...'

Which was why she'd accept his kisses—which was why, tonight, she would shut out the fact that this was temporary. Because tonight maybe she just needed to escape, and maybe he did too.

And even if he wouldn't admit it, even if he chose not to share his feelings, Niklas felt as if he'd just stepped out of hell's inferno into heaven as his mouth met hers.

Her mouth was bruised, but very gently he kissed it. Her cheek was hurting and her legs were grazed where she'd fallen. She knew she could never keep him, that for now guilt and fear would drive his kisses, and that later this man she didn't really know would return to a life she had never really been in. This wasn't love they were making. It was *now*.

Over and over she told herself that.

She thought he'd make love to her in the water, but he took her wet to the bed and dried her with a towel, every inch of her, and then he kissed her bruises, up her legs, and he kissed her *there* till she was crying and moaning in frustration. His hand was over her mouth again, because there were still guards outside, but she wanted him—wanted all of him. Then he slipped inside her, and it was incredibly slow, a savour in each thrust, but the words she needed were not in her ears. She bit down as she came, and gave him her body while trying to claim back a heart this man didn't want but already had.

CHAPTER TWELVE

MEG WOKE IN the night, crying and scared, and Niklas held her tightly before he made love to her again.

And he would have had her again in the morning—was pulling her across the mattress when the phone rang to tell them that Rosa was on her way up.

'Later!' he said, and kissed her. 'Or just really, really quickly now?'

She looked into black eyes that smiled down at her and simply could not read him—couldn't be his sex toy any more.

'Later,' Meg said, and climbed out of bed.

She let Rosa in. She had brought fresh clothes for both of them. Surprisingly, she gave Meg a hug and told her that she would accompany them to the police station.

'I am very sorry for the way I spoke to you,' Rosa said.

'What way?' Niklas checked.

She looked at Niklas. 'I gave her a hard time.'

'You weren't the only one,' Meg said, and then went purple when Rosa laughed. God, was that the only place minds went in Brazil? 'What I meant,' she said in her best cross voice, 'was that I do understand why you said what you did.'

'I am grateful,' Niklas said to Rosa. 'To all three of you, but especially to you. I will repay you just as soon as I get my assets back.'

'Hopefully it won't be long now,' Rosa said, and then smiled as she scolded, 'But did you *have* to drink the most expensive champagne in the fridge? I just paid your room bill.'

'*You* paid?' Meg blinked. She wasn't talking about the champagne. 'That was your money?' Meg had assumed it came from Niklas's funds, but of course she now realised that while he was being investigated they would all be frozen.

'I put up my home,' Rosa said. 'I believed in him.'

'You're the richest one of us in the room,' Niklas said to Meg, and even Rosa laughed.

'I'll buy you all a coffee on the way to the station.' Meg smiled, but it was strained. She headed to the bathroom to get changed and thought about Rosa's belief in Niklas. It was clear to Meg that in the past Rosa and Niklas had slept together, but it wasn't that fact that riled her. It was the friendship they had that ate at her—a friendship that would not waver, one that would always last.

It was the longevity that riled her.

Meg opened the bag of fresh clothes and noticed that Rosa had chosen well for her. There was a skirt that was soft and long and would cover the grazes on her legs, a thin blouse and some gorgeous, albeit completely see-through, underwear. Meg inspected the underwear more closely and saw that there wasn't an awful lot of it, and when she pulled the knickers on she was silently mortified to realise that there was a hole in the middle—which was intentional. They were the most outrageous things she'd ever worn, but she could hardly complain to Rosa.

There were sandals too, because hers had broken yesterday.

She dressed and brushed her teeth, and combed her hair, and looked in the mirror and examined her solemn face. She should be happy and celebrating, except she couldn't quite rise to it. Memories of yesterday were still too raw, and she didn't understand how Niklas and Rosa could be smiling and chatting.

Didn't understand how Niklas could just turn his pain off.

But she had to learn how to, because soon she had to go home.

Had to.

She could not hang around and watch as his guilt for what he had put her through and the attraction he clearly had for her faded. She couldn't bear the thought of his boredom setting in as she waited for the news that she was to be dismissed from his life.

If Niklas didn't want for ever, then she couldn't carry on with it being just for now.

'Ready?' Niklas checked, looking over as she walked out of the bathroom.

'I guess so.' There was nothing to pack, after all.

'Do you want me to take your clothes and have them cleaned?' Rosa offered.

'I'll bin them.' Meg headed back to the bathroom to do so. 'I never want to see them again.'

'Okay.' Rosa hitched up her bag and headed off. 'I'll go and make sure the car is ready.'

When she'd left Meg picked up all the clothes from the wet bathroom floor and took them through to the bin in the lounge, but as she went to throw them in he stopped her.

'Not those.'

She looked at the denims he was retrieving and he turned and smiled.

'You might want me to shave my head again one day...'

She wasn't smiling back.

'It's all a game to you, isn't it?'

'No, Meg.' He shook his head, and he wasn't smiling now. 'It's not.'

But as they took the lift down she noted that he was holding a bag. He hadn't binned the denim clothes he'd worn in prison.

He pulled her into him and shielded her from the press as they left the hotel, did it again when they got to the police station, but she was actually shielding herself from him. He gave her a thorough kiss before she headed in to give her statement, but all it did was make her want to cry, because she wanted more than just sex from him.

'You'll be fine.' He wiped a tear with his thumb. 'Just tell them what happened. Rosa will be there...'

'I know.'

'It's nothing to be scared of,' he said. 'And then I'm going to get you right away from here—just us...' He smiled as he said it, gave her another kiss to reassure her.

She returned neither.

The statement was long and detailed, and she felt as if she were going over and over the same thing.

No, she had never met Miguel, and nor had Emilios mentioned him.

She didn't know who had called Emilios, but it had been after that call that he had suggested they go for a walk.

'They ask,' Rosa said, 'when did you realise it was not Niklas?'

'I never realised,' she said again.

'But you said you started to panic long before you saw the gun?'

She nodded, but Rosa told her she had to answer.

'Yes.'

They made her go over and over it, and she tried to explain things but it was so hard. It was hard to understand herself. She didn't want to say in the police station that she was surprised he hadn't taken her to bed, that perhaps that had been the biggest clue that it wasn't Niklas—which for Meg just rammed home how empty their relationship really was.

'So what made you panic?' Rosa checked again.

'I realised what a mistake I'd made marrying him,'
Meg said, in a voice that was flat as she relived it. 'That
there was no real basis for a relationship, that he'd always said it wouldn't last. All I wanted was to be away
from him.'

'From Emilios?'

She shook her head. She remembered her swollen
eyes and flinging things in a suitcase, the pleasure and
pain of the last year, mainly the pain, and still, *still* he
delivered it.

'From Niklas.' As she said it she saw Rosa's slight
frown.

And then they took her further back, to her first
meeting with Niklas on the plane and their late-night
conversation.

'I asked how he'd been orphaned and he said he
wasn't sure.'

'You asked if he had ever tried to look for his family?'

'Yes.'

'And what was his response?'

'He said that he had got Miguel, his lawyer, onto it,
but he had got nowhere.'

'He said that?' the police officer checked via Rosa.
'He definitely said that?'

'Yes.'

The officer looked long and hard at her, and then
Rosa asked if Meg was sure, as this was from a conversation a year ago. 'He asks if you are sure this is not the
conversation you had with Niklas last night.'

Meg blinked.

'I told the police.'

'You remember this conversation exactly?' the officer checked, and she said yes, because she had been replaying every second of their time over and over for close to a year now.

'Exactly.' She nodded. 'And then I asked what it had been like, growing up in an orphanage, but he didn't respond,' Meg said. 'He told me he didn't want to speak about that sort of thing.'

But the police weren't interested in that part.

Only Meg was.

She went over and over everything again. She said that, no, she hadn't been aware she was being followed at the time, and looked to Rosa for explanation, but she gave a brief shake of her head. Then her statement was read back to her. She listened and heard that basically they had had an awful lot of sex and just a few conversations, but he had definitely mentioned that he had asked Miguel to look for his family. She signed her name to it.

'That is good,' Rosa said as they walked out. 'You have a good memory. They will jump on that part in court if Miguel denies that he was asked to find Niklas's family,' she warned. 'Just stay with that.'

'Am I free to fly home?' Meg asked. She saw the brief purse of Rosa's lips. 'My family's worried about me.'

'It might be better for Niklas's case if you were here.'

'What case?' Meg asked. 'It's clear he's innocent.'

'To you,' Rosa said. 'And it is to me. But dead men

can't speak.' She gave a thin smile. 'I correct myself. When I said that Niklas never makes mistakes, he has made one—he hired Miguel, and he is a brilliant lawyer. He might say it was both of them that were conning people. He might insist he believed it was Niklas giving him instructions, or that the directions came from both of them...'

'No!'

'Yes,' Rosa said. 'I will fight it, but it might look better for Niklas if his wife was here beside him—not back home, counting the money his legal team has placed in her account.'

'You know it isn't like that.'

'Tell the judge,' Rosa said, and she was back to being mean. 'I get that your family is worried about you, but if you can pretend for a little while longer that Niklas is a part of your family...'

'Niklas doesn't want me to,' Meg retorted. 'Niklas doesn't want a family...'

'He doesn't even know what one is!' Rosa shouted. 'Yet he has done everything right by you.'

'Everything *right* by me?' It was Meg who was shouting now. 'Are we talking about the same man?'

It wasn't the best choice of words, given the circumstances—especially as Niklas appeared then.

'My mother had triplets, maybe?' he quipped.

It was her poor choice of words, perhaps, but his response was just in bad taste. She did not understand how he could be so laid-back about it. How could he have his arm around her and be walking out of the police station as if the nightmare of the last year hadn't even happened?

It was the same circus of cameras as before, and then they left Rosa to give the press a statement. A car was waiting for them. It's driver handed the keys over to Niklas, who sat behind the wheel as Meg sat in the passenger seat. The moment she was seated Niklas accelerated away at speed—away from the crowds of press. After a while the car slowed, and the drive was a long one, taking them out of the city and through the hills. There was little conversation, just an angry silence from Meg, whereas with every mile the car ate up Niklas seemed more relaxed.

'You're quiet,' he commented.

'Isn't that what you want me to be?'

Sulking didn't work with Niklas. It didn't bother him a bit. He just carried on driving, one hand on the wheel, the other out of the window. Any minute now he'd start whistling, just to annoy her further. She was still bristling from Rosa's words. The first thing she would do when she got back to Sydney was send back all the money that she had been paid.

He looked over at her tense profile. 'We'll be there soon.'

She didn't answer him.

Nothing made sense: the policeman's questions had confused her, Rosa had angered her, and as for him… She turned and could not fathom how calm he was after all that had happened. He was fiddling with the sound system now, flicking through channels. She did not need background music, and her hand snapped it off.

'The police said I was being followed. That it wasn't the police who shot him…'

'It was a bodyguard.'

'Bodyguard?'

'Just leave it.'

'No,' Meg snapped. 'I will not.'

'He will not do any prison time. I have my lawyers working for him. I had a couple of people following you when I realised you were still here—when I guessed I had a twin. I did not know exactly what was happening, but I knew you would not be safe, so I arranged to have people protect you.'

'How?'

'I owe a favour to a very powerful man,' Niklas said. 'He got a message to the outside after you rang me.'

And then he stopped talking about it, and she felt his hand come to rest on her leg, and she could not understand how easily he dismissed the fact that it was a bodyguard *he* had arranged who had shot his twin.

Did nothing get to him?

He gave her thigh a squeeze, which she guessed meant they were nearly at their destination and would be off to look at another bedroom any time soon.

'We're here.'

It was the most stunning house she had ever seen, with dark wood, white furniture and screens on the windows so the sun and the sounds of the mountains could stream in. It was gorgeous and, Niklas said, the place he had dreamt of when he was on the inside.

'You like it?'

'It's gorgeous.'

'Look…'

He took her by the hand and led her to the bedroom, then walked and opened huge glass doors, revealing lush grass that rolled towards another mountain. The sound of birds was all that could be heard. In a place like this, Meg thought, you could start to heal.

'There are servants, but I have told them not to come till I call them. They've left us lots of food…'

And there were her things, hanging in the wardrobe, and there were his arms around her, and again he was holding her close.

She started crying and he didn't seem surprised at all.

'You're exhausted,' he said.

She was.

From nearly a year of loving him.

'Are you about to suggest we go to bed?'

'Meg…' He saw her anger and he didn't blame her. 'I don't care how cross you are. You deserve to be. If you want to shout, go ahead. I have put you through hell and I am just trying to make you feel better, to say the right thing. I'm probably getting it wrong, but for now you are here, and safe.'

It was the 'for now' part that was killing her, but she wasn't going to go there again. 'I don't know what's wrong,' she said. 'I'm so angry! I'm so confused…'

'It's shock,' he said. 'You were nearly kidnapped. You saw a man shot.'

'I saw your *twin* shot!' she shouted. 'I thought it was you.'

He did not react—he just held her.

'Shouldn't it be the other way round?' She pulled away from him, so angry. 'Shouldn't *you* be the one crying? He was your brother.'

'That's for me to deal with,' Niklas said.

'Can't you deal with it with me?'

'I prefer to do things like that alone.' He was nothing if not honest. 'I don't want to talk about me. Right now I want to be here for you.'

He said all the right things, but they were the wrong things too. He took all of her, but didn't give himself back, and maybe she had better just accept it. He felt nothing for anyone, and as she looked out to the mountains she hoped here she might find a little peace before she left him.

'I hope the press don't find us here.'

'Not a chance,' Niklas said. 'I told you that.'

'If they know that you own it they soon will.' She looked down the mountain and hoped there were no cars loaded with press following them up, because she was beyond tired now, could not face moving again. She just wanted a moment to gather her thoughts. 'They'll be going through all your assets...'

'I don't own it,' Niklas said. 'It's not listed in my assets. This is in your name...' He lifted up her face and kissed her frowning forehead. 'I bought this for you before I got arrested. I wanted the divorce, I knew I might be going away for a very long time, and this was to be part of your settlement. The sale went through the day before my finances were frozen…' He gave her a smile. 'They could not seize this because it is yours…'

'You bought this for me?'

'It is big enough for a bed and breakfast…' He shrugged. 'If that is what you want to do with it. I knew you would probably sell it…'

He had known he was about to be arrested and go to prison and yet he had still looked after her—had come to this place and chosen it. It was more than she could take in.

'Why are you crying?'

'Because of this.'

'I said I would take care of you.'

'And you have…'

He had kept every promise he had made, had listened to all her dreams.

They walked through the house and he showed her every room before he took her into the kitchen, with its massive ovens and benches, and huge glass doors that opened to let in the sound and the breeze of the mountains. He had chosen the perfect home—except he hadn't factored that he might live in it.

'I might have to stay here a while,' Niklas said. 'You can be my landlady.'

He came over for a kiss, because that was what he always did.

'I'll send you the rent I owe when I get it.'

'Send it?' Meg said.

'You need to go back.'

He did care about her. She knew it then—knew why he was sending her away. 'And you can't come with me.' It wasn't a question, she was telling him that she knew why.

He tried to hush her with a kiss.

'You can't come to Sydney even for a little while because you're still on bail.'

'Meg…'

When that didn't work, she was more specific. 'And you won't let me stay because you think you might go back to jail.'

'More than might,' Niklas said. 'Miguel is the best legal mind I have met…' He smiled. 'No offence meant.'

Always he made her smile, and always, Meg knew then, he had loved her—even if he didn't know it, even if he refused to see it. Rosa was right. He had always been taking care of her and he was trying to take care of her now.

'I'm on bail,' he said, 'and I doubt the charges will be dropped. Miguel will not simply admit his guilt. There will be a trial, there could be years of doubt, and then I might be put away again. You need to go back to your family.'

'*You're* my family.'

'No…' He just would not accept it. 'Because as much as I might want you here, as much as I thought of you here in this home while I was in that place, as much as a three-weekly visit might keep me sane, I will *not* do that to you.'

'Yes.'

'No,' Niklas said. 'We will have a couple of nights here and then, as I promised your father, I will make sure you get home. By the time you are there I will have divorced you.'

He was adamant.

And she both loved and loathed that word now. She wanted to kiss the man she was certain now loved her, yet she wanted to know the man she loved. He kissed her as if he would never let her go, yet he had told her that she must.

'You're so bloody selfish…' She could have slapped him. She pulled her head back, would not be hushed with sex. 'Why don't I get a say?' She was furious now, and shouting. 'You're as bad as my parents—telling me what I want and how I should live my life…'

'What?' he demanded. 'You *want* to be up here, living in the mountains, coming to prison for a screw every three weeks?'

'Your mouth can be foul.'

'Your life could be,' Niklas retorted. 'Barefoot and pregnant, with your husband—'

She didn't hear the next bit. It was then that Meg remembered—only then that she remembered what she had been preparing to find out before Emilios had come to her door. He watched her anger change to panic, and in turn she watched the fear that darted in his eyes when she told him that she might already be.

It was not how it should be. Meg knew that.

He just stood there as she walked off, as she walked into the bedroom and went through her things. Yes, there was her toiletry bag and, yes, Rosa had packed everything. The pregnancy testing kit was there.

She kicked off her shoes when she returned to the kitchen, because barefoot and pregnant she *was*.

'You need to go home to your family.'

'That's all you have to say?'

'That's it.'

She couldn't believe his detachment, that he could simply turn away.

'You'd let us both go, wouldn't you?'

'You'll have a far better life…'

'I probably would,' Meg said. 'Because I am sick of being married to a man who can't even talk to me, who sorts everything out with sex. Who, even if he won't admit it, *does* actually love me. I'm tired of trying to prise it out of you.'

'Go, then.'

'Is that what you want?' Meg persisted. 'Or are you telling me again what I *should* want?'

'I could come out of this with nothing!'

And if Meg thought she had glimpsed fear before, then she had no idea—because now that gorgeous mouth was strung by taut tendons. His black eyes flashed in terror as he saw himself searching bins for food—not just for himself but for the family she was asking him to provide for. Meg knew then that she had never known real fear…would never know the depth of his terror.

She would not die hungry.

She would not leave the earth unnoticed.

She would be missed.

'I might not be able to give you anything…'

She glimpsed the magnitude of his words.

'We might have nothing.'

'We wouldn't have nothing,' Meg argued, with this man who had no comprehension of family. 'We'd have each other.'

'You don't know what nothing is.'

'So tell me.'

'I don't want to discuss it.'

'Then I *will* leave, Niklas, and I *will* divorce you. And don't you dare come looking for me when the charges are dropped. Don't you dare try to get back in my life when you think the going can only be good.'

He just stood there.

'And don't bother writing to find out what I have, because if I walk out now I will do everything I can to make sure you can't find out. I will write "father unknown" on the birth certificate and you really will be nothing to your child.'

And she was fighting for the baby she had only just found out about, and the family she knew they could be, and as she turned to go Niklas fought for them too.

'Stay.'

'For what?' Meg asked. 'Shall we go to bed?' she demanded. 'Or shall we just do it here? Or…' she looked at him as if she'd had a sudden idea '…or we could talk.'

'You talk too much.'

He pulled her to him and kissed her mouth, running his hands over her, down her waist to her stomach. He pressed his hands into it for a second and then, as if it killed him to touch her there, he slid his hands between her thighs and moved to lift her skirt. He tried desperately to kiss her back to him, but she halted him and pulled her head away.

'And you don't talk enough.'

She would not let him go this time, and he knew he could not kiss her back into his life. And she *would* walk—he knew it. She was a thousand times stronger than she thought, and so must he be—for without her and his baby he was back to nothing.

'Don't waste time in fear, Niklas,' Meg said. 'You told me that.'

So he stood there and slowly and quietly told her what it had been like to be completely alone, to be moved on to yet another boys' home when he caused too much trouble, to boys' homes that had made living on the streets preferable.

And she *was* stronger than she'd thought she was, because she didn't cry or comment—just stood in his arms and listened. She'd asked for this, she reminded herself a few times at some of the harder parts.

'You would make a friend and then you would move on. Or he would steal from you and you would decide to go it alone. Then you might make another friend, and the same would happen again, or you would wake up and he would be lying dead beside you. But you keep on living, and you get a job, and it turns out you are clever—more clever than most—so you start to make money and you start to forget. Except you never do. But you make a good life for yourself, make new friends, and you would not change it, this new life, but still you taste the bitterness of your past. You make more money than you can spend because you're scared of having nothing again and, yes, you're happy—but it still tastes bitter.'

He didn't know how to explain it neatly, but he tried. He looked at her and could not fathom why she wanted to get inside his messed-up head.

'You never forget—not for one minute. You remember eating from bins and beatings, and running away, and the smell of sleeping on the streets, and you trust no one. You remember how people will take from you the second your back is turned—would steal from a beggar who sleeps on the streets. So you relish each mouthful you take and you swear you will never go back to being nothing. But always you fear that you will.'

And then he stopped.

'You want to hear the rest?'

'Yes.'

He paused, took a deep breath before continuing. 'Then you meet a woman on a plane, and this woman feels worried because in living her own life and following her dreams she might hurt her family, and you know then that there are people who do worry about others, who do care. And this woman changes your life.'

'I didn't.'

'More than that—you saved my life. Because when

I did go back to having nothing I survived. More than I should have, I thought of you. Every night I saw the sun, and it was the colour of your hair. Then last night I got to hold you, and look back, and I realised that it is a good world. There are people you cannot trust, but there are also people you can—people who help you even if you don't know it at the time.'

She didn't understand.

'That a woman you only dated for a while would put up her house…' He hesitated. 'Rosa and I…'

'I worked that out.'

'It was before she was married, and there has been nothing since, but her husband is still not pleased that she works for me. That she should go to him, that Silvio should trust her and me enough—that is real friendship,' he said. 'That does not let you taste bitterness.'

And that part she understood.

'Then you look back further and realise that the nun who taught you Spanish, the woman who named you, was the one good thing you can properly remember from your childhood and will end up saving the life of the woman you love—how can you not be grateful for that?'

'You can't not be.'

'And that woman you met on the plane—who your gut told you was right—who you married and then hurt so badly—would fly into Congonhas Airport to come and have paid sex with me…'

She thought of his anger in the prison, and the roughness of the sex, and then his tenderness afterwards, and she was so glad that he'd known he was loved, that she'd told him.

'I'd have done it for nothing.'

'I know,' he said, and he was honest. 'You loved me when I had nothing, and you will never properly appreciate what that means. But I might again have nothing, and I thought that was my worst nightmare, but to have nothing to give you or my child…'

'We've got a home that you chose for us,' Meg said. 'And I can work, and I have parents who will help me. Your child—our child—will never have nothing, and neither will you, so long as we have each other.'

He still could not really fathom it, but maybe he was starting to believe it.

'It might not mean prison…the charges could be dropped…' he said. 'Rosa thinks they have enough already to prove I was not involved. They are going through the evidence now.'

'And, unlike your wife, Rosa's got a good legal brain!' Meg said.

He didn't smile, but he gave a half-smirk.

'Rosa thinks it was Miguel who suggested the plan to my brother.' He tested this new thing called love. 'I want him to have a proper funeral. I want to find out more about him. I want to know about his life. Do you understand that?'

'Yes.'

'I might not talk about it without you.'

And still he said all the wrong things, but they were the right things for them.

'Whatever feels right for you.' And now she understood him a little better. She didn't have to know everything, didn't have to have all of him—just the parts that he chose to give. They were more than enough. And when he did choose to share, she could be there for him.

'Can you accept now that, even though I don't tell you everything, there are no secrets that might hurt you between us?'

'Yes.'

And then he did what Niklas did when he had to: he simply turned the pain of his past off. He smiled at her, held her, and then for the longest time he kissed her—a kiss that tasted deeper now, a kiss that had her burning.

But, unusually for Niklas, he stopped.

'And just to prove how much I love you,' he said, 'there will be no more sex for a while, so we can talk some more.'

'I didn't mean that.'

'No.' He was insistent. 'I can see what you were saying. We can go for a walk in the mountains.' He smiled and it was wicked. 'We can get some fresh air and we can talk some more...'

'Stop it.' His mouth had left her wanting.

She tried to kiss him, tried to resume, but Niklas shrugged her off and found a basket, started loading it from the fridge.

'We're going to have a picnic,' Niklas said. 'Is that romantic?'

He was the sexiest guy she had ever met, Meg re-

alised, and she'd been complaining because they were
having too much sex...

'Niklas, please.' She didn't want a picnic in the
mountains, didn't want a sex strike from her Brazilian
lover, and she told him so.

'Husband,' he corrected. 'I married you, remember?'

'Yes.'

'How can you say it was all about sex? I was nothing but a gentleman that day...I could have had you on
the plane, but I married you first!'

'Hardly a gentleman,' she said. 'But, yes, you *did*
marry me, and I get it all now. So can you put the basket down and...?'

'And what?' Niklas said.

Seemingly shallow, but impossibly deep, he was gorgeous and insatiable, and he was hers for ever.

His sex strike lasted all of two minutes, because now
he was lifting her onto the kitchen bench even as he
kissed her. His hands were everywhere and his mouth
was too, but so were her hands before he slapped them
away. '*I'm* doing this.'

He was the most horrible tease.

He whistled when he lifted up her skirt. 'What are
you wearing?'

She writhed in embarrassment at his scrutiny.
'They're new.'

'You didn't buy these, though.' He smiled, because
he couldn't really imagine his seemingly uptight girl
buying knickers you didn't even have to take off.

'I might have.'

'Meg…' He was very matter-of-fact as he pulled down his zipper. 'You wore sensible knickers the day I met you. You even wore sensible knickers when you came to visit me in prison.' And then carefully he positioned her. 'Watch.'

And when he slipped straight into her the outrageous knickers she was wearing seemed like a sensible choice now.

'Never think I don't love you.' He would say it a hundred times a day if he had to. 'Never think that this is not love.'

And she knew then that he *did* love her, and that what they shared was much more than just sex. He was very slow and deliberate, and it was Meg who couldn't stop. He kept going as the scream built within her, and she waited for his hand to cover her mouth, waited for him to hush her—except they were home now, as he told her, and he pushed harder into her.

'We're home,' he said again, and moved faster, and for the first time she could scream, could sob and scream as much as she wanted, could be whoever and however she pleased.

And so too could he.

He told her how much he loved her as he came, and over and over he told her that he would work something out, he would sort this out.

And as he looked over her shoulder to the mountains he knew how lucky he was—how easily it could have been him lying dead on the pavement instead of his brother. His twin who must have tasted so much bitterness in his life too and been unable to escape as Niklas had done. When still he held her, when he buried his face in her hair and she heard his ragged breathing, for a moment she said nothing.

And then, because it was Niklas, he switched off his pain and came to her, smiling. 'Do you know what day it is today?'

'The day we found out we—' She stopped then, and blinked in realisation as her husband moved in to kiss her.

'Happy anniversary.'

CHAPTER THIRTEEN

SHE LOVED BRAZIL more and more every day she spent there, but it was the evenings she loved the most.

Meg lay half dozing by the pool, then stretched and smelt the air, damp from the rain that often came in the afternoon, washing the mountains till they were gleaming, and thought about how happy she was.

The charges had been dropped, but it had taken a couple of months for them to get back on their feet. They had paid Rosa back her money and lived off Meg's savings, but only when the nightmare of his returning to prison had stopped looming over them and Meg's pregnancy had started showing had Niklas really begun to think this was real.

There were now regular trips into São Paulo, and Niklas came to each pre-natal visit, and she loved that her family adored Brazil as much as Niklas did Australia when they were there.

She saw her parents often—they had only just left that day—and, thanks to a few suggestions and more than a little help from their new son-in-law, business was going well in Sydney.

They had surprised her—after the shock of finding out had worn off, they'd been wonderful. Niklas had flown them over to Brazil and the first day he'd met them he'd begun to work out why sometimes you couldn't just hang up the phone or shut someone out. He'd started to get used to both the complications and the rewards of family.

They hadn't shared their good news about Meg's pregnancy on that visit—it had seemed all too new and too soon to give them another thing to deal with, and there had also been a funeral to prepare for.

She had thought Niklas would do that on his own, except he hadn't.

Only a few other people had been invited. Meg had met Carla for the first time, and she was, of course, stunning, and there had been Rosa and her colleagues, and Rosa's husband Silvio too. And, even if they hadn't wanted to attend at first, her parents had come too, because they loved Meg and Niklas, and Niklas had told them how much it was appreciated. There had been flowers sent from Fernando—a fellow *paulistano* who knew only too well how tough it was on the streets, who knew that sometimes it was just about surviving.

Meg had been a bit teary, saying goodbye to her parents that morning, but they'd reassured her that they'd be returning in a month's time, so that they could be there for the birth of their grandchild.

If she lasted another month, Meg thought as she felt a tightening again and picked up her baby guidebook.

No, it wasn't painful, and they were ages apart. So

she read about Braxton Hicks for a while. But then another one came, and this time she noted the time on her phone, because though it didn't quite hurt she found herself holding her breath till it passed. Maybe she should ring someone to check—or just wait because Niklas would be home soon? It probably was just Braxton Hicks…

Her pregnancy book said so…

Meg loved being pregnant. She loved her ripening belly, and so too did Niklas. And she loved *him* more than she had thought she was capable of.

No, she'd never fully know him. But she had the rest of her life to try and work out the most complicated man in the world.

The nightmares had stopped for both of them and life had moved on, and more and more she realised how much he loved her.

There was plenty of happiness—they had friends over often, and many evenings she got to do what she adored: trying out new recipes.

Meg looked at her phone. It had been ages since the last pain, so she should be getting started with dinner really. They had Rosa and her husband and a few other guests coming over tonight, to cheer Meg up after saying goodbye to her parents.

They had such good friends. She could even laugh at things now, and she and Rosa had become firm allies. Rosa would sometimes tease Meg about the earlier conversations they had shared—not to mention the outrageous knickers.

God, she'd been such an uptight thing then.

She lay blushing in her bikini at the thought of the lovely things they did, and then she felt another tightening. She looked at her phone again, noting the time. They were still ages apart, but as she heard the hum of the helicopter bringing Niklas home she was suddenly glad he was here. She walked across the lush grounds to meet him and picked a few ripe avocados from the tree to make a guacamole. As she did so she felt something gush.

It would seem the book was wrong. These weren't practice contractions, because there was real pain gripping her now—a tightening that had her blowing her breath out and feeling the strangest pressure.

Niklas saw her double over as he walked towards her. He could hear the chopper lifting into the sky and was torn between whether to ring and have the pilot return or just to get to her. He walked quickly, cursing himself because they had been going to move to his city apartment at the weekend, so that they could be closer to the hospital.

'It's fine...' He was very calm and practical when he found her kneeling on the grass. 'I'll get the chopper sent back and we will fly you to the hospital. Let's get you into the house...' He tried to help her stand but she kept moaning. 'Okay...' he said. 'I will carry you inside...'

'No...' She was kneeling down and desperate to push—though part of her told her not to, told her it couldn't be happening, that she still had ages, must keep the baby in. And yet another part of her told her that if she pushed hard enough, if she just gave in and went with it, the pain would be gone.

'It's coming!'

She was vaguely aware of him ringing someone, and frowned when she heard who it was.

'Carla?'

She wasn't thinking straight, the pain was far too much, but why the *hell* was he calling Carla?

'Done,' he said.

'Done?'

'Help is on the way...'

She could see him sweating, which Niklas never did, but his voice was very calm and he was very reassuring.

'She will be ringing for the helicopter to come back and for an ambulance...'

He saw her start to cry because she knew they would be too late—that the baby was almost here.

'It's fine...' He took off his jacket and she watched him take out his cufflinks and very neatly start to fold up his sleeves. 'Everything will be okay.'

'You've delivered a lot of babies, have you?' She was shouting and she didn't mean to.

'No,' he said, and then he looked up and straight into her eyes, and he turned her pain and fear off, because that was what he did best. 'But I did do a life-skills course in prison...'

And that he made her smile, even if she was petrified, and then she started shouting again when he had the gall to answer his ringing phone.

'It's the obstetrician.'

She must remember to thank Carla, Meg thought as he pulled down her bikini bottoms. From what she could make out with her limited Portuguese he was telling the doctor on speakerphone that, yes, he could see the head.

She could have told the doctor that!

But she was sort of glad not to know what was being said—sort of glad just to push and then be told to stop and then to push some more. She was *very* annoyed when he said something that made the obstetrician laugh, and she was about to tell him so when suddenly their baby was out.

'Sim,' he told the doctor. *'Ela é rosa e respiração.'*

Yes, her baby was pink and breathing. They were the best words in the world and, given he had said *ela*, it would seem they had a baby girl.

The doctor didn't need to ask if the baby was crying for it sang across the mountains—and Meg cried too.

Not Niklas—he never cried. Just on the day he'd found out she was safe she had seen a glimpse, and then the next day she had guessed he might have been, but he was in midwife mode now!

He did what the doctor said and kept them both warm. He took his shirt off and wrapped his daughter in it, and there was his jacket around Meg, and then he got a rug from beside the pool and covered them both with it. He thanked the doctor and said he could hear help arriving, and then he turned off his phone.

'She needs to feed,' he told her, and he must have seen her wide eyes. He was an expert in breastfeeding now, was he? 'The doctor said it will help with the next bit...'

'Oh...'

'Well done,' he said.

'Well done to you too.' She smiled at her lovely midwife. 'Were you scared?'

'Of course not.' He shook his head. 'It's a natural process. Normally quick deliveries are easy ones...'

He said a few other things that had her guessing he'd been reading her book—the bit about babies that come quickly and early.

'She's early...' Meg sighed, because she had really been hoping that this would be a very late baby, that somehow they could fudge the dates a little and she would never know she'd been made in prison.

'It will be fine,' he said. 'She was made with love. That's all she needs to know.'

They had a name for a boy and one for a girl, and he nodded when she checked that he still wanted it. She tasted his kiss. Then she saw him look down to his daughter and thought maybe she glimpsed a tear, but she did not go there—she just loved that moment alone, the three of them, just a few minutes before the helicopter arrived—alone on their mountain with their new baby, Emilia Dos Santos.

The Portuguese meaning, though.

From the saints.

* * * * *

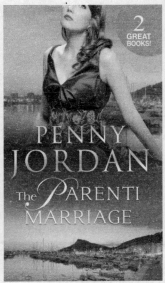

Two fabulous stories full of drama and passion
from Mills & Boon® favourites

Lynne Graham and
Penny Jordan

Now available from:

www.millsandboon.co.uk